VAMPIRE-TECH 3
OUTBREAK

Bryan Romer

VAMPIRE-TECH 3
OUTBREAK

Fiction4All

Chapter One

Viktor Tiranul smiled in satisfaction at his handiwork even as his body transmuted back into human form. The crumpled and broken corpse of Don Salvatore Morello lay at his feet, the dead man's blood streaming off of his hands, repelled by the alien nanites, which were actually more like an intelligent colony, that resided in his bloodstream and which made him a werewolf. In fact, the entire luxurious living room was a charnel house, with great splashes of blood defiling the walls, ceiling and floor, and soaking the human bodies that lay all around, some of which were mostly whole while others were dreadfully torn and shredded. Not all of the dead bodies belonged to Don Salvatore's Mafia family. Slumped beside the main door was a man in a suit who looked to be Russian. Bullet wounds blossomed red and wet at the side of his neck and to the left of his chest. Diagonally across the room, splayed awkwardly over the end of a sofa was a Chinese man, his torso shattered by several hits from a shotgun.

"The house is clear, Viktor. They're all dead," Jenny Smith said, pressing her naked body against Viktor's side. She preferred to undress before changing into her werewolf form in order to preserve her clothes. The nudity didn't bother the pretty ex-prostitute. "This is the last bunch of holdouts. We control every bit of the London underworld, and probably most of the country. So what's next?" she asked. She knew Viktor well enough to be sure that this success would not be the end of her lover and leader's ambitions.

Viktor put his arm around the female werewolf, touching her with a familiarity that would have gotten any other man killed. He chuckled. "All of this is just the start, the mere foundation. These criminals will supply the cash and manpower to carry out the next step."

"Which is?"

"Taking over the country, of course," Viktor said, his human smile every bit as savage and merciless as when his face had a muzzle and fangs.

"Oh good! I'm assuming we get to kill lots more people?" Jenny said eagerly. She had grown to love killing with an almost sexual passion.

'Of course my darling. It wouldn't be fun otherwise," Viktor replied. He kicked the Don's body and laughed at the mushy sound of cracking bones.

***

"Why do I have to get naked?" Tara Harker asked, hands on her hips and head tilted quizzically. "I know you've seen me in the buff before, but a girl has to maintain her standards, you know!" She assumed John Seward had a good reason for his request, and she trusted him enough that if they had been in a life or death situation she probably would have obeyed without question. But since they were in his private gym, she felt justified in asking. To her surprise, instead of replying, John began to undress himself.

"What I'm going to show you can be done with your clothes on, but they tend to be worse for wear afterwards. Honestly, I don't even know if I can teach you to do it or if you have to just find out how to do it yourself. I discovered I could do it when some unpleasant people set fire to a tower I was in. But I think that simply knowing it is possible will help."

"Knowing what?" Tara said, exasperated by his mysterious manner.

"This!" John said as his trousers fell to the floor, leaving him nude except for his underpants. Then in a flowing movement of his body that was almost too fast to see, his human form was gone and in its place was a vaguely bat-like form, still bipedal, but with longer, more delicate arms and a fine membrane wing stretching between the underside of each of his arms down to his legs. At the same time his body shrank and lightened, although the overall appearance was of compact strength rather than fragility. With a thrust of his legs John sprang into the air and took flight.

Tara stared in shocked amazement as John flew in a short arc towards the far end of the hall, rolled in mid-air, and bounced off the wall like a swimmer to fly back and land where he started. "You ... " Speechless, she waved her arms at his changing body and then in the air, as if to mime his aerial performance.

Once more in human form, John calmly smiled at her as he dressed. "If we are to meet with the representatives of the other vampires in Britain, I thought you needed to at least be aware of this potential capability." He raised an eyebrow. "It took me decades and a life and death situation in order to discover how to do it. But given your ability to um, communicate with our little guests, it's quite possible you can accelerate the process."

Tara was still so stunned at what she had just witnessed that she undressed without further comment or hesitation. John's gaze was speculative and analytical, and she wasn't sure if she was pleased or disturbed by his lack of sexual response to her nudity. They had become close during the recent weeks, but his ability to seemingly turn off his emotions at will still bothered her. She had wondered more than once whether it was his natural personality or something the alien medical system had done to him – and whether it would do the same to her. "So what do I do now?"

John rubbed his chin and frowned. He had mentored new vampires before during his long life, but never one that had the potential capability to interact with the alien nanites like Tara did, thanks to her father's own far more primitive nanite based command interface. "I'm not really sure. Different people have reacted to different stimuli. Most had to be provided with an incentive."

"Should I ask?" Tara said raising an eyebrow.

"Being thrown off of the roof of a barn often worked," John replied. Then he grinned. "In your case let's try something less dramatic for a start. Flex your knees, get up on your toes, spread your arms out, and imagine yourself lifting up into the air."

Feeling like a schoolgirl asked to imitate a chicken, she did as he said. Despite the absurdity of her position, she had seen what John had done and was well aware of the capabilities of the awesome and as yet barely understood alien technology that had been implanted in her body. To her surprise, the internal HUD which originally functioned with her father's experimental aircraft faded into view in front of her eyes. The alien medical implant had somehow found a way to communicate and even control the HUD and used it to interact with her. The "flight systems check" symbol flashed, followed by the "undercarriage retracting" symbol, followed by the "standby/hold" warning icon. She had grown better at interpreting the alien AI's attempts at communication and guessed that it was trying to tell her that it understood her desire to morph the way John had, but that it would require some biological changes that couldn't take place instantly. At the same time she felt subtle tingling feelings in her limbs, and more alarmingly, twisting and shifting sensations within her body. The things that the medical nanites did to her body never seemed to hurt, and both she and her father suspected that it was blocking the pain rather than everything being actually painless. She turned her head to look at John. "I think it might work, but it could take some ti – " She stopped talking because her face, along with the rest of her body was suddenly changing. Not just her form but the very composition of her flesh, bones and internal organs. The alien medical system was unleashing its full power to mould and transform her body into the image of the original alien that it had been designed to serve and protect, or as close to it as possible. Despite her test pilot training, her iron will, and all that she had seen and experienced since becoming a recipient of the alien medical nanite system, she still felt a rush of primal terror and a near irresistible impulse to scream in horror. Unlike John's transformation, hers was slower, more gradual, as if the medical system within her body was carefully mapping a vast wave of alterations that had to radically alter her body without killing her in the process. And then just as suddenly, it was done. Tara looked at herself in shock and amazement. If it hadn't been for her experience in melding with her father's aircraft, she might have gone mad from the radically different sensory input.

"Don't try to talk. Just relax and get used to how your body feels. Stay calm and focused," John said in a brisk commanding tone that demanded obedience. He distinctly recalled how he had felt when the change had first come upon him. "Remember who you are, Tara. If you lose that anchor you can become as lost as the poor sods who turn werewolf."

His words cut through the fog of panic and confusion, replacing it in Tara's mind with a greater concern of being lost in the instincts and thought patterns of the alien form. Fortunately, the bat creatures were social and omnivorous, and even had two distinct sexes, so the mental and emotional conflict wasn't as great as when a human took on the form of a werewolf. Instead she focused upon the alien creature's ability to fly, treating her new form as if it was an aircraft that she now controlled. The "All Systems Ready" indicator brightened on her HUD, followed by the "Autopilot On" icon. Then suddenly she was in the air. "I'm flying!" she cried, or at least she tried to. What came out was a garbled mixture of English and a rapid pulsed set of squeaks and high-pitched barks. Flying wasn't at all how she imagined it would be. The flapping of her arms and wings happened without conscious thought, as did all the other fine movements of her body that were required for her to fly and to glide in a circle around the huge exercise hall before landing back where she had started. The "Autopilot" symbol went dark in the HUD just as she landed, and she staggered when she was given full control of the alien body. Before she could fall, the change started to reverse itself and in the time it took for her foot to take a step to the side and rear, it and the leg it was attached to, had returned to human form. The speed of the transformation was both shocking and disorienting.

John reached out to support her with his arm. "Careful! I fell on my arse the first time. Not very dignified at all. It completely spoils the whole 'Creature of the Night' thing.

Tara leaned gratefully against him, still trying to mentally grasp what had just happened. "That was … incredible! Terrifying, but incredible. Do you think that is what the aliens are actually like?"

"I think so. I've studied every case of vampire transformation I could find and according to all records and reports, the result has always been the same shape and form. I've also seen some poor bastards whose bodies or minds somehow resisted the change. Some went insane during the change and became trapped in a half-way state. These were the creatures that became known in legend as Nosferatu.

"You mean there's a chance I won't be able to change back again?" Tara asked in alarm.

John shrugged. "Do I look like a bat? But there is always a possibility of error when dealing with something that was never meant to happen. The alien system knows it's in the wrong kind of body, and is just muddling along as best it can. My hypothesis is that the more cooperative the host is, the better the thing works.

Viktor seems to have embraced the nanites from the very beginning, while you have the advantage of your own built in interface. At any rate, I'd advise not changing except under the most extreme circumstances."

Tara realised that she was leaning against John's body in a most familiar fashion and that she was still completely naked. She liked him, but there were still so many questions lurking in the background that she wasn't ready to be physically intimate with him just yet. Trying to be casual, she pulled free of what was close to being an embrace and turned away to get dressed. "I don't think I'll be trying that again anytime soon, although I'll have to tell my father about it and he may want to run some tests." No longer naked, she said, "Why didn't you tell me about this earlier? What else are you hiding from me?"

John stiffened and frowned, a trace of the ancient nobleman appearing in his expression and posture. "I'm not hiding anything, not in the manner that you're suggesting. You already know that you are now capable of physical changes, and the werewolves are a very clear example of how far it can go. Are you suggesting that the obvious conclusion never occurred to you?"

"Of course not!" Tara snapped angrily. "I .... " Then she sighed and nodded. "You're right of course. I was simply avoiding the thought that I might become ... like Viktor."

He put his hand on her shoulder and gently squeezed. "You're not like Viktor in any way. Many, most, people are incapable of handling the truth of the transformation and I suspect that they mentally shut down when in werewolf form, leaving their bodies to be run by the werewolf form's basic instincts. Some may even develop a form of protective amnesia when they return to human form again and may truly not know what happened and what they have done. The fact that we are even talking like this proves that you're not one of them."

Now that she was dressed she felt more comfortable with allowing him to embrace her, and she leaned her head against his chest. "I need you to keep telling me that. I still have nightmares of – " Her words cut off when John kissed her. She stiffened and pressed her hands against his chest as if to push him away, but then just left them there as she kissed him back.

***

"I don't like it," Rowland Harker said, sending an insect sized drone buzzing towards the large TV screen on the wall with a gesture of his hand. "New Belmarsh is nothing more than a concentration camp for undesirables. Out of sight, out of mind."

Emily Palmer touched a control on the virtual keypad that was projected into her eye from the headset she wore like a pair of slim framed glasses. The video camera on the drone turned to focus on Rowland and his image appeared on the TV screen. "What do you want the authorities to do with the captured werewolves, Rowland? They have no cure for them, so filling up the hospitals with extremely dangerous patients who can't be treated is pointless, and they can't just put ankle bracelets on them and send them home."

"I'm more concerned with security," Tara said. "A single lapse and there could be a terrible incident. Having some civilian visitors and guards ripped apart would panic the public just when the tranquilliser darts that John is providing the police and armed forces is starting to turn the tide."

John shook his head. "I've studied their security, and it's as good as it can get without sealing the inmates into their cells. Basically the detention areas are completely separated from the public and administrative areas. They are being treated more like psychiatric patients than criminals, and those who show good control are allowed a great deal of freedom of movement within the detention areas." He sighed. "Although the media is putting a brave face on it, the rate of take down and capture of new werewolves isn't accounting for all the reported incidents and sightings, let alone the ones nobody sees. That means that a small percentage, the stronger, more intelligent ones more like Viktor, are disappearing into the population, or worse being recruited by Viktor's people."

"Then shouldn't we be doing something? We could go after Viktor again," Emily said.

Tara tossed her head in frustration. "You know I would love to have another chance at Viktor, but Commander Blair has warned us several times that there are many in the government and military who see us as a threat on par with the werewolves. A private war between us and the werewolves would give them the reason they need to put us on the take down list as well. All it would need is for one of us to accidentally hurt a bystander."

"Unfortunately, Tara is right. We have to let Viktor and his allies strike first and wait for Blair and his superiors to ask for our help … for now at least. I suspect that things are going to get much worse before long. Viktor isn't going to be content with skulking in the background. My contacts tell me that he has been creating a huge upheaval in the criminal underworld, but I doubt that he will be content with that. And we have our corporate friends in the US to consider. I think my warning will make them tread softly for the time being, but they will want to strike back eventually. Of course, none of this means that we don't prepare to defend ourselves."

Karen Duncan, the ex-mercenary and head of John's security force nodded. "The assault rifles and silver impregnated ammunition, plus the tranquilliser guns are in the armoury and the guards have started training on them. But per your orders they won't be issued unless there is an attack or threat." She rubbed the back of her neck. "I understand the need for the control of access, but I wish it wasn't necessary. All the guns in the world won't help if we can't get to them during a surprise attack."

John nodded. "Pick half a dozen of your people, the most steady and reliable. I'll set up a separate arms cabinet in the Security office that you and your number two can access. Just don't shoot anybody that I wouldn't."

Duncan grinned and saluted. "Yes sir. I'll try not to."

For a second, the faces of the thousands of brave and loyal soldiers who had saluted him, the man the world had known first as Vlad Tepes, and then as Dracula, over the centuries scrolled past his mind's eye. All of them dead now, many because of decisions that he had made. Then John smiled. "I'll hold you to that." Then he turned to Tara. "All of this ties back to the need to meet with the vampires."

"Is there a High Council, or Clan Elders?" Emily asked excitedly. John had been aggravatingly reticent regarding the other vampires in Britain.

John laughed. "Sorry to disappoint you. There are a few groups of ... well you could call them friends, there isn't any kind of organisation amongst the vampires. Most of those who have survived all the assorted perils of our situation tend to be introverts, although there are a few couples. The only reason I even have any contact with them at all is because of the synthetic blood substitute I invented and have been supplying free of charge to those who have agreed to refrain from attacking humans."

"Then how do you know they'll agree to help?" Tara asked.

"As a group, probably not. But I'm hoping some

will volunteer, out of self-interest if nothing else," John replied. "Have you ever been to Edinburgh?"

"That's where we're meeting them?" Tara asked.

"I've arranged for a product exposition and corporate convention there, which will provide a good excuse for us to travel and to meet with the public. Our vampire friends are understandably paranoid," he said. "We'll take the corporate jet, not the batplane."

Rowland groaned. His experimental aircraft was his pride and joy, second only to his daughter. "I wish you would stop calling her that. She's already been named."

John, who had been teasing the brilliant scientist, bowed. "I stand corrected. We shall not use the Vampire. We want to look like normal travellers, and landing an advanced jet in a field somewhere in Scotland won't help."

***

Jenny tapped the screen of her notebook's display. "That's the last item confirmed. Everything's ready to go, Viktor."

Viktor tapped his fingers against the arm of his chair. Because he had allowed his werewolf claws to form, his tapping produced a rapid and somewhat sinister clicking sound. "Not yet. We have one more thing to take care of."

"Tara?" Jenny said warily. She felt almost jealous over how often that bitch seemed to be on Viktor's mind.

Viktor nodded, seemingly unaware of Jenny's tone. "And her friends. If anyone can interfere with the plan it's them. Even they can't stop us, but they could prove to be an inconvenience. Besides, I just want to see the bitch's head hanging from a pole." He pressed his hands flat against the table. "And one more thing, Jenny …. "

With her mind focused upon the pleasant thought of decapitating the disgusting vampire woman who Viktor almost seemed to admire, she replied absently, "Yes, Vikt- "

Before she could finish her words, Viktor sprang up from his chair, changing even as he moved, his fur covered, and clawed tipped hand locking around Jenny's throat like a bear trap.

Jenny stiffened in terror, knowing that he could rip out her throat and decapitate her if she tried to change herself.

"Never insult me by using that tone, or insult me even more by thinking I wouldn't notice," Viktor growled into her ear, his head changing back enough for him to speak clearly. He gradually changed back to human, the hand around her throat changing last. Gripping her jaw he turned her around to directly face him. "Tara is going to die. Don't make me include you on that list."

Seeing that he wasn't going to kill her, Jenny licked her dry lips and smiled. "I was just jealous. I'm sorry. It won't happen again." She stiffened when the tip of his claw broke the skin just beneath her jawbone. The tiny wound healed inhumanly fast, but a single drop of blood ran down her neck to stain her blouse.

"I know it won't, my dear Jenny," Viktor said, his words a promise as well as acceptance of her apology. He took his hand from her neck and brushed the back of his hand down over the front of her blouse. "Now go and find out from our underworld informants what Tara is doing. This John Seward that she has befriended is rich and well connected. I think it best we arrange a convenient accident for them."

Jenny's smile was wide and almost sexual. "Yes, Viktor." She would have liked to feel Tara's throat in the grip of her fangs, but the vampire woman's death would have to do.

Chapter Two

"Join? Join what? I'm locked up in this giant hamster cage with no chance of parole." Ed slammed his fist against the thick glass-like perspex that separated him from his visitor. Due to the unusual status of the inmates the meeting rooms of the New Belmarsh Detention Centre were reminiscent of confessional booths, designed to provide privacy but also safety for the visitor in case the inmate suddenly changed into werewolf form.

"Calm down. We can't talk if you're drugged into a coma," the visitor, who had signed in as Ivan Ivanovich Ivanov, said nodding at the automatic injection device strapped to Ed's arm. Based upon the technology of the popular fitness watches, it monitored the wearer's pulse rate and triggered an injection of the werewolf tranquilliser whenever the wearer's heartbeat and blood pressure rose above a pre-set level. "You have friends outside. People who don't agree with the way you are all being treated."

"And these friends want to help me just out of the goodness of their hearts?" Ed said suspiciously.

"They want what you want. A chance for people with special abilities to be able to live in peace and freedom," Ivan said blandly.

"But?"

Ivan nodded, acknowledging Ed's unspoken question. "But nothing of such importance ever comes without the willingness to fight for it."

For a moment Ed's eyes flushed red. He looked around the compartment. Then his eyes narrowed. "What would I have to do?"

Ivan smiled. "Relax. The authorities have been very careful not to violate your civil rights more than they already have. There are no hidden listening devices or cameras. Several NGOs have verified it. And so have I."

He pulled a security scanner from his coat pocket and showed it to Ed. "For now, what I want you to do is to talk to the others. Find people who are willing to act to regain their freedom."

Ed raised an eyebrow. "Act?" He nodded towards the device on his arm.

"We'll take care of that. And you," Ivan said.

Ed began to smile.

***

"Private jets do have their advantages," Tara said as they drove away from the private terminal of Edinburgh Airport in the corporate limousine. She had noticed that John seemed to know the chauffeur by sight, a sign of how seriously he was taking matters of security. W.A.R Corporation had not taken any new hostile moves against them ever since John had paid their CEO a personal visit in the US, but that didn't mean they wouldn't try again.

"I would have thought that as a test pilot you've had your share of private flights," John said, even as his senses scanned the surroundings for observers and following vehicles.

"Only in prototype aircraft, and fighter jets aren't the height of luxury and comfort. When I and my father travelled it was normally by economy. How do we find the people we're supposed to meet at the Assembly Rooms?" Tara said.

"I've sent them all invitation cards to a private product briefing to be held in one of the smaller conference rooms. It will be all set up with Powerpoint displays and glossy brochures. They'll be able to stay hidden in the crowd until the meeting, and leave the same way," John replied.

Tara frowned. "You've taken a lot of precautions. Are you expecting trouble?"

He shook his head. "I'm simply being careful. I wouldn't put it past MI5 or some other spooks to have eyes and ears at the convention. I trust Commander Blair to be discreet, but he may have said enough to make somebody curious about us. I can't put the other vampires at risk by exposing them. And there is W.A.R. They might not be actively trying to kill us, but that doesn't mean they aren't watching."

***

Tara walked beside John through the grey stoned arch of the Edinburgh Assembly Rooms and into the cream and gold interior, filled with display boards, small booths, and banners, as well as visitors and convention goers with their lanyards and pass cards. The hall was filled with the hum of conversation and recorded voices coming from video displays. She could smell the scent of coffee and tea, pastries and sandwiches, which were being given out free to convention members and the public who had paid the entrance fee. She almost missed a step when her HUD sprang into life in front of her eyes, the combat information display active, a glowing green sphere indicating a globe of space around her, scaled to the size of the hall. In the centre of the display were icons representing John and herself, but in addition, there were four more glowing icons which she had come to recognise as signals from people bearing the alien medical nanite technology. "They're here. Four of them," she said softly to John.

He smiled as if responding to a joke. "Yes, I sense them too. The meeting room is that way." His smile faded and changed into a puzzled frown. "There's – " He spun around taking on vampire form even as he moved.

Tara had just noticed the "Incoming Missile" warning flashing on her HUD when John's shoulder hit her abdomen with pile driver force, lifting her off of her feet. The pressure didn't let up and she found herself flying backwards, knocking other visitors out of the way even as she and John shot through the doorway and out of the building at an angle to the entrance. She immediately realised what he was doing and allowed herself to go limp while simultaneously transforming into vampire form herself. Her feet had not yet touched the ground when the catering box filled with C4 explosive detonated. The stone and brick walls of the building were solid enough to channel most of the blast through the doors and windows, and if they had been directly in front of the door, even their amazingly tough and resilient vampire forms would have been burned and shredded by the heat and force of the explosion. Even then they might have survived, although the recovery would have been long and agonising and would have required a huge amount of blood, which might not have been forthcoming if they had been taken to a local hospital. As it was, both Tara and John were struck by granite fragments and the general concussion of the explosion flung them across the road. Tara rolled to her feet through sheer instinct, her ears ringing and blood dripping down over her eyes from a wound on her forehead. She realised that one sleeve and shoulder of her blouse and coat had been ripped completely off her body, exposing her bra. The flesh of her shoulder had not escaped unscathed, but despite the blood streaming down her back, her vampire body had prevented her arm from being ripped off entirely, and the wound itself was rapidly healing, while the medical implant was suppressing the pain that would have incapacitated her. Ignoring the dizziness she looked towards John, and cried out in horror at the raw and bloody wounds that covered one side of his body and the awful and unnaturally twisted shape of his spine. "John!" she cried, moving to kneel down beside him, ignoring her own wounds. She could see his body healing, but the wounds were so severe that it was happening agonisingly slowly, especially his broken spine.

His voice barely a whisper, John said, "Blood. Car …. " He stopped speaking to cough up blood and bits of tissue from lungs damaged by the overpressure of the explosion and broken ribs.

Tara barely heard him over the ringing in her ears, but realised he was telling her that there was a supply of artificial blood in their car. "Blood in the car. I understand. I'll be right back." She stood up, head ringing and still feeling wobbly, and slowly turned around towards their car, only to gasp in shock. The limousine had been parked on the cobbled car park space directly across from and facing the main entrance. The blast had flipped the vehicle on its back and its front end was a shredded tangle of metal and loose parts. When she bent down to peek into the passenger compartment, she saw that the windscreen had been smashed and hurled into the driver's face and body like a shotgun blast, ripping him into shreds of raw flesh. But the rear of the vehicle was still relatively intact. Although her ears were still stuffed with cotton wool, which she guessed was the result of damage to her ear drums, her sense of balance had recovered enough for her to run towards the car without staggering too wildly. With the car upside down and its front end smashed, it was tilted with its rear end touching the ground, which meant opening the boot would be a problem. She looked around to see if anyone was watching, but everybody's attention was focused on the broken and blasted building and the horrific casualties. Things had happened so quickly that there were still no sounds of sirens, simply the shouts, cries, and screams of both the injured and the people rushing to the scene to help or simply gawk and take videos. Squatting down, she jammed the diamond hard claws at the end of her fingers into the seam between the lid and the body of the car where she judged the lock to be and pulled downwards, while pushing against the car with her other hand. The metal creaked and groaned, and for a moment Tara feared that her claws would simply rip furrows through the thin steel. Abruptly, there was a loud metallic pop and snapping, and the rivets holding the lock broke free. She glanced around once more, then shifted her hands to the rear bumper and heaved as she straightened her legs, lifting the rear end of the car up into the air. The broken lid dropped and the contents of the boot spilled out and rolled onto the cobbled street. She let the car drop again when she was sure that all the luggage and cases had fallen out. Scanning the items spread across the ground, she rejected her own luggage and the ones she had seen John check in at the airport. That left two cases. One was long and metal with a lock, which she guessed contained weapons, and the other looked like a large picnic ice-box. A push of her hand revealed that it was filled with packs of liquid, and without further hesitation she snatched it up and dashed back to John with almost no stagger in her stride this time.

In the brief time Tara had been gone, John had healed sufficiently to be able to turn his head and smile at her when she dropped the container next to him. "Clever girl," he said, his breath wheezing from the cracked ribs and the one that had pierced his lung. The medical nanites were working to seal the puncture, and the rib was slowly easing out of the lung and back into its normal position, but for the moment the injury still hampered his breathing. He winced as his spine twisted and popped. Even the alien medical implant couldn't block all of the pain without shutting down his autonomic functions. Despite the agony, his smile widened when Tara ripped the top of the container off and brought a plastic sac of synthetic blood to his lips. Despite centuries of research, it wasn't as efficient as real blood in giving his body strength and healing, but for now it would do. He bit down on the tube-shaped outlet and sucked hard. The alien nanites greedily sucked up the nutrition, the building blocks they needed to do their restorative work, and most of the blood never even reached John's stomach.

Tara desperately fed bag after bag of the synthetic blood to her injured friend, mentor, and perhaps lover, and watched the miracle of his smashed and twisted body repair and rebuild itself faster than any living thing on Earth could accomplish – except the werewolves, the humans who had been given, or infected by, the medical nanites designed for the wolf-like aliens that had been the allies of the bat creatures, like Viktor, Tara's ex-test pilot, betrayer, and would be murderer.

John's body shuddered and convulsed, quivering and arching as if he had been subjected to a high voltage electric shock. With a series of fluid popping sounds his spine straightened and his legs kicked and flexed. "Ahh! That's better," he said, his voice sounding almost normal. "Help me up. We have to get out of here before we're noticed."

Tara didn't waste any time asking questions and helped John to stand up. She imagined a paramedic or reporter finding them and seeing their wounds visibly heal, although probably no one would believe it. His arm went around her shoulders and she used her inhuman strength to take most of his weight as they walked down the street away from the partially destroyed building and the terrible casualties. She knew the deaths had to be especially terrible for John because so many of them were his friends and employees. Legend would have people believe that Dracula was a heartless monster, but she knew he was fiercely loyal to those that depended upon him. It was fortunate that the main convention events had been scheduled to start only on the next day, today being reserved for the public and press, so the huge conference halls had not been packed with

23

attendees. "I wonder if any of the other vampires survived?"

John nodded. "The vampires who were meeting us were old ones. People like us only grow old if we are very hard to kill. They saw me moving and dived for the nearest door or window. I'm afraid that they might be less scrupulous in taking human blood if they need it under these circumstances, although none of them would deliberately kill, or I wouldn't have been dealing with them." He guided them into a doorway, glanced around, and then downed another packet of blood which he had pulled from a pocket of his ruined coat. By the time sirens and flashing lights filled the street and a military helicopter thumped and rumbled by in the air, he was walking normally and had donned a hoodie that Tara had managed to buy for him.

Tara had discarded her own ripped jacket and covered her ruined dress with a large pink t-shirt sporting images of small bright yellow creatures from a popular film franchise. John had taught her that being glaringly obvious was often the best form of camouflage.

When they had gone far enough to be out of the likely area that the police would be cordoning off, John took out his smartphone, a toughened and waterproof model designed by one of his companies for use by the military which had gratifyingly survived the explosion, and called for transport and a crate of more synthetic blood. Then he called the contact number for the vampire group that he had been supposed to meet. An anonymous voice at the other end informed him that all of the vampires at the meeting had survived, although one had been severely injured. He promised a fresh supply of synthetic blood and hung up. "Unsurprisingly, our friends are having second thoughts about working with us. However, it isn't hopeless. The attack probably served to demonstrate how serious the situation really is."

Tara voiced the question both of them had been thinking. "Who planted the bomb? Do you think it was the Americans?"

"I don't think so," John said, his eyes constantly scanning their surroundings for threats. "Mass destruction of this kind isn't their style. They're businessmen, and pissing off the British authorities for such an uncertain result doesn't make sense. They would have found a way to put a bomb in our car or even use a drone with a Hellfire missile. An assassination is quite different from a terrorist attack. I'm sure Werner could have found a way to make our government cover it up, but it would have meant using up influence and goodwill for no compelling reason."

"Then who ... Viktor! It has to be him. No one else knows enough about us to try something like this," Tara said. For a moment her eyes reddened in rage before she regained control of herself.

"It's possible the bomb was meant for me, either as John Seward, industrialist, or Dracula, but I suspect you're right. But why now?" He slammed a fist against the wall he was leaning against, cracking several bricks. "We need to find the people responsible for the bomb. Not just for vengeance, but for intelligence. Whomever they were targeting, no one would have done something like this without a very compelling reason unless they were insane, and whatever Viktor may be, he's definitely not mad."

Just then an unmarked and unremarkable car pulled up to where they were standing. The driver was a woman, who lowered the passenger window and said, "An old friend of the family."

Without looking in the direction of the car, John replied, "A sharpness on the neck." Neither the driver nor car belonged to any of his companies or employees.

The driver nodded and smiled. "I'm supposed to give you a ride. The package is in the back seat."

Tara, who had recently been studying all things vampire, recognised the passwords and chuckled as she got into the vehicle. "Really? Saberhagen titles?" The ride didn't take them very far at all, to the luxury shops of Multrees Walk, where she and John could clean up and obtain respectable clothing. A generous tip got her an emergency session with a hairdresser and her make-up redone, while John was similarly groomed. In hardly any time at all she was in a replacement corporate limousine identical to the one destroyed by the explosion, and they were headed back to the scene of the bombing.

The street in front of the Assembly Rooms was filled with emergency vehicles, firemen, paramedics, as well as police officers, many in tactical combat gear, and bomb disposal personnel, and was blocked off by yellow tape and armed officers. The presumption was probably that it was a terrorist attack. But as soon as John identified himself he and Tara were ushered through the perimeter to the mobile command centre that had been set up near to where the two of them had fallen after the blast. As John had guessed, the investigators focused on him and the reason why he had appeared to have suddenly departed from the convention just before the bomb went off. Since Tara wasn't officially an employee of John's businesses, she allowed them to assume that she was simply arm candy and was soon dismissed, allowing her to discreetly wander around much of the site of the attack. She watched as a group of explosives experts and crime scene investigators found and gathered up fragments which they suspected were part of the bomb. Acting bored and idly curious, she drifted close to the tent that was being used to gather the evidence. It was hard to ignore the screams and moans of the injured and the terrible scent of torn and ruptured bodies, but she forced herself to focus on the task at hand. She drifted behind a nearby van, and when there was no one in the tent she dropped to the ground and scuttled on all fours, lizard like, under the edge of the tent's side wall. Once inside she quickly scanned the various notes that lay around on the folding work tables before darting over to the gathered evidence, where she photographed whatever she could with her mobile phone. She was not an expert on explosives, but she did have a working knowledge of them that was necessary to safely test the weapons systems of her father's fighter aircraft. More importantly, she had an advantage over the police and military experts. She could actually smell not only the chemicals making up the explosives, but the scents that clung to the box and even the casing and components of the bomb itself. The bomb maker may have wiped off his fingerprints, but not his scent. Her vampiric sense of smell was even more keen than that of a dog and she quickly discerned the scent of two people, a man, whom she guessed was the bomb maker since the scent was older and clung to the internal components, and a woman, likely the person who had packed and delivered the device. Just as importantly, she detected a combination of scents from the location where the bomb was built, as well as the vehicle which transported it. She wished that John, who had vastly more knowledge and experience, could have done this part, but they were lucky to have had the opportunity at all. The sound of approaching footsteps made her drop to the ground and scuttle out of the tent. Her sonar told her no one was in a position to see her and she sprang upright. She brushed herself down and checked for grass stains and dirt before strolling casually back towards the command station. She arrived just in time to see John coming out of the tent and saw him turn to face her as if he had known she was coming up behind and to the side of him, which she knew he did. She waved and smiled, trying to look as clueless as possible.

John gave her a hug and a peck on the cheek as if

apologising for the inconvenience. "Find anything useful?" he asked as they walked back to the car.

Tara nodded. "A fragment of a label."

John glanced around as he spoke, searching for anyone who might be paying him and Tara more than normal attention. "The event security wouldn't have allowed a crate or package into the convention unless it was delivered by an approved vendor or caterer. Even if it was placed into a delivery by some outside party, knowing where it came from is a start. Anything else?"

Tara smiled. "A human scent. Male. From inside the box. It didn't match any scent on the outside of the box fragments or those of the investigators."

John's smile was as bleak as an Arctic wind. "Let's get to work then. I badly desire to have a … word with this person and his compatriots," he said as they walked past the ambulances and the triage tent, filled with torn and broken bodies. Rescue workers and sniffer dogs, along with bomb disposal and fire investigators were crawling all over the wreckage of the shattered main entrance to the building. One of the dogs passed close enough to catch his scent and it whined, puzzled by his odour and the rage that seemed to emanate from the strange human like a black flame. When it came to those who worked for him and looked to him for protection, John had not changed very much over the centuries from the Romanian warlord who had defended his people against the Turks and made his very name a thing of fear to his enemies, or the legendary aristocratic monster the world knew as Dracula. He looked out across the devastation and suffering and he vowed a terrible death to those who had caused this to happen. But as a medieval ruler he had also learned to hide his true feelings from the world so that they couldn't be used against him. Instead he put his arm around Tara's shoulder and looked shocked and sad, even though in his mind he could see a field of impaled bodies.

**

A check with the Edinburgh office of John's holding company quickly revealed that the logo belonged to a caterer with an office in Great King Street. After a quick stop at his Edinburgh apartment to change into less formal clothing and to pick up his own car, an Audi with a secret compartment under the rear seat that held a variety of weapons, John drove them to the caterer's office. The police investigators had already been there, so the manager was not surprised to have people asking questions. "Since the attack happened during an event organised and run by my companies, you can see why I want to know what happened and whether I should take any actions to protect my employees," John said to the manager, who was already worrying about accusations of working with terrorists and of potential law suits.

The manager was almost wringing her hands in distress, and was more than happy to cooperate. "As I told the police, this is just our office and where the administrative staff and planners work. We have a workshop and commercial kitchen at another facility to the north of the city. That's where the … package must have come from. But I can't believe that any of our people could have done such a terrible thing. We've never – "

John calmed her with an easy charm and said, "I'm sure no one thinks you have anything to do with this tragedy. But you must see that the more I know about the situation the better I can see to it that no adverse publicity or accusations come your way."

Despite the grimness of the situation Tara was amused. "You charmed the pants off of her in there."

John chuckled. "She was just looking for reassurance and for someone to tell her things would be all right."

"I'm sure the fact that you're tall, good looking, and rich didn't play any part at all," Tara said dryly. "So, did you get anything from her other than her telephone number?"

"As a matter of fact, I did," he replied, holding up several pieces of paper. "The address of the facility from where the box was transported to the convention, and a complete list of employees and their duties, as well as details of all their vehicles and the ones used in the delivery."

Tara nodded. "In case one is missing or there was an extra unidentified van or something."

"We don't know who might have been bought off or threatened into cooperation, or might be working for Viktor or whoever was behind this atrocity," John said as they got back into the car.

***

As the car neared the small stand-alone industrial facility Tara said, "There's a car parked at the side of the road about ten metres further down to the other side of the entrance of the place we're headed for. Her hawk-like vision zoomed in and she added, "The driver's holding a camera and there's a pair of binoculars on the dashboard."

"Then let's have a chat with him," John said, maintaining speed and driving past the facility as well as the parked car, carefully ignoring the watcher. He slowed the vehicle and nodded to Tara. "Go!"

Tara opened the door of the still moving vehicle and threw herself out, her inhumanly quick reactions and physical speed allowing her to land on the road and run towards the observer's parked car without stumbling. She heard John bring their car to a screeching halt behind her, but by that time she was already level with the observer's door, which she yanked open with a whoosh of rushing air.

The man inside the car was still trying to pick up a sawn-off shotgun from the seat beside him when Tara hauled him bodily from the vehicle. The shotgun went off, blasting a hole through the windscreen, and the recoil breaking the man's awkwardly angled wrist. His scream of shock and pain was abruptly cut off when he slammed against the ground, the impact knocking the breath out of him.

The weapon, and his readiness to use it was all the proof Tara needed that the man was no innocent bird watcher. She caught his fist when he tried to punch her in the throat and drove her fingertips into his sternum in retaliation, very carefully limiting her strength so that her hand didn't drive right into his chest cavity. It also took a conscious act of will not to extend her claws and rip him open as her vampire instincts wanted to, or to extend her fangs and bite out his throat.

The man grunted in pained shock, and went limp.

John ran towards them, keeping his speed to a human level just in case there were witnesses or cameras. He could see that Tara seemed to have the situation under control, but although she had accumulated a lot of unarmed combat experience since they had met, she still didn't have the training or field experience of a professional. Even the AI of the alien nanites linked to her implanted human combat control couldn't warn her of something her senses didn't detect or her mind and reflexes didn't correctly interpret – such as the knife the man beneath her was sliding out of the sheath inside the waistband of his trousers. He could have sprinted forward at full vampire speed and pinned the man's hand down before the knife was drawn, but instead he just yelled "Knife!".

Before she could lower her head far enough to see the man's hand and the handle of the blade, her vampire sonar involuntarily pulsed and her HUD lit up with an outline of the man's body and a red triangular threat icon flashed over the figure's hand. Her incessant training with John had taught her to make the best of her new strength and speed, as well as the muscle memory to use them effectively. Rather than trying to grapple with the man for the knife, her left hand shot straight down, the heel of her hand striking his shoulder joint with bone crushing force, something that would have been impossible for her before becoming a vampire. There was the sickening sound of breaking bone and tearing ligaments as her blow smashed his shoulder against the ground like a sledge hammer.

The man tried to scream in agony, but the sound was choked off by Tara's grip around his throat. His other hand went to her wrist but then went limp when he felt her claws puncture his skin. His employers had warned him that these people were dangerous, but he realised that they had grossly understated what he was facing. He turned his head to the side and threw up weakly, spat, and said, "I give up. Don't hurt me anymore."

By that point John was kneeling next to them and he pulled the man's knife out from the sheath and tossed it into the shrubbery that lined the road. "Any other weapons? If I find so much as a paper-clip I'll take your eyes."

The man took one look at John's face, groaned and said, "Ankle holster, left leg."

John's smile would have made a shark look for somewhere to hide. He tapped the man between the eyes with a fingertip, making him start and blink. "Wise choice." When he had retrieved the compact automatic pistol strapped to the man's ankle and emptied it of cartridges, he returned to stand next to the man's head, very deliberately looming over him and forcing the man to squint as he looked up towards the sky. "Now then. Who do you work for, and what are you doing here?

"I don't know. I got a call and picked up a package with details. Your photos and names. I was supposed to come here and wait. Find out what you knew and ... kill both of you. Money was transferred to one of my accounts. That's it," the man said.

In a blur of motion John dropped into a crouch, and grabbed the man's crotch. His claws extended, pierced the man's clothing, and dug into his genitals. "One more lie and you will lose your manhood. Now, a call from whom? I'd bet you don't have your number posted on social media. Think carefully before you speak."

The man was a professional. He would have taken a beating rather than betray his manager and his clients, but he was also a pragmatist. He didn't know what his captors were, but he had heard rumours of something or someone terrible who had torn through the toughest gangs in the underworld like they had been children, and he already knew these two weren't ordinary people. If he needed any further proof of that, he could feel what had to be claws digging into the flesh of his crotch and the familiar feeling of blood leaking from his flesh. The mental image of his genitals being ripped from his body made him shudder, and he didn't have to struggle hard to come to a decision. Jackson had put him in this shit, let him answer to these creatures, whatever they were. "Jackson. Jackson Smith. He's my agent and manager. He gets the jobs and negotiates the fees. If anyone knows something about the client, it's him. His number and address are in my phone. Right trouser pocket." He shuddered when the woman slit open his trousers with a razor-sharp claw and lifted his mobile out. "The details they gave me are in an envelope in the glove compartment. That's all I know, I swear."

Tara had been content to let John perform the interrogation, until she noticed the smell. It had been drowned out by the scent of the man's fear and blood, but now she caught it. "You were with the person who delivered the bomb." She knew she was right when the man's face grew even paler and a display of his vital signs, all revealing panic, popped up in her HUD. Although the alien medical system could only work with the information supplied by her own senses, except for very special circumstances involving other people who were also carrying the alien nano devices, it was able to analyse and interpret the data in a way that she could not have done without seeing all the readings set out in charts and numerical displays on a computer. John had developed this ability to detect lies and truth to an almost supernatural level, but she was rapidly learning too, aided by the ability of her father's nano interface to allow the alien nanites to communicate with her. "You were with the bomb and the man who delivered it. That means you know more than you're letting on."

The man yelped in shock and terror when he felt the clawed grip on his penis and testicles grip and wrench, accompanied by the sound of tearing fabric. "Wait! Wait! You didn't ask about the bomb. I was just the driver and helped with the heavy lifting."

"But you knew it was a bomb, didn't you?" Tara said, fighting not to let her fangs extend.

"I … yes, I knew." He felt John's grip tighten and he groaned when a panicked movement jarred his broken shoulder. "Don't! I can tell you where the bomb was made."

***

John glanced across the car at Tara as he drove down the road. "Don't worry, I'll have someone phone in an anonymous report. He'll be found and taken to hospital before anything really bad happens to him. Unless his employers send someone to find out why he hasn't reported in."

Tara shook her head, still frowning. "That's not it.

34

He was party to a massacre and nearly the deaths of both of us. I could care less what happens to him now. And that's the problem."

"Ah yes, I think I see. It's what you wanted to do that bothers you." John took his hand off of the wheel to touch her hand. "The desire for vengeance and retribution is very human. The more power you have, the greater the temptation to indulge in it. It doesn't require alien technology meddling with your mind and body to create that urge. But the fact that you didn't do it speaks well for your humanity."

"But what if I – " Tara said.

John cut her off. "You may make mistakes, but the fact that you're asking these questions shows that you're going to do the right thing." His fingers tapped the steering wheel and his brow furrowed in thought. "We're going to have to split up, now that we have two leads to follow. Since you have the bomb maker's scent, you should take the place in Leith Walk, and I'll pay a visit to Jackson Smith."

Tara couldn't completely forget her misgivings, but she knew John was right and that they had to strike back swiftly before their leads grew cold. Besides, if she was going to hurt anyone, it would be the person that had made the bomb. Suddenly her doubts faded and were replaced by a fierce, predatory anticipation. She wasn't sure if it was her or the alien creature's instincts, and she honestly didn't care.

***

It wasn't hard for John to find Mr Jackson Smith. His supposed business consultancy firm had its office in Hill Street, which was close enough to the Assembly Rooms to have heard the explosion. It was harder for John to find a parking space, but he finally did and strolled down the street which was lined by plain grey stone buildings, many of which displayed discreet company logos. As he walked he debated with himself over the best way to approach Mr Smith. Since the job details had been collected directly by Parker, the gunman they had questioned, it was likely that Smith wouldn't know who he was by sight. That being the case, he could simply walk into the man's office and talk to him. Being a modern industrialist and not a medieval warlord, it behoves him not to leave a trail of dead bodies in his wake. It wouldn't be politically correct in the most literal sense. If he was recognised however, then he would revert to the old ways. That thought made him smile. He strolled briskly up to the correct doorway, entered, and followed the sign on the wall up the stairs to the first floor. The plastic sign on the door told him that he had found the right place. He knocked once and pushed the door open without waiting for a response. Stepping into the office, he smiled urbanely at the startled looking secretary. It was obvious that the so-called consultancy didn't entertain many walk-in customers. "Good afternoon. My name is Seward, and I have a business proposition for Mr Smith."

The secretary, who was female and looked as if she spent a lot of time at the gym said, "Is Mr Smith expecting you?"

"No, but he'll want to see me, I assure you," John said. He had spotted the tiny video camera above the inner doorway as soon as he had entered the room and he looked up at the lens.

The secretary's telephone buzzed and she picked it up. "Yes, Mr Smith," she said into the mouthpiece and stood up as she returned the handset to its cradle. "Mr Smith will see you, Mr Seward. Please go in."

John nodded to her and went to the door. His nostrils flared minutely and he smiled as he went past the secretary and pushed down on the door handle. The ultrasonic pulses of his vampire sonar gave him a three hundred and sixty degree image of his surroundings and he effortlessly detected the woman moving silently up behind him, her right arm extended towards his back. As soon as he was through the doorway he darted to the side in a blur of speed. His left hand shot out and gripped the woman's wrist. His fingers clamped down with bone crushing force and he caught the small snub-barrelled revolver with his right hand as it fell from her nerveless fingers. He yanked hard on her arm and the woman flew diagonally across the room to smash against the wall. She rebounded from the solid brick surface and fell limply to the floor.

Open mouthed in shock, Smith's hand dipped into his desk drawer where a heavy automatic pistol, a .40 calibre Beretta 96, lay on a velvet pad. His shocked silence became a scream of agony when his forearm was raked by knife-like claws that cut through the sleeve of his coat and sliced skin and muscle to ribbons.

"I think you have something to tell me," John said, touching his bloodied claws to the man's cheek. He would have settled for simply asking questions or even paying the man for information, but he couldn't deny that he was happy it had worked out this way.

Smith whimpered and wet himself when he saw the fangs.

***

Tara knew that she didn't have the option to simply walk up to her target. Not unless she wanted to enjoy the effects of a second explosion in the same day. Simply kicking the door down was out as well for the same reason. If the bomb maker was at home and working, a sudden shock like the appearance of a vampire might cause an unfortunate accident. She would have to be sneaky. Fortunately, the premises at Leith Walk turned out to be a huge old abandoned station building set right beside the road, and the iron gate and wall enclosing it had no barbed wire, so access wasn't a problem, not that barbed wire would have hindered her anyway. It would have been better if she could have waited for nightfall, but she had no idea whether the bomb maker would still be there, or if the site might already have been cleared of all useful evidence by then, so she couldn't afford the time. There wasn't a lot of pedestrian traffic near the dilapidated red brick building, so there was little chance of being observed. The entrances on the ground level were too exposed for her to risk, so she decided to make her entry from an upper storey window or the roof. When she was sure there was no one looking she sprang up and over the rusty gate and into the grounds, landing silently on the grass and gravelly soil. She dropped low and darted over to press herself against the wall of the huge building. There were large arched windows lining the side of the abandoned station and all temptingly void of glass, but the risk of being spotted was too great, especially since she didn't yet know how many people were inside. She went still and listened, filtering out the ambient noises in her mind. She had discovered that her sonar could work even when she couldn't project bursts of ultrasonic sound due to an obstruction like the very solid wall in front of her by passively analysing the sounds of her environment. It was far less effective and the images were just crude blobs, but it could detect moving bodies well enough to be useful. This mode wasn't actually something new or different and had always been part of her bat-like sonar, but she had previously not thought to use it this way, the bursts of ultrasonic sound coming instinctively. After several minutes of concentration she was fairly sure that there were three people inside, and from the way they were moving she guessed that they were packing up. It seemed that she had arrived just in time. She dropped to the ground on all fours, arms and legs outstretched like a lizard and scuttled rapidly past the gaping, broken windows and around to the rear of the building. An adjoining building had been demolished, leaving the corner of the building jagged and irregular, providing the perfect climbing surface. She could have climbed a smooth concrete wall, but now she went up the wall in a four-limbed sprint, hidden from any observers in the street or across the road. Seconds later she was perched on the roof like a gargoyle and she peered down into the cavernous interior. To her surprise she discovered that the bomb makers had set up a large yellow marquee or tent inside, and just a moment later she detected the scent from the bomb materials that matched the residue at the site of the attack. There was only one person in sight, loading boxes onto a warehouse trolley. When he disappeared into the tent she went down the inner wall, moving so fast that she was almost in free-fall. Her claws left deep pits in the old brick as she slowed at the last minute and dropped silently behind the tent.

"How much longer before you're finished? We need to get out of here before the pigs find us," said a man's voice from inside the tent.

Tara's sonar allowed her to pinpoint the positions of the three occupants of the tent, two standing and one sitting at some kind of work bench. There were lights inside the tent, but no sign of any connection to a power supply or generator, so they had to be using battery powered lighting. That meant a surprise attack in a sudden darkness was out. She smiled. She was in the mood for some gratuitous violence anyway, at least as far as these mass murderers were concerned. She edged her way around until she was at the side of the tent and the work table wouldn't be an obstruction, and then darted under the bottom edge of the tent wall. She was spotted almost immediately and sprang at the man standing closest to the entrance.

The large burly man shouted wordlessly in alarm

and grabbed for the pistol in the holster clipped to his belt, but he was far too slow. His cry turned into a gruesome gurgle when knife-sharp claws ripped his throat open and sent him spinning towards the floor in a spiral of crimson spray.

The second standing man had the time to draw his gun, a battered looking revolver, but Tara was on him before he could raise his weapon. She had hesitated for a fraction of a second, fighting the urge to rip out the man's throat with her fangs, and to disembowel him with an odd raking movement of her claws, which she realised was the natural method of attack of the alien bat creature for which the medical nanites had been intended. In her white-hot rage she had almost given in to the desire, the raw need, to rip her opponent apart like a prey animal. She was willing to kill if necessary, but not to give in to such mindless impulses. Instead, she grabbed his hand and squeezed it hard against the metal of the gun, until she heard his bones crack. But before she could grab the man's throat to finish him, her sonar and the alien technology in her body made her twist her torso sharply, even while her HUD flashed an "Incoming Fire" warning. She felt a sharp tug at her sports jacket and a momentary searing pain across her chest just below her left breast before the nanites neutralised the pain and began to heal the wound. If the semi-intelligent nanites had not dampened her hearing at the same time, she would have been deafened and stunned by the explosive roar of the pistol that had fired the bullet. Her hand shot out to drive the heel of her palm into her opponent's chest, cracking his ribs and extracting an agonised grunt from the man. She pulled him around like a dance partner, putting his body between the gun and herself. A darting glance around his body revealed that the seated bomb maker was a woman, who snarled and fired again, the bullet hitting the man squarely in the back and remaining lodged inside his body. Tara placed both her hands against the badly injured man's chest and shoved with all her augmented strength, sending his body hurtling and flailing backwards like a rag doll towards the bomb maker. She threw herself forward, desperate to get to the bomber before the woman could recover from having the man's entire weight slam down on top of her, and possibly detonate the explosives on the table.

The bomber was viciously determined. She thrust her pistol around the body of the man that crushed her against her chair and fired blindly in Tara's direction.

Tara dodged the wildly fired bullets and snatched the pistol from the woman's hand, ripping off the bomb maker's finger when it became caught in the trigger guard. Tara ignored the raw bloody groove on her chest, trusting the nanites to handle the injury. She hauled the dying man's body off of the woman. "We need to have a chat." The woman's scent confirmed that the bomb that had gone off at the Assembly Rooms had been her work.

Using her left hand the bomb maker snatched a thick cylinder from the breast pocket of her overalls. Her thumb mashed down on the red button at the top end. "Touch me and I'll blow us both up! This is a dead-man's switch connected to the detonator in five kilogrammes of C4 on the table. You broke my hand, bitch! I should blow you to hell," she said, her knuckles white around the device.

Tara didn't have the experience that allowed John to tell if someone was lying better than any lie-detector, but in this case her gut and her heightened senses told her the woman was bluffing. Rather than grabbing for the detonator, her hand shot out and she dug her claws into the woman's belly, causing five circular spots of blood to stain the fabric of the bomb maker's overalls. She leaned her face closer and willed her fangs to extend. "Go on. Let it go. But if nothing happens I'll rip your guts out and leave you here to die. Just remember that I've already survived one of your bombs. Well?"

The woman went pale as she stared into Tara's red tinted eyes. "Wh-what are you?"

Tara smiled, baring her fangs even more. "Do you really want to find out?"

The woman slowly shook her head, her hand and the dead-man's switch starting to tremble. Her every instinct screamed that she was facing something totally inhuman, a nightmare made real. She sighed and took her thumb off of the button. "It's not connected to anything. I didn't have time to set up a remote detonator. Don't kill me. I'm just doing what I was paid to do."

Hiding her relief, Tara said, "Tell me everything you know about the people who hired you and about their plans. Your bomb killed a lot of innocent people today and you really need to give me a reason not to hurt you very very badly." She didn't need to fake the rage she felt and the powerful desire to tear this person limb from limb, and her sincerity blazed from her eyes.

The woman shook her head desperately. "You don't know who you're dealing with! If I talk they – " Her shrill agonised screamed filled the tent when her captor pulled her uninjured hand up and out with irresistible force, and bit off her thumb.

Tara spat out the bloody digit and snarled. "I don't care. If you don't talk, I'm going to tear you apart right now, starting with your fingers and hands." She felt slightly shocked at her own viciousness, but she was too angry to care. The memory of John crawling painfully on the ground with a broken spine made her want to do terrible things to this mass killer, and for the first time she thought she dimly understood the impulses that had made John infamous as Vlad The Impaler. She didn't even realise that her face had twisted into a fanged horror mask.

Staring aghast at her mutilated hand and the inhuman visage looming above her, the bomb maker nodded convulsively. "A-anything … I'll … don't hurt me …. "

***

"What did you do with the bomb maker?" John asked. They were seated in a private meeting room in the Edinburgh office of his holding company, with tea and sandwiches prepared by a private chef on the polished table.

Tara sighed. "I tied her up and then called the police with an anonymous tip after I managed to find a public telephone. I … I was really tempted to …. "

"Take matters into your own hands?" John said softly. When she nodded he reached out and took her hand. "But you didn't. Which probably makes you a better person than I."

Tara looked up. "You mean you – "

John nodded, remembering with satisfaction the look on Smith's face when he had used the coat stand as an impromptu impaling stake. At times his concept of justice was still quite old fashioned. "He was the willing participant in an atrocity. He confessed as much and his records confirmed it." They had both made notes regarding what they had individually discovered and John tapped the papers on the table. Though the details varied, both their notes had one name in common – Roy Brodie. John had called a friend in the police for a favour and soon possessed a copy of the man's record. When he and Tara read it, something immediately stood out. Until a few months ago he had been just an ordinary low-level criminal. He had shown signs of being ambitious and on his way up, but still a long way from being a real player in the underworld. Then abruptly he was the head of one of London's biggest firms, with hardly a ripple being caused. No gang war, no burned drug houses, nothing. "This Brodie person obviously has powerful support.

43

Powerful enough to overcome any competitors."

"Viktor!" Tara said, speaking the name as if it had a bad taste. "In which case it means he, Viktor, is up to something more than being a run-of-the-mill criminal. Something bad enough to justify mass murder as a distraction."

Chapter Three

"The bomb failed, and Brodie says he's lost contact with the bombers, so it looks like the second bomb isn't going to be planted at Tara's hotel," Jenny said, not trying to hide her disappointment.

Viktor chuckled. "Don't look so gloomy. I didn't have very high hopes that the bomb would actually rid us of those two, although hopefully they were hurt … a lot. Tara has proven herself annoyingly hard to kill. But it will make them angry and preoccupied with hunting down those responsible for the attack, which means they won't be looking in our direction until it's too late.

"What if they find their way to Brodie?" Jenny asked.

Viktor's grin was more a baring of fangs. "Then we'll find out if he's the right man to hold his position." He leaned forward, elbows on the table to either side of the steaming cup of coffee Jenny had just made him. "And what about the main event? Where are we with the Belmarsh recruitment?"

Jenny tapped on the screen of her notebook computer with a flourish. People who knew she had been a prostitute before meeting Viktor were always surprised that she was very good with computers and was an avid gamer. "We have the two main teams filled, and enough volunteers for the secondary teams. Our own people are prepared to move on Belmarsh. We're ready to go," she said with an almost sexual excitement. Blood turned her on.

Viktor chuckled. "Patience, Jenny. After all, we can't interfere with tradition, can we?" Viktor said.

Jenny's laugh was a predatory growl. "No, of course not. We'll just kill the fuckers. Kill them all."

***

"That's a nice house," Tara said. "At least what I can see of it," she added as the car drove slowly along the opposite side of the road to the Georgian style mansion in Murrayfield. In the distance, the towers of Edinburgh Castle were visible. The secluded mansion sat in the middle of a generous patch of land. Although there were no armed guards in black suits and dark glasses like in the films, there were discreet security cameras and motion detectors covering the approaches to the mansion and undoubtedly guards and alarms inside. However, the wooded grounds bordering the property on two sides made it easy to approach. It also meant less nosy observers.

John's eyes went wide and dark as his vision zoomed in on the details of the mansion while his inhumanly amplified and sensitive hearing scanned his surroundings, listening to frequencies ranging from the supersonic to subsonic, and building up images of his surroundings in his mind like a three-dimensional sonar which was immensely better than anything human technology had managed so far. "I think the roof is the best option for an unseen approach. Much as I would enjoy it, kicking down the door isn't a viable choice in this case, not if we want to keep Victor ignorant of our efforts. I'm sure he has considered the possibility that we might find out about Brodie, but he can't be certain of it."

"Do you think it's a trap then?" Tara asked, her eyes narrowing as she studied their immediate surroundings. She wouldn't put it past Viktor to somehow have arranged for land mines to be placed under the approaches to the mansion. When she didn't find anything her mind focused on what he had just said. "The roof? How are we going to … oh!"

He nodded. "Do you think you're up to it? You can wait here if you don't feel confident about a flight."

The mention of flying woke Tara's test pilot

instincts. For as long as she could remember she had wanted to fly, and the risks were just a normal part of it as far as she was concerned. Shaking her head she said, "I'm not going to just lurk in the bushes." She raised an eyebrow and stared at him accusingly. "But you knew that already, didn't you?"

John just smiled, and then looked up at the sky. "We'll wait a little longer. The sky will be a bit greyer then and we'll be harder to spot."

Tara looked down at herself. "Um, what about – " she said, pointing at her clothes.

"Tie them in a bundle and we can carry them with us," John said and chuckled. "I've had to abandon my garments on more than one occasion. I remember often meeting some rather surprised ladies where I landed."

She sniffed. "I bet you did that on purpose."

"Would the Prince of Darkness do such a thing?" he said, avoiding a reply. "I think the gloom is sufficient for our purposes."

Tara sighed and began to undress. "You're enjoying this, aren't you," she said accusingly.

"Beauty should be admired," John said with a slight bow. Then he joined her in taking off his clothes and tying them into a bundle along with his shoes. "Are you ready? You go first, so that I can keep an eye on you."

"I bet you will," Tara said, rolling her eyes. Then she let her test pilot persona assume control and focused upon the feeling of changing and taking to the air. Nothing happened. But she was acutely aware of John's eyes watching her and she refused to admit failure. She focused and concentrated so hard that she felt close to blacking out, and her body shook as if she had Malaria. Then totally without warning she felt every fibre of her being twist and change. She managed to snatch at the bundle of clothes with the elongated toes and claws that now tipped her feet, and then she was soaring up into the air. There was a moment of vertigo, the fear of falling, and then alien instincts took over, and she was flying. Her sonar, which seemed even more sensitive and powerful, told her that John was flying just behind and above her, ready to grab her body if she fell. But the air was her medium, the place where she had always felt most alive, and with the aid of the alien technology in her bloodstream and the human nano interface in her brain, it was like she was flying an invisible version of her father's aircraft. Her arms stroked the air with a power and flowing grace that she didn't even have to think about, while the wind rushed past her face and into eyes that were now protected by nictating membranes. She fought the urge to climb higher or to dart around in a jinking, unpredictable pattern and flew straight for the roof of the mansion. Her sonar and amplified binocular vision gave her the precise distance from the grey tiled surface and the vertical boxes of the chimneys. Her clawed feet touched down and gripped, while her arms and wing membranes flapped to fight the momentum that threatened to throw her off the edge of the roof. A moment later she sensed John landing beside and up-slope of her. There was a repeat of the strain and near panic as she tried to change back to human form, and then a fresh panic when her centre of gravity rapidly altered and rose, which nearly caused her to slip and topple because her bare foot was resting on the bundle of her clothing. She dropped onto all fours for balance, feeling silly with her naked bottom in the air, especially with John watching her. Gingerly lowering herself into a sitting position she got dressed, pretending to ignore the inhuman, but nonetheless handsome legend sharing the roof with her, but unable to resist preening a little anyway. She shocked herself when she realised that she rather hoped he liked what he saw, followed by a rush of insecurity about how her body looked. Men staring at her figure had never bothered her before because she had never cared. When she looked over her shoulder John was already dressed, and the look on his face made her blush. "How do we get in?" she said, changing the unspoken subject. "I'm not going down a chimney, if that's what you're thinking."

John held his finger to his lips and then went down on all fours as well. He crawled across the roof until he reached the edge where it dropped down to an inset balcony which served a room built into the loft. Peeking over the edge, he saw that there were French doors which led into the interior. He closed his eyes and listened, tilting and turning his head slowly from side to side like a curious dog. If there had been anyone in the room he would have heard their heart beat, and he was about to signal for Tara to join him when he heard the inner door open. It was followed by the sounds of two people, which he guessed to be one male and one female. He heard the woman gasp, followed immediately by the sound of a body hitting the floor, and then the door closed again with a click of a lock. He continued to listen, and unless the man was standing absolutely still and not breathing, it seemed that only the woman was inside. Then there was the sound of movement and more gasping, but no footsteps. John cautiously lowered his upper body over the edge and peeked, only to find his eyes meeting those of the woman, who was staring at him in surprise through the French windows. Her hands were tightly tied behind her back, which explained why she hadn't gotten up off the floor yet. He held his finger to his lips and then made a "wait" signal with his palm. When she nodded he pulled himself back up onto the roof and waved to Tara.

She crawled silently over to his side, and listened as he explained the situation, speaking in an ultrasonic frequency inaudible to normal humans. She nodded and peeked over the edge as well to exchange glances with the increasingly confused woman inside the room. She looked at John, and when he nodded back, both of them sprang lightly and almost silently onto the balcony. The tall glass-paned doors were locked, but John stopped her before she could use her vampiric strength to break the lock.

John pointed at a set of small metallic contacts between the leaves of the doors. "Alarm," he said ultrasonically. He extended a single claw and used it to unseat four of the glass panes and snapped the wooden frames separating them, leaving a hole large enough from them to step through. He scanned the floor in front of the hole and then the ceiling, searching for pressure or movement sensors, but there was nothing, so he stepped through and strode swiftly past the bound woman to the inner door. He pressed his ear to it and listened for any indication that there was a guard outside, but he heard nothing. He nodded to Tara and silently gestured to the bound woman and then at the door. He didn't use ultrasonic speech because the bound woman would see their lips move, and that would only serve to confuse her more.

Tara immediately understood that he wanted her to distract the captive while he broke the door lock. Kneeling down, she smiled reassuringly and lifted the woman into a sitting position, making sure that she was facing away from both John and the door.

"P-please don't hurt me," the woman said, obviously shocked and terrified.

"Don't be afraid. We're the good guys," Tara said, pretending to study the handcuffs that held the woman's wrists. Behind her she heard the crunch of snapping metal and breaking wood.

"Are you the police?"

"Not exactly. You could say we're private investigators. The owners of this house are bad people. How did you end up here?" Tara extended a claw to shim the ratchet of the handcuffs, letting the cuff slide open.

"I don't know! I'm not rich and I don't work in a

50

bank or anything," the woman replied in a desperate tone. "They just snatched me off the street. I haven't been raped either."

"Were they wearing masks?" Tara asked

"No, they weren't," Monica said. Then her eyes widened. "They were going to kill me, weren't they?"

When the handcuffs came off Tara helped the woman over to a chair and stroked her shoulder soothingly. "Why don't you tell me your name and what you do," she suggested. The woman wasn't unattractive, but not so young and beautiful as to inspire a major criminal like Roy Brodie to bother kidnapping her solely for her sexual appeal. If Brodie was working for Viktor, then she wanted to know why Viktor needed this woman.

The woman wiped her nose with the back of her hand, sniffed, and said, "My name is Monica. Monica Dobson. I'm just a tour guide from London. I'm on leave, visiting a friend in Edinburgh."

Over the woman's shoulder Tara saw John open the door and peek out into the landing and down the stairs. Returning her attention to the woman, she ran her fingers through her hair in puzzlement and asked, "Tour guide? What kind of tours? Do you visit anything valuable? Art collections or jewellery?"

Monica shook her head. "Nothing like that. I just do the Main Hall."

John's head popped back into the room. "We need to learn more," he said to Tara, pointing down stairs.

Tara gripped Monica's shoulder. "Stay here. We'll be back and we'll get you out of here."

"Can't we just go now?" Monica asked.

"Too much security covering the grounds. You'd never make it out without being detected, and we'd lose the element of surprise. Trust us." Tara said. She smiled when Monica nodded and followed John out into the dark hallway. The sun had gone down and the house was a patchwork of bright light and deep shadows. She moved silently down the stairs, her sonar making her movements sure and graceful.

John signalled for Tara to halt at the bottom of the stairs. There was another door at this point and once again he listened. When he didn't hear anything he tested the lock, which opened smoothly under his hand, and stepped out like a shadow sliding across a wall.

Tara followed, and then tapped him on the shoulder. It still felt odd to speak in ultrasonic frequencies and she had to concentrate so as not to drop back into her normal voice. "We can't just peek and run now. Brodie will know something is wrong if Monica disappears." Then her brow furrowed. "But if Viktor loses touch with Brodie and his people, he'll still know something is wrong."

"Let's reconnoitre first. Then we'll do whatever's necessary," John replied.

***

Roy Brodie stood with his hands behind his back, staring out of the window into the well-manicured grounds which were now lit by banks of artificial lights. When he heard the door open he said, "What is it Charlie? Have you heard from – " His eyes narrowed when he saw the reflection of the person behind him. Whoever it was, he could tell that it definitely wasn't Charlie. Keeping his hands clear of his body, he slowly turned around. "You're much better looking than Charlie. Is he still alive?" He tensed imperceptibly when he recognised her face. This was the woman that Viktor had warned him against, and the same one that the clearly incompetent specialists he had hired were supposed to have killed with the bomb. Viktor hadn't specified what made this woman dangerous, so although he didn't see a gun, or hair and fangs like Viktor and his disgusting crew, he wasn't inclined to be rash.

Tara could have rushed in and put the man down before he was even aware of her presence, but there was no guarantee that he wouldn't have been killed or seriously injured in the process. John had favoured that approach, but she had convinced him to let her try talking to the man first. "If you mean the man who was guarding the door, he's a bit worse for wear but still alive. Both of you can remain that way if you're reasonable."

Brodie casually lowered himself into his chair. There was a pistol in the half open desk drawer next to his left hand, but he didn't reach for it. However, he did press the concealed button beneath the arm rest of his chair which sent out an alarm to all his men in the house. "So what can I do for you? It must be something important for you to take all this bother just to see me."

Tara raised an eyebrow as she took a step closer to him. "It seems to me that you came knocking at my door first. Rather loudly too."

Brodie smiled. "Ah, that. Well, I suppose I could say that I was only doing someone a favour, but I don't suppose that would make any difference. Since you're here, I take it that I won't be making use of that particular contractor again?"

"She's alive, if that's what you mean," Tara said. "But I think she'll be out of circulation for quite a while. The authorities take a rather dim view of terrorists." She returned the smile. "But just because I didn't kill her, or your bodyguard, it doesn't mean I won't take great delight in killing you."

The muffled crack of gun shots filtered through the door and Brodie's smile widened. "I think that means your friends outside are dead or dying." He snatched for his gun, lifted it, and fired twice across his polished desk.

But Tara had been expecting something of the sort, and she hadn't been distracted by the fear that John had been killed. He wasn't immortal, but it would take more than a few low-level thugs to kill Dracula. She was moving around the table even as the gun fired, the bullets zipping past her side and smashing into a bookshelf next to the doorway, sending books and torn paper flying in a cloud of dust. It appeared that Brodie didn't read very much. It was hard, harder than she expected, not to tear into him with fangs and claws. She could smell his fear and anger, and her fangs itched in anticipation of the sweet copper taste of blood. But she wasn't like Viktor, or the other werewolves. Human or bat, she was a thinking, civilised being. It took all of her will and self-control, but she halted her plunge towards his throat and slapped the gun from his hand. She didn't want him injured. At least not now.

To Brodie it had all happened in a confusing blur. In one moment he had aimed and fired at the centre of the woman's chest, and in the next his hand was stinging, and his gun was half-way across the room, while the Tara woman was looming over him, an inhuman look of rage twisting her features. For a second he thought he had seen fangs, but when he blinked they were gone. He tried to push himself back and away from the table, so he could stand up, but a slap that twisted his head around made him slump in his chair, the room spinning crazily around him. He fell out of the chair, but he wasn't one to give up so easily. Hidden by his body he drew a folding knife which was clipped to his trouser pocket and flicked it open while pretending to be more stunned and disoriented than he really was. Through half-open eyes he watched the woman approach and when she was close enough he threw himself over and slashed at her with the razor-sharp blade, using all his strength and momentum to whip the edge across her throat.

He caught her totally by surprise and if it had not been for the accelerated reflexes of her vampire state combined with the military grade alien nanites, her throat would have been slashed wide open. As it was, she felt a brief, intense sting where the steel edge sliced her skin as her body pulled back in an involuntary motion. But the very force of the man's slashing motion left him open, and the knife dropped to the floor when she grabbed the back of his hand, sharply bent his wrist and pulled his arm towards herself with the sound of tearing tendons. With carefully controlled force she slammed the heel of her palm into his sternum.

The blow drove all the breath from Brodie's lungs, making him turn green and retch. But he still didn't give up and grabbed her arm, trying to use his superior weight and strength to wrestle her down onto the floor with him.

The man's superior mass might indeed have dragged her down, but Tara braced her knee against the ground and wrenched his left hand away from his grip on her other arm. Fed up with Brodie's stubbornness, she twisted his hand around with superhuman speed and force, breaking his hand and wrist with a sickening snap and crunch of carpal bones. "Unless you want me to do the same to your other wrist as well as your ankles, stop struggling. I just want to have a civilised chat with you. You'll regret it if you piss me off further."

The grim expression on the woman's face, along with the agony that racked his entire body, especially his chest and wrists, convinced him to capitulate. He nodded reluctantly. "I give up. I swear."

John had silently entered the room and now leaned over the man's head. "You know why we're here. Tell me all you know, and I might consider being merciful. I warn you not to lie to me."

Brodie shrugged. "Someone asked me to do them a favour. People ask me for favours all the time," he said.

John sighed. "I warned you not to lie."

Brodie sneered. "Sod off. I'm not afraid of you. You two are the walking dead. Just as soon as my people find you."

Speaking to Tara in ultrasonic tones, John said, "Tie him up while I search the room. It will be easier to question him if we know more." He ripped a curtain down and tore the fabric into strips as if it was paper. He saw his reflection in the glass of the window and grinned. It would have been truly inconvenient if vampires actually didn't have reflections. Just one more bit of misdirection he had suggested that Mr Stoker place in his book. He handed the makeshift ropes to Tara then turned to searching Brodie's desk. None of the documents on the desk top or in the drawers were of much interest, although he found an expensive hunting knife to supplement the gun. "I need the password for this notebook." He heard Brodie utter an obscenity which was cut off by a scream of pain, followed by the grudgingly given password. "Thank you." He rapidly went through the notebook's hard disk, his fingers a blur on the keyboard. It would have been an easier job with the assistance of the computers, hackers and technicians in his employ, but he suspected that they didn't have much time. He had been a keen student of computer technology since the science's baby steps in the second world war, and combined with his inhuman abilities, he was able to strip all the information from the device at seemingly impossible speed, transferring files to a thumb drive and making written notes. When he was done, he frowned and began looking around the room again. Although Brodie was unaware of it, John was using his sonar in a very focused and concentrated form to search the walls for signs of a cavity.

Brodie, his hands tied behind him and his ankles bound together, watched in amazement when John got up and walked over to a glass cabinet mounted on the wall that appeared to be a display case for a small sculpture. "What are you doing? Be careful, that thing's valuable."

John ran his fingers around the wooden back of the

transparent case, and smiled when he found a small circle of metal that could have been mistaken for the head of a nail. But when his finger touched it, the cabinet clicked and swung away from the wall on concealed hinges to reveal a wall safe. The safe was secured by an old-fashioned dial and not a biometric scanner or key pad. "What's the combination?"

"Fuck you!" Brodie said, hiding his dismay.

"The hard way it is then," John said, unperturbed. He leaned closer to the door and turned the dial. Even without a stethoscope or more modern device the clicks of the tumblers were perfectly clear to him, and a minute later the door swung open.

Jaw gaping in amazement, Brodie said, "How the fuck did you do that? Who are you people?"

Ignoring Brodie's questions John rifled through the contents of the safe. He found many documents that would have been of interest to the police, but nothing that related to his immediate concerns. However, he also found a high capacity thumb drive. He turned and held it up. "What's in this, I wonder," he said. His vision zoomed in on Brodie's face, and the man's apprehension was unmistakable, at least to him. "I wonder … " He plugged it into the notebook and nodded when a window popped up demanding a password. He glanced at Brodie, who grinned triumphantly back at him. "Yes, I know, fuck me." He switched to ultrasonic frequencies and said, "We need to see what's on this drive. Perhaps you should leave. I can handle this."

Tara shook her head. "I agree that Viktor must be up to something dire, and Brodie was the one directly responsible for what happened at the Assembly Rooms. If I agree to torture, then I need to be able to watch." She was surprised at how angry and vengeful she felt, and wondered how much of it was due to the alien instincts that had been grafted onto her own. "Do it."

John walked towards the criminal leader lying on

the floor. "I'll give you one chance. Give me the password."

"Or what? I've been beaten by experts. Do your worst. You'll not get anything from me." Brodie replied.

John chuckled, the sound a deep rumbling in his chest. The lines of his face shifted, making his face more gaunt and chiselled. "Many of the Turks were courageous men too."

"Turks? What the fuck have Turks got to do with anything?" Brodie said.

Ignoring the crime boss, John looked around and focused upon a conference table at the other end of the room. Going back to the desk he picked up the hunting knife in the drawer and strode over to the table, grabbed one of its thick wooden legs and flipped the massive object upside down with a single movement of his wrist, smashing two chairs under it in the process. Using the big blade he whittled the end of one leg until it had a tapered point, but leaving it rounded at the tip. When he was satisfied with his handiwork he paced back to the desk and rammed the knife half-way up its blade into the desk top, and then picked up another strip of the torn curtain before turning to Brodie.

The crime boss began to struggle when John grabbed him by the collar and effortlessly dragged him towards the overturned table. "What are you doing? Let go of me you sodding bastard." His shouting became incoherent with fear and rage when his trousers and underpants were pulled down over his hips and to the middle of his thighs. He tried to kick when John grabbed his ankles, but a slap to his face that made his head ring silenced him.

John leashed Brodie's ankles to his thighs with the curtain fabric, preventing the man from completely straightening his legs. Squatting down, he picked the burly man up like a child and held the madly squirming gangster over the improvised impaling stake.

Brodie screamed in horror when he felt the point of the stake touch his buttocks and finally realised his assailant's intention. He screamed even louder when the point entered his body.

When the stake's tip was firmly lodged in the man's rectum John let go and stepped back. He patted Brodie on the cheek and said, "Password."

Panting and shivering with pain and terror, Brodie stared uncomprehendingly when John walked away and sat down in his chair. His toes braced against the floor were the only things preventing him from sinking further down the stake, and the muscles of his thighs were already trembling from the effort. "Y-you can't do this ... you c-can't .... "

Tara watched the impalement with a strange mixture of horror and satisfaction. The man was a mass murderer and held the key to discovering possibly worse planned atrocities. Her heart felt hard as stone as she watched the man scream and writhe. Any horror she felt was at the fact that she felt that way.

According to John's watch it was less than five minutes before Brodie shouted out the pass code, a mixture of numbers and letters, yelling them out over and over as if it was some kind of magical spell that could relieve his suffering. John lifted the man off of the bloodied stake and dropped him on the floor.

Tara darted to the computer, but paused before she entered the code. It was still possible that what Brodie had given them was a fake, something that might delete all the information on the hard disk instead of unlocking it. Any complete deletion process would be necessarily slow, so she could stop it by ripping out the battery, but that would leave them back where they started from. She glanced at John inquiringly and then entered the pass code when he nodded. She sighed with relief when the list of files on the thumb drive appeared on the file manager. She copied the files to the notebook's hard disk so that they couldn't somehow be encrypted again on the thumb drive, and then began to browse through them along with John, who peered at the screen over her shoulder. There was no super villain's guide to world conquest amongst the documents, but tantalising fragments, references, dates, and times. "Look!" Tara stabbed a finger at the screen, her voice filled with loathing.

"Viktor!" John said, reading the word at the bottom of a document. "So he really is behind this. But behind what, apart from killing people?" He continued to scan the documents. There were documents that contained references to groups, transport, and even the word "strike", but the locations were all designated with just a single letter, the main targets being described as "B" and "P", with all dates being plus or minus "D" except for a passing reference to "QT". John tried questioning Brodie, but the man swore he didn't know anything more.

"I'm not one of Viktor's lieutenants. I just get instructions now and then. I know something big is coming. We were told to be on standby in case we were needed. Like the bomb. But that's all," the gangster said, between groans of pain.

Tara slapped the desk in frustration. "There's got to be something here that will tell us more."

John rubbed the back of his head, and then frowned. "Perhaps there is." He looked upwards.

Tara's eyes widened. She had been so concerned with Monica as a victim to be rescued that she had not asked herself why the woman had been kidnapped in the first place. "Monica? Oh my god, you're right! Who would know routines, directions, and security better than a tour guide. And she's on leave, so no one would notice if she disappears." She got up and headed for the door. "I'll go and talk to her."

60

John was surprised when Tara came running back just moments later. "What's wrong?"

"Parliament House! The Palace of Westminster! That's where Monica works. That's the target!" Tara shouted urgently.

John slapped his forehead. "QT. Question time. That's ... tomorrow! Viktor's going after the Government. Wiping out the Prime Minister, the Cabinet, and most of the MPs would throw the country into absolute chaos."

Tara shook her head. "Even with his werewolf followers, he can't have enough people to handle the security present and who will turn up in minutes of an attack. There's got to be something more."

"We need to get back to London. But first, I have to call Commander Blair to warn him. Without more evidence, no one else would listen to us." He took out his smartphone and called up the contact list.

"Without more definite information, they're not going to cancel a sitting of Parliament just on our say so," Tara said.

"I know. But we have to try. Go and fetch Monica, and we'll leave," John said while shutting down the computer and pocketing the thumb drive.

"There might still be more of Brodie's men outside," Tara replied.

"I'll take care of them. Go." He had been reluctant to harm the men and women who followed or worked for Brodie, but time was of the essence now, and if they got in his way, they were his enemies, and the enemies of Dracula seldom lived long. He swept out of the front door like a dark phantom, disappearing into the night.

Tara's super sensitive hearing caught the faint sounds of bloody death coming from the grounds and her lips thinned. Apparently John had met with opposition.

Despite all that had happened, she didn't kill as easily as John, especially not ordinary humans. But they were a threat to Monica, who would be completely vulnerable to a bullet or shotgun blast as she left the house, and carrying her in vampire form was out of the question, as it would scare her witless and they needed her cooperation if they were to convince Commander Blair to take action. Monica was more than eager to leave when assured that there was no danger, and Tara led her downstairs and to the front door, where she found John waiting.

"It's all clear outside. You take Monica to the car and I'll fetch the notebook and tidy up here before I join you," John said, stone faced.

Tara froze for a fraction of a second when she realised what he intended, then nodded and silently led Monica out of the house. The spotlights created glowing patches on the lawn, and in contrast actually made the other areas seem darker by contrast as she walked down the driveway towards the main gate. They were almost at the gate when she heard a high-pitched screaming coming from the house. She guessed that John had placed Brodie back on the stake. She glanced at Monica, but realised that to the woman's normal hearing it would have been barely audible. In any case it was obvious the tour guide was much too concerned about getting away from the place of her captivity to pay any attention to distant peripheral sounds. They were almost at the main road when John caught up with them, and she looked him in the eye. "You took care of everything?"

John studied her expression for a moment and then nodded. Using ultrasonic frequencies he said, "His men may get free and break out of the room in time to save him. Or perhaps not. That's more of a chance than the people at the Assembly Rooms were given."

"Did you get hold of Commander Blair?" Tara asked in her normal voice, changing the subject.

"I did. I told him everything that we had learned, and he promised to do his best to warn the authorities. But as I feared, without concrete evidence, or at least some idea of the actual threat, he doubts anyone will act on it, other than tightening standard security. Blair says he will put his own anti-werewolf unit on standby, but he can't just hang around the Houses of Parliament either," John said. "I'm tempted to go after Viktor directly, but conducting a running battle through London against someone who hasn't done anything provably illegal would put us on the wrong side of the law ourselves."

Tara sighed in frustration but nodded. "The best we can do is to get back to London as quickly as possible." Then she nodded towards Monica and grinned. "Perhaps we can use Viktor's idea and go on a tour in the morning."

Monica suddenly spoke up. "Do you really think that there is a threat to the Parliament?"

John nodded. "We're almost certain, although we can't prove it."

"I can get you in on a private tour. That way no one will say anything if you don't follow the official tour itinerary," Monica said eagerly.

"Are you sure? It could get you in trouble, and there might be danger," Tara said.

"I would most likely have died back there if not for you two. It's my turn now," Monica said, giving Brodie's mansion and its occupants two fingers.

Chapter Four

With the change in purpose of Belmarsh Prison, the regulations had changed too. Although security was even tighter than before, visiting hours were now six in the morning to midnight every day, since the inmates were technically not criminals and thus had to be allowed as much opportunity to interact with loved ones and friends as possible, just as the detention centre held both male and female inmates. Even though there were separate wings for the sexes, they were allowed to meet and even have sex. Rape was not a big issue, since the changes in pulse rate and blood pressure involved in an act of aggression would also trigger the sedative armbands, although there was the occasional unfortunate lusty couple found drugged and asleep by the guards as well. There was even a free shuttle bus service that ran from Woolwich Arsenal Station to New Belmarsh every half an hour, and the parking facilities outside the prison had been expanded. There was even a row of fast food restaurants, coffee shops, and a gift (approved) cum bookshop that had sprung up next to the car park to cater to the visitors. Since the inmate section was completely sealed off from the visitor's section by steel lined reinforced concrete walls and thick bulletproof glass, there was little necessity for elaborate security measures on the visitor's side. Gifts and other supplies were taken by guards into a secure room with thick steel doors on either side like the airlock of a space ship. One door would only open when the other was fully closed and locked. Guards, catering, and janitorial staff only entered the inmate section when all the werewolf inmates were locked into their individual cells. The guards on the public side were friendly and relaxed. After all, the authorities had reasoned, who in their right mind would try to break into a jail full of people who might turn into ravening werewolves at any moment. Viktor fully intended to make use of this vulnerability to break New Belmarsh wide open and to free every last one of the werewolves confined within. Resentful, angry, and frightened, they were just what he needed. He glanced over his shoulder at the occupants of the shuttle bus.

"Don't worry, they all know what to do," Jenny said, stroking his shoulder with her fingers.

Viktor smiled at her. "I know. It's just so good to see how everything has gone according to plan and that the stupid government has done exactly what I wanted them to." He laughed. "By supplying the werewolf tranquilliser, Tara's industrialist friend actually helped to accelerate my plan. Originally I thought it would take longer for the police and army to work out an effective way to capture newly turned werewolves, and conveniently gather them up." He leaned towards the driver. "Remember what will happen to your family if you screw this up for us," he said, his voice low and rumbling.

The driver's face was pale and glistening with sweat, but he nodded vigorously while facing straight ahead, thinking of the live video of the werewolf's clawed fingers gripping the throats of his wife and daughter. He wasn't part of the prison service and had no desire to be a hero. "Th-they know my face, and I n-normally go in and out dozens of times a day. J-just don't hurt them … please."

Viktor saw that Jenny was about to say something mocking so he squeezed her arm and gave her a flat, warning stare. When he was sure that she would keep quiet, he turned back to the driver. "Just do as you're told, and everything will be all right. If I could have been certain that you would have gone along, I would have offered to pay you, but this is too important for me to risk you developing a sudden bout of conscience. All you have to do is your job. Once we're all off of the bus, you can turn around and drive away. Jenny will accompany you until you're out of the prison compound and on your way down the road. Then she'll get off, and she'll phone my people to tell them to leave your home." He smiled and slapped the man comfortingly on the shoulder. He didn't want the driver to look visibly upset when they got to the security gate. Once they were in, he would leave the driver to Jenny's tender mercies.

***

Viktor obligingly handed over the bag of grapes he was carrying and stepped through the metal detector gate, and the officer with a hand-held detector wand waved him on when the gate was silent. The grapes went through a scanner similar to those used at airports, and he picked the bag up at the other side. What first struck any new visitor was the cheerful décor and relatively good quality furniture. There were helpful signs on the walls, and painted lines on the floor guided visitors to appropriate areas, making the main visitor's entry hall resemble a modern hospital rather than a prison. He went up to the guard at the counter. "I'm here to visit Ed Barlow. I'm his friend." He handed the bag to another guard and picked up a pen to fill in the Visitor's Book. While he was doing so, he watched the other guard attach a name tag to the bag of grapes and put it on a trolley, joining several other packages and bags of gifts from other visitors. Just as the Russian mobster who had acted as his go-between with Ed Barlow had reported, the guard waited until the trolley was full before pushing it over to a locked steel door that led into the interior of what the authorities preferred to call the Holding Facility, rather than a prison. He watched with approval as the selected members of his pack drifted towards the door that led to the guard's control room and ultimately to the inner gate that opened into the detention area. But they couldn't make their move until the inmates had been notified of their visitors over the PA system and had gathered in a row to be allowed into the assigned meeting cubicles. He needed the help of the inmates to overcome the guards in the rest of the facility as well as the armed reaction team that would respond as soon as the alarms went off. But once he and his pack made their move, New Belmarsh would turn into Hell on Earth for the guards and other visitors – a hell that the rest of the country would soon share. The thought made him smile with genuine happiness.

***

General werewolf sightings and captures were now handled by the local constabulary SC&O19 units on hand, who had all been re-trained to use the high-power dart rifles and pistols which had been issued throughout the country. However, every notification of a sighting or report of werewolf attack was copied to Commander Blair's special unit, who were the most experienced in dealing with werewolf incidents. The official stance was still that werewolves were some kind of viral infection that made the sufferers extremely aggressive and unusually strong, similar to the worst effects of rabies combined with the taking of PCP. The government had not admitted that some of the afflicted could function and think normally, and to some extent control the changes that the supposed infection brought about. When an organised attack by werewolves occurred, Commander Blair's team was called in to handle the situation. The day had started off normally enough, although Blair had put his armed special response team on standby alert. He trusted John Seward, but without real evidence he couldn't justify sending his men to Westminster without receiving a request from the SO17

Security Command unit stationed there. Then his attention was drawn to the large electronic map on the wall. In the few minutes since he had entered the room, red and blue icons had begun to blossom all over the map of London and its surrounds. The blue were reported sightings of werewolves, and red meant a confirmed sighting or attack. Usually there were about a dozen sightings a day, mostly false alarms, and on average about three confirmed incidents in a week. But now there were red and blue dots appearing all over the map. "That's impossible!" Commander Blair said. "Is there something wrong with the system?"

"No sir," the female constable in charge of the monitoring system replied. "I've checked with the reporting stations."

The icons continued to blossom and spread, and Commander Blair's eyes widened and he cursed under his breath. He retreated to his office and shut the door. Trying not to appear agitated, he dialled the contact number given to him by John Seward. When he heard Seward's voice answer, he said, "The city is going mad with werewolf sightings as well as actual attacks. But none of the attackers were on site when the police arrived. These are obviously distractions designed to have us running all over the map chasing shadows while they hit their actual target, whether it is the Houses of Parliament or elsewhere. I'm not going to be able to hold my team back when I'm called to respond. If you're right and they are going to hit Parliament, you're going to be on your own until I can get there from wherever I happen to be at the time. The best I can do is to warn SO17 to expect private security contractors and to request they work with you. But they are an elite team and I doubt they'll welcome non-police amateurs, so I'll leave it to you to decide if you want to approach them. Good luck." The government had attempted a number of euphemisms instead of using the word "werewolf", but the public and press quickly started using that name, and it soon became useless and embarrassing for the authorities to pretend otherwise. Once the effectiveness of the tranquillising darts had been proven, the initial public panic had subsided to some degree, but the atmosphere in the city and elsewhere in Britain was similar to when the IRA had been actively making bomb attacks. So far the public had avoided mass panic, but it wouldn't be hard for a rash of sightings and attacks, let alone a major werewolf strike against the government itself, to create uncontrolled hysteria and even a state of civil war between the werewolves and the rest of the population. Worse still, it appeared that some non-infected people had chosen to work with the werewolves. Commander Blair had to struggle in order to suppress his own feelings of panic. It was now clear that the werewolves had an actual agenda, even though he had no idea what it was, other than to attack the government and perhaps social order itself. His head jerked towards the closed tempered glass door of his office when he heard someone knocking. He nodded. "What is it?"

"Call for you sir. It's the Commissioner," the constable said through a gap in the door.

Blair took a moment to calm himself, and then picked up the handset. "Good morning Commissioner."

Not bothering with the niceties, the Commissioner said, "I assume you're aware that the city is rapidly turning into a disaster area and that the Metropolitan police are running from pillar to post looking like bloody fools with their thumbs up their arses?"

"I'm aware of the sudden outbreak of reported werewolf sightings, if that's what you mean sir," Blair replied calmly.

"You know perfectly well that the approved term is Infected Victims, Blair," Commissioner Beckett snapped. He had only been appointed Commissioner a month and a half ago, after the previous Commissioner had resigned for reasons of health.

"If you say so sir. I haven't had the time to stay up to date with the approved terminology. But you were talking about the current situation sir?" Blair said.

"Indeed I was. Why the blazes aren't you out there helping to keep the situation under control? Isn't your unit tasked with handling things to do with these Infected Victims?" the Commissioner said.

"I'm not running around out there because no one has yet requested my assistance, Commissioner."

"Well I'm ordering you and your team of so called experts to get stuck in. Handle the situation, or I'll get someone else who will," the Commissioner said, almost shouting.

"Where exactly should I go, Commissioner?" Blair asked, determined to place the responsibility for this insane waste of his unit's time and resources on the Commissioner. But before the Commissioner could answer, there was another tap on his door. The look on Sergeant Murphy's face told Blair that something bad had happened. "Commissioner, I have to go. You want my team to do something, well I think you've just got your wish." He put down the phone without waiting for the Commissioner to reply. It was bad politics, but sucking up to his new boss was the least of his concerns at the moment. "What?" he said to his waiting sergeant.

The sergeant shook his head. "It's bad. An ARV was despatched to a confirmed sighting near the Baker Street Tube station. Upon arrival the officers spotted an injured female civilian, but as soon as they exited the ARV they were attacked by two werewolves. All three officers were killed."

"How do you know that?"

"You should see this, sir," the sergeant replied, holding out a tablet computer.

Blair took the tablet and touched the screen to

activate the video player. He gasped. "Bloody hell!" The video was clearly from a police body camera, but from the angle and height it was also obvious that it wasn't in its usual place on a constable's vest. For about ten seconds the video simply displayed an empty street, with an unusual dearth of moving cars or pedestrians. Then without warning a werewolf stepped in front of the camera with the limp, shredded body of a woman in the remains of a police tactical uniform hanging from its clawed paw. Blair involuntarily recoiled from the screen when the monster tossed the constable's ruined corpse towards the camera. The last shot was of the dead bodies of all three officers lying in a jumble of limbs and exposed organs. "It was an ambush!" As soon as he said it he realised the consequences of the massacre. Every sighting, confirmed or not, would now have to be treated as a possible trap and combat zone, instead of just diverting the nearest constables to check up on the unconfirmed sightings. The entire force would soon be dragged into the effort, and even worse, it might force the government to approve the deployment of British Army troops on the streets in support. Although such a use of troops had been considered and even planned for in the case of an overwhelming terrorist attack, it had always been rejected because it would appear to the public that the police, and by implication the government, had lost control of the situation. However Blair wondered if the consequences of not deploying troops might not be even worse for public morale.

"Similar videos of the incident taken by the public have already appeared on the Internet and have gone viral," the sergeant said grimly.

"We need to take the videos down, and quickly. The werewolves want to show that they're in control and we're helpless. Unless we can stop them there'll be mass panic," Blair said as he strode out of his office.

"But those bastards could be anywhere by now,"

Sergeant Murphy said.

Blair pointed at the grinning fanged face of the werewolf leering out of the large monitor screen on the office wall. "They're going to want to do it again, and we're going to give them the opportunity," he said, slapping Murphy on the shoulder.

The sergeant grinned and cracked his knuckles. "I'll get the lads loaded up and ready to move out sir."

***

Despite being vouched for by Commander Blair, John didn't think that the SO17 security detail would allow them to bring bags full of weapons and body armour into the Palace, so the first thing that he and Tara did upon arriving in London was to gather up their field kits, consisting of body armour designed specifically to resist powerful stabbing and ripping attacks, although they were also quite effective against non-armour piercing bullets, electro-magnetic mass driver rifles that hurled hypersonic, heavy silver bullets, and silver impregnated swords, all technically prototypes developed and made by John's own companies. In addition, Tara's father Rowland had added another bag that resembled an oversized briefcase. Printed on the side in black and yellow was *Swarm MkII*. "We'll cut through Victoria Tower Gardens and then Black Rod's Garden. There's a blind spot in the security camera coverage there and an easy climb up onto the roof. Easy for us, at any rate."

"You seem very familiar with the place," Tara said as they flitted through the pre-dawn gloom, taking advantage of the deep shadows of the trees and monuments.

"I was here when the original Palace burned down and this pile was built. Over the years there have been many times that I've had reason to pay discreet visits to

72

Westminster. For instance, in late 1941 the SIS received a report that the Germans had recruited a very special undercover operative code named 'N', tasked with assassinating Churchill and the Royal Family. A team of agents were sent out to investigate, but none ever reported back, except for a single incomplete message that read, *Nosferatu*."

Tara's head snapped around to stare at him. "The Germans knew about vampires?"

John nodded. "They were very open minded, exploring both science and the occult. Of course no one in the SIS believed that the message referred to an actual vampire. It was assumed that it was the assassin's code name or the name of the operation itself. However, I had allies within the government, and when Churchill and the King were informed about the potential threat, word reached me as well. Then as now, I didn't meddle in the affairs of government, at least not directly. But I wasn't going to tolerate another vampire intruding into what I considered to be my territory, if that was indeed the case. In any event, my investigations eventually led me to a confrontation with this Nosferatu person on the somewhat damaged roof of the Palace."

"You killed him?" Tara asked, fascinated by this unexpected glimpse into the history of both John and of wartime Britain.

John's eyes met Tara's with a measuring gaze. "I killed *her*," he replied, emphasising the last word.

Tara froze for a second, pressing her back against the bole of a tree. "The German vampire was a woman?"

"She was indeed. She was well trained and fought skilfully, but it quickly became obvious that she had not been a vampire for more than a few years. With her special capabilities, her vampirism made her very formidable against ordinary humans, but I had the advantage of hundreds of years of training and experience over her. I destroyed her body and the SIS eventually dismissed the whole affair as a non-event." John's gaze shifted into the distance. "She was a beautiful and accomplished woman. I've often wondered over the years what might have been if we had met under different .... " He shook his head and pointed. "The security cameras are there and there. Stay close and follow my footsteps."

Before she had been injected with the alien medical nanite system, John would simply have disappeared into the darkness. But now with her vastly improved vision and the bat-like sonar that painted a detailed three-dimensional map of her surroundings in her mind, she was able to follow him at a gliding run without missing a step or tripping over any of the myriad of small obstacles on the ground, even when he climbed up the ancient stonework of the Palace without breaking stride. Diamond hard claws extended from her fingers and toes, and allowed her to grip and climb the wall as if it was covered with deliberate hand holds. She saw him bound over the crenelated edge of the roof and followed suit, landing on the roof on all fours, distributing her weight and reducing the chance of damaging the roofing. She followed him across the dark grey roof, surrounded by a forest of stone towers big and small as they headed towards the mass of the Central Tower.

John stopped near the base of the Central Tower at what looked like a service hatch that was locked or bolted from the inside. But when he reached under the rim and probed with a claw, there was the sound of metal sliding on metal and a moment later he lifted the service hatch to reveal a ladder-like staircase. "You can always rely on buildings this old to have its little secrets," he said before disappearing into the dark opening.

Again Tara followed him down into the depths of the old, history filled building, walking and climbing along and down ladders, stairs, and even vertical walls when locked doors and gates barred the way. Finally they reached the Central Lobby, the huge arched space that linked the various main areas of the Houses of Parliament. The massive chandelier wasn't illuminated, and the smaller light sources left most of the huge space in shadow. Running up and recessed into the walls were columns of statues, and it was here, metres above the ground that John indicated that they should hide their equipment bags.

John said, "This is as good a place as any, in roughly the centre of the building and more accessible than most. I hope to god we can stop whatever Viktor is planning without resorting to weapons, but given what he has done simply to divert our attention, I'm afraid that it's going to be bad."

"Do you really believe Viktor is going after the entire government, or the elected portions at any rate?" Tara asked as they made their way back out equally unseen.

"It doesn't make sense that he would simply strike at the Prime Minister or someone else in such a high-profile way. Viktor doesn't think small. You know that. In addition, the longer he is a werewolf, the more aggressive he will become. Nothing but blood will satisfy him. Remember, we're dealing with the primal form of the werewolf creature, not the civilised version that built a space going culture."

Tara sighed. She knew Viktor better than John and she knew he was right. Viktor had never been one for half measures. If he was going to reveal himself and his people so openly, he would go for the throat. "That's what bothers me. I have a nasty feeling that this isn't anything as simple as another Guy Fawkes day."

Chapter Five

If it had been possible, Commander Blair would have replaced every team responding to a confirmed werewolf sighting with his own people, but that was impossible. He only had enough manpower to set up two response teams, each with a standard marked police car with two openly armed officers serving as bait, and a second unmarked vehicle with four more officers wearing jackets or other garments to hide their special stab-resistant vests that sported high collars and protection for the shoulders, upper arms as well as the groin and thighs, which the men of CC01, Blair's covert anti-werewolf unit, jokingly called Legionnaire gear, referring to the armour of the ancient Roman legions. Blair himself led one team, while the other was led by Sergeant Murphy. Another team which drove a large heavily armoured confinement vehicle remained on call in case any werewolves were captured. However, Blair knew that since the werewolves in question were apparently planning ambushes and killing policemen, his men were in no mood to try to capture them alive. He was sitting in the team's unmarked vehicle, a white Mercedes Citan van, when he received the report of the second ambush.

"Three constable's dead sir. The video's on the net too. They've tried to take it down, but it's gone viral like the first," the constable said, looking ill.

Blair slammed his fist against the side of the van, making the others jump in alarm. He shook his head. "Sorry." He took a deep breath and tugged on his body armour which had shifted uncomfortably. "Don't let what's happening make you lose focus. The next call could be the one, and we're going to be the people doing the ambushing." The men growled in agreement and he nodded. Like the others, he was armed with a semi-automatic dart rifle, but he also had a Glock G19, 9mm automatic pistol and, contrary to regulations, a heavy Chinese War Sword strapped diagonally across his back. Its relatively short sixty-one centimetre blade and long double-handed grip made it easy to perform an over-the-shoulder draw, and was perfect for decapitating a werewolf. He had paid for the swords that each of his field officers carried with his own money and they officially didn't exist. All the men went for training to use them on their own time. Normally both pistol and sword were nearly useless against a werewolf, but it was a different matter if they had been hit by a dart containing the compound created by John Seward's people. Because John had patented the drug, no one could question how or why it worked, especially since he was charging a pittance for it. But most important of all, it worked. So far, nothing else the government researchers tried had worked, not even things that were so toxic the users had to wear hazmat suits. The radio crackled and his attention snapped to the front of the van, which was being driven by a constable in plain clothes.

The driver listened for a moment and then looked into his rear-view mirror. "Confirmed sighting in our area sir! King Street."

Blair shared a horrified look with the others. "Covent Garden ...." He had to grab the back of the seat for support when the car in front turned on its siren and accelerated, followed a moment later by their van, throwing all of the heavily loaded and top-heavy team towards the rear. The van couldn't keep up with the front car without being obvious, but since the van's driver knew where they were going that wasn't a problem, even when a traffic light separated them. He called out to the front car on his Airwave radio. "Bravo Two, remember, stay in the vehicle until we are in position to support you. Do not allow yourselves to be lured out."

"Roger Bravo One. Stay in the vehicle.

Understood," the constable in the passenger seat of the front car replied. "Turning into King Street now. I can see people running away from the area of Covent Garden. Nearing the end of the road. Bodies sighted. Injured or dead. Blood everywhere."

Hunching forward as if he could will the van to greater speed, Blair said, "Do you see the werewolves?"

There was an irritating crackle, and then the same officer's voice said, "Wait! I think … yes, I have a werewolf in sight. It's in the courtyard in front of the main entrance to the market. It's growling and roaring at the crowd. People are running in all directions."

The van skidded around the corner and Blair was thrown against his seat belt. "We're turning into King Street now. Keep the werewolf in sight. Do not engage!" All around him the rest of his team were checking each other's armour and gear, and then their own weapons, one last time. The men next to the rear doors of the van prepared to fling them open.

Another crackle and message from the radio made Blair's eyes narrow. "It hasn't moved. Wait, it sees us! It's pointing at us and it looks like it's smiling." The officer sounded slightly unnerved. They had all faced werewolves before, but almost without exception they had been confused and angry, lashing out wildly, driven mostly by blind instinct. To see this werewolf behave in such a calm and deliberate way, made the hairs on the back of the officer's neck bristle. He pressed the button on the Airwave unit clipped to his shoulder so hard that his finger hurt. "Fuck! It's grabbed a child. A girl. A young girl, about eight! The bastard is holding her up, showing her to us. It looks like it's going to … no!" There was the sound of the car door unlocking and opening. Then the transmission cut off.

Blair slammed his fist against his thigh. "Bravo Two! What's happening?" Then the van pulled up behind the lead car and Blair saw what was happening for himself through the windscreen. Both of his men had left their vehicle and were running towards the werewolf and its hostage, clearly not daring to fire from a distance for fear of hitting the hostage. The massive dose of tranquilliser would be instantly fatal to a person the size of a child, and even to an adult. Despite what was portrayed on TV and in films, there was no effective, one-size-fits-all tranquilliser dart for humans.

"Sir, should we assist?"

Blair held up his hand. "Hold. If it's just one of the creatures, they can handle it. If it's an ambush we risk scaring them off. But get ready to move." He glanced up at the small video monitor suspended from the roof of the van that displayed a wide angled view of the area behind the van, a precaution against opening the doors right into an attack. His head swivelled back to the windscreen when the driver called out. Following the driver's pointing finger he saw two more werewolves sneaking up behind the uniformed constables who were completely focused upon trying to rescue the child. "It's an ambush. Move! Move!" Slapping on his riot style helmet with its full-face visor, he scrambled out of the van and ran after the others even as he spoke into his radio. "Bravo Two, behind you!" He saw the leading man of his team fire his dart rifle as he ran and cursed breathlessly when the targeted werewolf moved with inhuman speed to bat the dart away as if it was a bothersome insect. In order to work as an injector and not shatter against the werewolf's body, the darts travelled at a much slower speed than a bullet or the pellets of a shotgun, especially when fired from near to maximum range.

Alerted to the approach of Blair and his team, the ambushing werewolves charged towards the first two officers, who hesitated to turn their backs to the first werewolf and its hostage. One of the constables started to turn and fire at the new threat, but the first werewolf roared and gripped the child's throat with its claws, drawing blood and causing her to scream, making both constables hesitate for a fatal fraction of a second. The nearness of the pair of charging werewolves to the two officers also forced Blair and his men to hold their fire as well. Both werewolves lashed out in what was almost a coordinated movement, their claws ripping into the unarmoured forearms of the constables who were finally and much too slowly turning to aim and fire their weapons.

One of the constables screamed in pain and threw himself to one side in an effort to avoid the follow-up blow from the werewolf's other clawed hand, splattering blood in a fan of crimson on the cobble stones that covered the ground. Even so, the creature's slashing claws managed to rake his side. The man's armour held, but the force of the blow spun him like a top, sending him crashing to the ground, stunned.

The second officer bravely ignored his attacker and took aim at the hostage-holding werewolf, but he was forced to jerk the muzzle of his rifle aside when the werewolf lifted the screaming child up like a shield, and the dart snapped harmlessly past the werewolf's shoulder.

Blair stopped running and took aim, but he suddenly found himself flying through the air to crash face down on the hard cobblestones, his back throbbing from the force of whatever had hit him. He realised that the sword across his back had saved him from having his spine broken. A clawed foot-paw appeared in the edge of his vision and he rolled frantically away, still clinging to his dart rifle. Huge fanged filled jaws snapped closed millimetres from his head, spattering his face shield with spittle as he continued to roll. He scrambled to his feet and saw in horror that several more werewolves had come out of hiding behind his team, and he realised that the werewolves had set a trap specifically for him and his men. He fired a dart and grunted in satisfaction when the werewolf holding the girl staggered and dropped her onto the floor. "Disengage and get into the market!" he shouted to his men who were desperately fending off slashing claws and fangs in a mad melee like something out of a video game. One of the men went down with a werewolf on top of him. Dropping his rifle to hang from its sling, Blair snatched the heavy bladed sword from its sheath with his right hand and swung it down double-handed with all his strength. The keen edge sank with a meaty thunk into the werewolf's shoulder, and the creature roared in anger and pain, but the wound began to visibly heal as soon as he pulled the sword out. However, the distraction allowed the bleeding constable to break away and stagger to his side. With the wounded officer following, he backed towards the columned market building. Blair handed the sword to his companion and threatened the werewolves with his dart rifle, forcing them to dodge and retreat, giving the rest of his men the chance to break away and join him too, except for one constable who lay in an obscenely huge puddle of blood that spurted and flowed from a gaping hole in his throat.

They would have still been overrun by the much faster and stronger werewolves before they reached the shelter of the building, except for a group of Japanese tourists, who, apparently unaware of the attack, came streaming out of the arcade following a flag-waiving tour guide. Some of the younger women in the group squealed in excitement at the sight of the werewolves, assuming them to be street performers of some kind. The entire group broke up into a confused mass and advanced towards the monsters with all sorts of cameras and smartphones raised, flash guns twinkling and sparkling in the daylight like ephemeral diamonds.

The werewolves flinched from the bright lights, and then realised that the tourists were not a threat but helpless prey. If the pack had been comprised of Viktor and his close followers, they would have retained enough judgement to keep their minds on the task at hand, which was to kill the men from the anti-werewolf police unit, but these were the new recruits, ones that Viktor had considered too unreliable to employ in the assault on New Belmarsh. They proved that now, becoming distracted by the sight of such easy and tempting prey. They hesitated and growled, torn between faint remnants of their humanity, and the base instincts of the werewolf creatures they had turned into. The most dominant of the pack sniffed, detecting the scent of growing fear and helplessness coming from the confused tourists who were still not fully aware of their peril. When he charged towards the tourists, the rest of the pack followed suit, duty submerged by the instinct to kill the tempting and unarmed prey.

Blair swore under his breath. His team, minus one man, had reformed at the entrance of the main market building, the walls and columns at their back giving them a chance to hold off the werewolves with their dart guns and pistols. He could see that the others were frantic to do something to help the tourists. But firing a barrage of darts in their direction might kill as many of the tourists as the werewolves could, and charging back into the open would be suicidal. Activating his Airwave he called out, "Charlie One, this is Bravo One. Do you hear me, over?" Charlie One was Sergeant Murphy who was leading the other bait and strike team.

There was a long silence, and Blair feared that the Airwave system had been overloaded by all the panicked calls flooding the city. He sighed with relief when the radio crackled. "Bravo One, this is Charlie One, over. Do you have something for us Gov'nor?"

Almost choking with relief, Blair said, "Sergeant, they were waiting for us. We're cut off from the vehicles and there are a lot more werewolves than expected. At least five ... no, make that seven of the bastards," Two more werewolves had appeared from the Southampton Street side of the plaza. "I need you to bring your team to Covent Garden via the Russell Street approach. Set up to provide cover fire when you arrive. We'll be coming to you in a fighting retreat and we'll need the cover fire to get across the open stretch of the plaza without being overrun, so be ready to pull out fast.

"Roger, Bravo One. We'll be waiting. You should know that there have been sightings of more werewolves headed in your direction from all over London, so don't stop for tea," Sergeant Murphy replied.

"We're on our way, Murphy. Just be ready when we get there," Blair said, fighting down a surge of panic. He didn't need to add that if Murphy's team and vehicles weren't there, he and his men would be dead. It was times like these that he was glad he wasn't married. When he ordered the team to begin edging back into the market hall, he could see that several of them were on the verge of rebellion, especially when a young woman began screaming and sobbing when a werewolf snapped at her and took a bite out of her thigh.

"Sir, we can't – "

Blair cut him off. "What we can't do is face so many of them out in the open without the benefit of surprise and with those civilians around them. There's a time to be a hero, and a time to die fighting. This isn't one of them. For the time being we're the closest thing to an effective defence the public have, who actually understand what we're facing. Throwing our lives away won't help them or all the other people of London. We've learned something important today. They, those creatures, are trying to kill us. Not just anybody. Us. We need to regroup and change our plans. But first we need to get out of here alive. Now move!" He was relieved when the team responded and formed up into single file behind him as he headed into the market building. They had just cleared the passage and entered the open space of the central market area when he heard the muffled screams from the tourists stop. "Get ready! They're coming! Watch the upper floor. Don't let them surprise you." As soon as he spoke they all heard the rattle of claws and heavy bodies moving on the roof, and low growls echoing through the huge space of the old market. The spilled stalls and abandoned shops, as well as ominous splashes of blood turning the normally cheerful marketplace into a maze of fear and death.

With Blair in the lead, the team snaked its way through the cavernous building, keeping a wall or a stall against one side at all times to reduce the possible angles of attack. The smell of fresh coffee and baked bread contrasted incongruously and sickeningly with the copper tang of spilled blood and the stench of ripped abdomens. They were just passing a stall filled with posters and framed photos when a werewolf crashed through the cloth and plywood backing of the stall, throwing the constable immediately behind Blair to the ground in a snarling, flailing, jumble. "Watch out for more of them!" he shouted even as he pressed the muzzle of his dart rifle against the werewolf's back and fired. Its powerful hairy arm lashed out and hurled him back into the remains of the smashed stall, crushing glass and wooden frames beneath him. Somehow he managed to hang on to his rifle, and lying on his back he spotted movement in the air above. He fired, missed, fired again, and another werewolf crashed to the ground a metre from him, twitching spasmodically as the powerful tranquilliser took effect, the silver compound in it causing a massive allergic reaction and temporarily disrupting the ability of the alien nanites to counter the tranquilliser. The man he had saved helped him up, and Blair drew his pistol and shot both werewolves in the head. Short of complete decapitation, it would not kill them, but the damage caused to the creature's brains would take much more time to repair than a wound to the body and thus keep them out of the fight. He heard dart rifles snap and crack behind him. "Come on, keep moving. We have to get out of here before they rush us in a group." He looked down and was shocked to see that the werewolf's claws had ripped open the armour over his abdomen, although it had saved him from being eviscerated. He holstered his pistol and moved forward, hugging the walls whenever he could.

***

Tara and John had just entered the Houses of Parliament, ostensibly on an early morning private tour when John's mobile phone chirped an ultrasonic tone that most people couldn't hear. She stopped walking and watched his face as he listened to the caller. Normally he would have used the speaker, but there were other people around them. When he ended the call she said, "Blair?" Although she hadn't been able to make out many details, she had identified the Police Commander's voice.

John nodded. "It's definitely started. Sightings and werewolf attacks are being reported all over London. Blair has no choice but to respond to them."

"Distractions. So we're on our own then," Tara said.

"Not entirely. There's still the SO19 detail," John replied.

"They've never faced werewolves, and it's likely Viktor and his followers will be here, and they won't be like the sad confused bite victims the police usually encounter," Tara said grimly. She wasn't sure if she feared or anticipated meeting Viktor again. Until just recently she would have definitely been more anxious than eager, but under John's mentoring she was rapidly gaining confidence in her own ability to handle the treacherous co-pilot who had tried to murder her more than once. Standing in the ancient building where laws had been debated and made for so long, the responsibility that fate or circumstance had placed on their shoulders suddenly felt crushing, and without thinking, she reached out and took John's hand. When she felt him gently squeeze her hand she almost pulled away again, but instead she moved closer and leaned her body against his. She had not forgotten that he had done terrible things in his long life and that he was the being the world knew and feared as Dracula, but the fact that he was standing here with her at this moment confirmed what she had been feeling for some time now. As far as she was concerned, he was a good man, and that it was entirely possible she was falling in love with him. A half-smile twisted her lips when she considered the idea that it was the attraction of one monster for another of her species that she felt. If that was true, then perhaps it was time to stop fighting it. Neither of them were immortal, and it was very possible that one or both of them might die today, and she wanted him to know what she felt. But when she looked up at his face, his gentle smile told her that he already knew.

Speaking in ultrasonic frequencies so that the tour guide couldn't hear him, John said, "We'll talk about it after were done here."

His total and unfeigned confidence banished Tara's fears, and she grinned and nodded.

"I think we need to get our equipment, and then Miss Dobson can take us around. We should be familiar with our battleground," John said, smiling at their new ally.

Monica bit her lip. "Do you really think it's going to come to that? Surely the police will stop them before they can do anything ... bad."

Tara put her hands on the guide's shoulders. "If we're right and this is something planned by the man we call Viktor, it's not going to be like some terrorist attack. It will be far, far worse."

"But what can you and Mr Seward do that the police can't? Are you secret agents or something? Like James Bond?"

Tara nodded. "Let's just say we have some special skills when it comes to werewolves."

John chuckled. "I always liked Ian Fleming."

Tara realised that he meant that literally and gave him a wide-eyed look. "That's another thing you need to tell me about." Turning back to the guide she said, "We need to get to the Central Lobby, quickly."

Monica nodded confidently to her left. "This way."

***

Jenny caught Viktor's eye and gave him a thumbs up. He felt an almost orgasmic rush of excitement and had to resist the desire to turn into werewolf form there and then. It was becoming increasingly easy for him to initiate the change, so much so that he had to be careful not to transform without consciously noticing. Her signal meant that the campaign of fake werewolf sightings and actual ambushes was operating as planned. With a little luck all police resources including that troublesome special unit CC01 would be drawn into running blindly around the streets and even falling prey to guerrilla ambushes by his least experienced werewolf recruits. They would suffer casualties too, but it wouldn't matter. Not after today. By concentrating every captured werewolf in Britain in this place, and creating what was in effect a werewolf community, they had done Viktor's work for him by allowing natural social forces, accelerated and magnified by the confined and cramped conditions, to reveal who were the dominant and effective ones, and who were the followers. By offering hope of freedom and even revenge, as well as material aid to their families in the outside world, Viktor had recruited an army. An army of very angry and resentful werewolves. And now he was about to unleash them on the unsuspecting country. In order not to draw attention to himself he gave a pre-arranged signal to Jenny, and then slowly drifted towards the metal entryway marked "Staff Only" that required a security pass worn by the guards plus a biometric hand scan to open. According to Ivan Ivanovich, there was a guard just inside the door armed with a shotgun and not a dart gun, since he was there to prevent human intruders from getting into the restricted area. When he casually glanced around, he saw that the others were in their positions, blocking panic buttons on the wall, standing near the other guards, and Jenny leaning against the wall near to the guard manning the reception counter. That guard would be the first to die when he made his move, and from the console built into the counter Jenny could prevent any alert being sent over the computer network system. He watched a fresh trolley of gifts for inmates which had been scanned and checked, being pushed towards the security gate and drifted closer, but still at a distance that wouldn't alarm the guard inside the door or the guard pushing the trolley. This was the critical moment. If one of the guards managed to close the gate before he got through, then his plan would fail, and he might never get a second chance. When the guard tapped his pass and began to place his hand on the scanner, Viktor triggered the change, timing it so that he was in full werewolf form when the gate buzzed and swung open. The guard pushed the trolley forward, blocking the gate from closing and totally unaware of the threat behind him.

The face of the guard inside twisted in horror when he glanced over his colleague's shoulder. He raised his shotgun, but froze when he realised that if he fired he would most likely blow the other constable's face off. He started to shout a warning and to pull the trolley inwards with one hand at the same time so he could slam the gate shut, but he was too late.

The powerful muscles of Viktor's fur covered legs thrust him forward with the force of a battering ram. He smashed into the back of the police constable pushing the trolley, which in turn propelled the heavily laden trolley into the armed guard like a runaway car. The shotgun went off, most of the shot hitting the unfortunate constable who was involuntarily shielding Viktor, pulverising the constable's shoulder. Several pellets hit Viktor, and though he growled in annoyance when a pellet ripped across his cheek, the wounds began healing almost before any blood could flow from the wounds.

The armed guard was not so fortunate. The impact of the trolley broke both of his legs and threw him backwards across the room. The back of his head hit the concrete with a ghastly sound akin to a smashing melon, blood and brains spraying out in a halo across the wall.

Back in the reception hall, the guard at the desk went down with Jenny's fangs locked around his throat, while other werewolves were ripping into the rest of the guards. Since the main entrance was locked and the guard who controlled it was lying on the floor with his abdomen ripped open, the visitors were trapped in the hall as well and were running around, fighting and trampling each other in a maddened attempt to find a way to escape. A couple of men picked up chairs and tried to attack one of Viktor's pack, but their bravery, or desperation, was rewarded by a gory and agonizing death under the creature's claws and fangs.

Four more werewolves followed Viktor into the secure section, split into two pairs and then loped down the corridors to either side of the entry room, eyes and noses sniffing for more guards to slaughter, while Viktor dealt with the badly injured constable who had been pushing the trolley, through the simple expedient of ripping his head off. Viktor then waited until all the other werewolves, including Jenny, had joined him in the access room.

"The front door is sealed and I've disabled the network connection from the rest of the facility. The security cameras in this area are down too. The rest of the cameras and coms are controlled from the main control room," she said, having changed completely back to human form. She pointed at the heavy locked door facing the entrance they had just forced, which bore a yellow and black plastic sign with the words "Central Control Room" on it. There had been a video camera that pointed at the spot in front of the door, but Victor had bounded up into the air and ripped the camera from its mountings.

The werewolf form was capable of speech, but not of forming human words and the transformation didn't come complete with alien language skills. Viktor had devised a set of simple commands that allowed him to give his pack orders without changing back into human form, but in this case he wanted to make sure that everybody remembered their roles. As soon as he could speak clearly he pulled a notebook out of the pouch he wore slung around his neck, and thus unaffected by his changes of form. "All the gates and cell doors are controlled from that room, except for the caged walkways that run up there just below the ceiling, and which are connected to the Emergency Response Unit's ready room. They have a separate access code for exactly this kind of situation. We can't lock them out. They'll be coming for us, so we need to keep some of the guards alive as hostages. Stay in control!" he said, glaring around at his followers.

Jenny touched his arm. "They know the plan, and they'll do what's needed."

Viktor grinned. "I know they will, or they'll answer to me. But this is important, so no one gets carried away. Understand?" He stared into the eyes of each of his pack of followers. Satisfied with what he saw, he changed back into werewolf form, dropped to his haunches and ripped the security card and lanyard from around the dead guard's severed neck. Then he lifted the guard's hand and bit it off at the wrist with a savage twist and shake of his head. He stood up, licked the blood from his fangs, and stalked over to the sealed inner gate, where he tapped the card against the sensor pad and then pressed the bloody hand against the biometric scanner. The scanner should have had a temperature sensor to defeat this trick, but the designers of New Belmarsh were on a budget and had chosen to save the cost of this feature. The LED light over the lock panel turned green and there was a mechanical click. Viktor dropped the card and hand, and threw his shoulder against the door even as his clawed hand pushed the handle down.

Although the guards in the control room had no idea what was happening outside, the shotgun blast had been an obvious indication that something was badly wrong, especially when the guards on the outside didn't reply to their radio or PA calls. Prison guards didn't usually go around armed, but there was a locked gun cabinet that contained both dart rifles and shotguns, but everyone considered them in the same way that people looked upon the fire axe in the glass case on the wall. If it really became necessary to use them, it was probably too late anyway. However, when the officers in the control room lost contact with the reception area and the security cameras went down at the same time, they began to get nervous. The sergeant in charge considered hitting the alarm that would call out the armed response team, but that would have also activated an emergency lock down of the entire facility and create a huge amount of bad press and administrative work. They were under strict orders to maintain a public-friendly atmosphere, and viral videos of men in full armour running around with machine guns and assault rifles would likely get people fired. He had finally decided to unlock the gun cabinet when the door leading to the reception area exploded inwards, swatting an unfortunate guard aside with a crunch of broken bones. The sergeant stared, mouth gaped wide in horror when a stream of werewolves burst into the control room. He reached desperately for a dart rifle, even though he knew he would never get it out of the rack and insert the magazine in time. He screamed in fear and rage when he felt claws tear into his shoulder and hurl him away from the cabinet. But his hand remained closed around the stock of the dart rifle he had just loaded even as he was flung back to crash into the main metal console. He tried to aim and fire as his attacker loomed over him, his mind whirling in shock. All the plans, drills, and precautions worked out by the designers of New Belmarsh had been predicated upon the risk of an attempted break out of the detainees, or at worst an escape attempt coordinated with people on the outside. No one had seriously considered the possibility of an organised attack from the outside, and especially not by a team of werewolves. Before he could fire, a sweeping blow of a hairy paw knocked the dart rifle out of his hands with force sufficient to bend the steel barrel. The paw reached down towards him and he closed his eyes, bracing himself for the agony of claws ripping into his flesh. Instead, he was thrown face down onto the ground and his arms twisted behind his back with irresistible force. He gasped in surprise when he felt the cold steel of handcuffs close painfully tight around his wrists, cutting off the blood circulation to his hands, but he had the feeling that a protest would be worse than useless. Still face down, he was grabbed by the collar of his uniform jacket and dragged across the room to be dumped in the corner with more of the guards. He was unable to see if all of the men and women in the control room were present and unharmed. A finger poked him in the back of the neck, and a distorted voice growled into his ear, "Move and I'll tear something off that you'll definitely miss." The sergeant was very familiar with the power and ferocity of werewolves. Despite the tranquilliser armbands worn by all inmates, there were incidents almost daily of an inmate transforming and committing horrific acts of violence in the time before the tranquilliser took effect, ranging from seconds to a minute or more. There were cases where the inmate had somehow managed to damage or disable his or her bracelet and as a result had to be taken down by a dart fired by the emergency response team from the caged walkways that passed above them. But in all those cases he had been separated from the werewolves by thick concrete and armoured glass. This was the first time he had been in the same room as a werewolf, let alone an entire group of them. Even more terrifying was the fact that these creatures seemed to be much more in control of themselves and disciplined than any of the inmates. He nodded convulsively and struggled not to wet himself.

Through careful questioning and bribing of the right people, Viktor knew that the response team had their own set of monitors that let them see every section of the inmate areas, allowing them to spot and analyse any disturbances or potential uprisings. However they didn't have a camera feed looking into the control room, which should have been superfluous. Nor did they have individual control of the cells or locked meeting rooms, since this was handled from the control room. But they could, as a last resort, seal off individual sections of the tunnel-like walkways as well as their ready room. In addition they had a duplicate of the emergency lock down switch located in the control room. He had to prevent the response team from triggering a lock down. Any attempt by his pack mates to charge the ready room would only result in them being trapped in locked sections of the walkway and shot down like sitting ducks by the response team. But he had a plan.

While Viktor and the others had been busy subduing

the guards, Jenny had been going over the computer system that controlled the individual cell doors, comparing them to a list that she had brought with her, and checking their video images against their photographs. "I've got them Viktor," she said.

Victor nodded and pointed at the guards lying on the floor. "Get changed." While his followers started to strip the uniforms off of the guards, Viktor knelt down beside the sergeant. "Listen carefully if you want to live, if you want your men to live. We're only interested in freeing our friends, five of them, nothing more. If we get what we want, no one else has to get hurt. But to free them, I need to disable the emergency response team, and to do that I need your help."

"Why should I help you?" the sergeant asked. "If they don't hear from us soon they'll activate the lock down and you'll be trapped in here until more police arrive to take you down."

Viktor let his hand change and dug his claws into the sergeant's scalp, pulling the man's head back and up off of the floor, baring his throat. "You'll cooperate for two reasons. Here's the first." He held out his hand and the ever-attentive Jenny passed him a mobile phone. He tapped the icon for the video player and held it in front of the sergeant's eyes as the video of the ambush and massacre of the police officers began to play. He grinned when he heard the sergeant utter a shocked gasp. "This is happening all over London, along with hundreds of false sighting reports. The police are much too busy to respond to an alarm from Belmarsh. And the second reason – "

Jenny dragged one of the other officers, now dressed only in underpants, to where the sergeant could see him. One paw held the man down by the throat, and when Viktor nodded she slowly raked her claws down the purple-faced man's belly, slicing skin and flesh like surgical scalpels, but only inflicting cuts less than two centimetres long.

Despite the clawed grip on his scalp the sergeant tried to struggle, but stilled when Viktor growled, "Move again and I'll let her gut him. I'm sure that if we start tearing your men apart, the noise will make the response team attempt a rescue, since they'll assume we're ordinary humans. If they burst in firing, I can't guarantee how my people will react."

The sergeant's shoulders slumped. "What do you want me to do?" From his tone it was obvious he was sorely tempted to add an expletive to his question but a glance at Jenny's eager grin crushed any thought of defiance.

Viktor lowered the sergeant's head gently to the floor and said, "I really have no desire to harm any of you, but one way or another, we're going to get our friends out of here. I'm going to offer the response team a deal. An exchange of hostages. They agree not to shoot at my friends and let them walk out of here instead of locking the place down, in exchange for all of you." He saw the flicker in the policeman's eye and grinned. "Of course your colleagues will attempt a double-cross of some kind, so when we make the exchange, you will be in front, and my friends will be behind you in borrowed uniforms. Once they unlock the security gate in the middle of the walkway, my people will overpower them just as we did with your men, and then we'll leave." He squeezed the sergeant's shoulder. "Jenny and I will remain here with your friends to ensure your good behaviour. Do we have an understanding?"

"You swear that you won't hurt anybody?" the sergeant asked, even though he knew he really didn't have a choice.

"I swear upon my honour, neither I nor any of my team will harm any of you unless attacked. We just want to get our friends out of here safely," Viktor said.

The sergeant could just see the pale shocked face of

the injured officer out of the corner of his eyes as he nodded. "All right. I'll do it. Just don't hurt anyone."

Viktor patted the sergeant on the back. "Good choice." He stood up and went over to the control panel. The internal communications controls were clearly marked out on the display screen, so it didn't require any particular familiarity with the system to open a direct channel to the response team. He touched the screen and the chosen channel lit up in a green highlight. "Hello, can you hear me? As you can see, I'm calling from the central control room."

There was a moment of silence, then the speakers came to life. "This is Inspector Crawford. Who am I talking to? What have you done to my men?"

"My name is … well you can just call me Viktor. There's no need to stand on ceremony. As for your men, they are all alive and unharmed, save for some minor nicks and scratches. And if you choose to be reasonable, they will remain that way."

"I assume that this is a prison break of some kind. Surely you know who we are holding here in New Belmarsh. Why the devil would you want to let any of them out?" Inspector Crawford replied.

"You're holding my friends here against their will. They've been convicted of no crimes, and the government has publicly said as much. This isn't a prison, it's a concentration camp!" Viktor said angrily. "But I'm not here to argue that with you. I have a list of five names, and I know which cells they are being held in. I propose an exchange. You let those five men go through the main gate unmolested, and in exchange we'll put our hostages into our end of the walkway, and then we'll leave. We'll jam the door to the control room, so by the time you break it down or go around through the alternate fire exit at the back of the facility we'll be long gone. As simple as that. Do we have a deal?"

"I can lock down the entire facility from here and

call for help. Why should I agree to anything like that?" the Inspector said. The fact that he had not already done so indicated that he knew the consequences, but he wanted to get Viktor's threat on the record.

Viktor nodded to Jenny, who picked up the sergeant as if he were a child and brought him over to the console. Viktor muted the microphone and said, "Tell the Inspector why. I'm sure he'll demand proof of life anyway. And before you're tempted to be heroic, think of your men. They're depending on you to keep them safe." He switched the microphone on again with the tap of his finger.

In a tired, defeated voice the sergeant identified himself and confirmed that all of his men were alive and generally unharmed. He then described Viktor's threats of retaliation and the fact that assistance from the outside would be slow in coming, if it came at all.

Viktor cut off the microphone and waited until Jenny had taken the sergeant back to his place on the floor, before tapping the microphone control again. "You have your proof of life and you understand your position. There's really no need for unpleasantness. Let my people go and I shall do the same for yours. You have ten minutes to decide." He cut off the connection without restating the consequences of non-cooperation. Viktor looked around at his followers, most of whom were dressed in their borrowed uniforms. Naturally the uniforms fit badly in some cases, but the Inspector would expect them to look dishevelled after their ordeal, and once they unlocked the security gate in the middle of the walkway it would be too late. The sergeant would be in front and they would hesitate to fire their dart rifles because they were instantly fatal to a human, or at least they would hesitate long enough. He glanced ostentatiously at his watch and then at the sergeant. "Eight minutes. Your inspector is testing my patience. Perhaps I should – " But before he could finish, Jenny pointed to the flashing red indicator on the screen. Victor waited a few seconds, and then activated the microphone. "Well? And before you say anything that might get your men hurt, there will be no negotiation, or time, or compromises. Yes or no? Choose now before I cut the line."

"Wait! I … yes. We have a deal. Give me the names of the inmates you want to be freed and I guarantee they'll be allowed to walk out of the facility. But before that happens I want to see the hostages gathered at your end of the walkway," Inspector Crawford said, trying to regain some semblance of authority.

Viktor read out the names and cell numbers from the screen of the security terminal. "I'm unlocking their cells now. You'll be able to see that only the five I have named have been released. When they are gathered safely at the main security gate I'll let your men leave the control room and step out into the walkway." He watched as Jenny unlocked the specified cells and instructed the inmates to walk towards the main detainee exit. Everything inside the main detention area was automated or operated by trustee inmates. When the five puzzled detainees were gathered at the airlock-style gate with its twin doors connected by a short tunnel, Viktor pointed at the sergeant. "Take the handcuffs off of him." Even in his human form, he could smell the tension in the control room. Everything depended upon the Inspector and his response team acting as Viktor anticipated. The security cameras showed a squad of armed officers gathered at the security gate in the middle of the walkway, which could only be opened from the Emergency Response Team's side. Viktor smiled and gripped the sergeant's shoulder. "Behave yourself, and everything will be over in a moment. Step through the door and walk slowly along the walkway. Remember, I'll be watching." He unlatched the heavy security door leading to the walkway and watched as the sergeant and his men dressed as guards filed through the portal into the wide metal tunnel. When the last man went through he pushed the door until it was almost shut but visibly unfastened. "Come on Jenny, let's get ready."

***

Dressed in full tactical gear and helmet, and carrying an SIG SG516 assault rifle, Inspector Crawford waited tensely at the gate. Looking past the approaching column of dishevelled officers he could see that the gate to the control room wasn't fully shut and guessed that someone was peeking through the gap, possibly with a firearm. Sergeant Owen's face looked shocked and pale, but that was only to be expected given the circumstances. When he judged that they were far enough from the control room, he said softly, "Unlock the gate." The moment the electronic lock clicked, he threw himself at it and charged out into the other half of the walkway, followed by the rest of the team save a single officer manning the control desk back in the ready room. "Down! Down! Down!" he shouted at the approaching hostages, and watched Sergeant Owen dive to the corrugated metal decking of the walkway, swiftly followed by the others. As soon as his line of fire was clear he let off a three-round burst at the control room gate to force whoever was behind it to move away from the exit, and sprinted over and past the prone hostages. Three seconds later he was at the gate. He dodged to one side and waited for the officer behind him to take position on the other side of the gate. Then he nodded at the next officer who kicked the door open. The Inspector threw himself diagonally through the open portal, sweeping the sector of the control room in his field of vision and fire for targets, the muzzle of the assault-rifle following the movements of his head. He edged along the wall and quickly leaned to peek behind a row of computer server racks, his rifle pointing accusingly like a steel and plastic finger. When he saw the huddle of near naked men tied up behind the workstations, he felt his skin go cold and he knew that he had been taken for a fool. He lifted the muzzle of his rifle as he spun around and pointed back towards the walkway. "Outside! It's a trap. Those weren't our men in the walkway. Cover the door, they'll be coming – " Before he could finish speaking, a hairy arm shot out from the opposite side of the steel firearms cabinet next to him. The clawed paw shot over his shoulder and around to grip his throat, lifting him up onto his toes. His rifle was ripped from his grasp and he felt hot, panting breath against the side of his head.

Viktor couldn't speak in his werewolf form, but the threat was obvious, and his jaw opened in a lupine grin when the other members of the tactical team all pointed their weapons at him. They were all carrying assault-rifles so it was nearly impossible for them to kill him, although so many bullets would definitely hurt, if it hadn't been for the fact that he was holding the Inspector in front of him as a shield.

For a tense, horrified moment it was a stand-off, and then the well trained tactical officers slowly began to move and spread out sideways across the room so that they could get a shot at the werewolf without hitting their leader. Their bullets wouldn't kill the monster, but they might force it to release its hostage in order to dodge the hail of fire. But in the excitement and tension of the moment, they had forgotten what the Inspector had been trying to tell them until one of the officers heard a low rumbling growl behind him. He glanced over his shoulder and despite his training, shouted out in terrified shock at the sight of the five werewolves standing right behind him, all of them draped in shredded pieces of the same tactical uniform he wore. The next thing he knew, he was flying through the air, hurled backwards by a raking blow to the chest that ripped the ceramic reinforcement plate from his body armour. His flailing body struck the backs of two other officers like a bowling ball and slammed them to the ground. A burst of gunfire from one of the falling men perforated a filing cabinet with an ear shattering thunder of sound.

The remaining two officers spun around with admirable speed and both fired at the charging row of werewolves. One of the werewolves, hit by two rounds in the upper part of its chest, staggered and fell into a crouch, but the other four werewolves kept coming despite being hit, moving with a speed that put any earthly predator to shame. If not for Viktor's commands, the policemen would have been ripped to shreds in seconds, but instead the werewolves disarmed the struggling men and handcuffed their hands behind their backs.

The entire encounter was over in seconds, and the Inspector blinked in disbelief. He had seen rampaging werewolves before, mostly inmates of New Belmarsh who had managed to break the automatic injector strapped to their arms. But this organised, coordinated attack was something he hadn't even thought possible. They had taken his superbly trained men as if they had been children, and even the werewolf who had been shot in the chest was back on his feet. Suddenly he realised that the hand holding his throat was no longer clawed and hairy.

"Impressive, aren't they?" Viktor said. "Please notice that your men are all still in one piece, even though you broke your word. However, that might change at any moment. For instance, if the man you left behind were to lock the facility down. That wouldn't make my friends happy at all."

The fact that the werewolves were calmly waiting, guarding his men after tossing them next to their other captives, instead of exhibiting the insane rage that he had grown to expect from his experience with the inmates, alarmed the inspector more than mere violence. "What do you want?"

"Right now, I want you to order all of your remaining men, including the snipers with dart rifles in the other sections of the walkway, to set down their weapons and to come here. If any one of them attempts to be a hero, your men here will pay the price." When the Inspector had obeyed his commands Victor used the Inspector's own heavy-duty handcuffs to secure his hands behind his back. The tactical team didn't use zip ties because they would be useless against the strength of a prisoner who could turn into a werewolf. He waited for all the officers to surrender and for one of his men to confirm that there was no one left in the ready room. He checked his watch and smiled. They were on schedule. He nodded at Jenny. "Do it!"

Jenny had already laid out the true list of the inmates that they wanted to release first. They were the ones who had been willing and eager to participate in the next part of Viktor's planned operation. She touched the screen and unlocked the gate to Ed Barlow's cell. Barlow already knew what to do, which was to collect and organise the selected inmates, and through several visits by the Russian contact, he knew the order in which they were going to be released. There were microphones in each cell, normally turned off for privacy, and she heard the triumphant eagerness in Barlow's voice when he confirmed that his cell was open. Speaking into the microphone, Jenny said "You know what to do. Confirm to me when you have each person on the list."

Viktor let her get on with the initial release of the selected inmates who had volunteered to take part in his plans and whom Barlow felt could be relied upon, a group of eight men and two women, while he kept an eye on the tactical team and made sure his own followers remained in control of themselves. Although unlikely, there was a slim possibility that a tactical officer or guard still hiding somewhere, and who still might trigger a lock down if there was a massacre. Even in human form his hearing was better than before and he heard the soft buzzing alert which indicated that the main door to the detention area was being cycled open. He also heard a chorus of confused babble coming from the other inmates.

"Team One is out, Viktor. Shall I proceed with the others?" Jenny asked.

"Make sure that Ed and his men are in the coach and then start with the others. I don't want to risk any confusion or clashes." His human underlings from the various crime gangs were waiting outside with a fleet of tourist coaches and private buses. Since the released inmates were still wearing their injector bands, he wasn't worried that they would change en masse and rip his human men apart. But if they became agitated they could still change, and in the seconds before the massive dose of tranquilliser took effect they could inflict a lot of damage to those around them.

"Others?" Inspector Crawford said in a horrified tone. "How many more are you releasing? Are you mad? Don't you know the kind of – " He abruptly stopped speaking when he remembered who he was talking to.

"Monsters? Creatures? Vermin?" Viktor said, his voice dangerously calm.

The Inspector went very still, acutely aware of how close he was to the edge of the precipice, and the fact that he might have dragged his men along with him. He blinked a drop of sweat from his eye as he mentally scrambled for the right words. "That's not what I meant at all. But surely you must admit that most of the … infected have little or no self-control when they suffer the change, unlike you and your um, companions." He flinched when Viktor dropped into a crouch beside him and he saw the man's jaws stretch and grow, and fangs begin to extend, before the change abruptly reversed and he appeared human once more.

"You shoot innocent people down, cage them like wild beasts with no hope of ever being released, and then call them monsters when they get angry?" Looking across the inspector's back he saw one of his followers give him a thumbs-up. The Response Team's ready room was clear and the lock down controls had been disabled. All the police staff had been accounted for and matched with the shift list on the control room records. New Belmarsh was completely under their control. "We're going to take all the prisoners who wish to go with us. I'm not going to force anyone to follow me. Now keep quiet. After all, you wouldn't want to antagonise a monster, would you?"

***

"I don't understand. Surely this Viktor person can't believe he can take over the country by killing the Prime Minister and the rest of the Cabinet?" Monica asked as they entered the Central Lobby.

Tara frowned. "I've been thinking the same thing. What could he hope to gain by attacking Parliament? Won't it just make the country even more aware of their existence and how dangerous they are?"

"Viktor's no fool. No matter how strong and powerful werewolves are as individuals, he knows they can't win in a straight out fight against humankind, or that he could somehow rule the country as superior overlords," John said. He had already thought about his opponent's choice of tactics and what Viktor's ultimate strategy could be.

"You think he's mad?" Tara said.

John chuckled. "Perhaps. But I believe he has a very sound reason for this. He knows he can't win a stand-up fight. Not yet anyway. At the beginning, it was to his advantage to work in the shadows, because he knew the authorities would reflexively deny the existence of werewolves or try to explain them away as some kind of disease or even an experiment gone wrong. But as their numbers grew and the Government was forced to act ever more openly to protect the populace, culminating in New Belmarsh, a tangible and undeniable confirmation of the reality of werewolves. But it also stands as a symbol of the Government's strength and ability to control them."

Monica nodded. "I think I see what you mean. By attacking Parliament he can prove that he and his werewolves are still dangerous and something to be feared. It's like when the zombies get into the army base or farmhouse. Everybody panics." She grinned. "I'm a fan of horror films."

John pointed at her with an approving nod. "Yes. Viktor's clever. He's realised that the monster's greatest weapon isn't fangs or claws, but fear. He wants the people to be afraid. To lock their doors at night and be frightened of the dark streets. He wants them to see that the Government can't even protect themselves. Terrorists try to do the same thing, but they don't have the advantage of being supposedly supernatural and unstoppable. If he plays his cards right he can force the Government to stop apprehending every werewolf that appears and sticking them in New Belmarsh." His brow slowly furrowed in a frown.

"What is it?" Tara asked, recognising the look on his face.

"New Belmarsh. Viktor knew they would have to build something like it. The Government couldn't just execute so many people, not without incurring worldwide condemnation, even if they officially revealed that Britain was infested with werewolves. Some countries would refuse to believe them, and others would seal their borders to all travel and trade from this country. Someone, perhaps the Americans, or the Russians, might even launch a nuclear strike to prevent the spread of the infection."

"They build a shiny new prison. So what?" Tara said impatiently. Then her eyes widened, and her mouth opened in a shocked "O". She realised that looking at it from Viktor's point of view, New Belmarsh wasn't a sign of the Government's strength, but a self-inflicted vulnerability. If he could successfully attack it and free the inmates, it would be like the storming of the Bastille, a symbol of werewolf freedom and defiance. "You've got to warn – "

But John already had his mobile phone out and was selecting Commander Blair's number. He activated the speaker phone mode and waited as it rang.

***

Only the shop fronts and overhanging walkway above them had allowed Blair and his men to make it this far. As it was, there were only three of them left, and Blair was bleeding heavily from a wound in his thigh and the other two officers were supporting each other as they backed towards the end of the market hall. Just two metres away lay the shaggy forms of three werewolves who had leapt down from the gallery above moments ago, landing too close for any of the police officers to aim and fire their dart rifles before the creatures were able to use their claws and fangs. If it hadn't been for their unorthodox body armour and the special tactics that Blair had worked out with the help of a private military specialist in close quarters combat, they would have all died right then. But because unlike a normal rifle, the dart guns didn't penetrate their target, so they were able to shoot even when another officer was right behind their target and with the muzzle almost pressed against the werewolf's body. Instead of each man taking on an opponent, they formed a tight formation and each officer covered the person beside him, a technique that required trust as well as practise. They responded as they had been trained, engaging the trio of attackers in a mad melee of growling, slashing combat. Blair was knocked to the ground by raking claws that ripped away a thigh piece of his armour and cut deep into his flesh, but he ignored his attacker and pressed the muzzle of his rifle against the side of the werewolf trying to bite into the back of the neck of the officer to his left. The snap of his dart rifle was closely echoed by the rifle of the officer next to him and the werewolf that had clawed his leg fell twitching madly before it could rip his leg off with its fangs. He climbed to his feet using his rifle as a cane, his heart pounding from his close brush with death, hardly feeling the pain of his injuries. Then he jumped when a man's agonised screams rang out from behind a stack of crates next to a stall. He looked around and realised that in the confusion, one of his men had been attacked and carried away by a fourth, unseen werewolf. More screams rang out and he ground his teeth in helpless rage. He knew that the werewolf was deliberately keeping the officer alive as bait, hoping to force them to retrace their steps back into the centre of the market building. But all of them were injured, and they were running low on darts, which were the only thing keeping them alive. "Keep moving." He looked out of the rear of the market hall and saw Sergeant Murphy's vehicles pull into the end of Russell Street, and he felt a surge of hope. "Murphy's here! We need to get to them and we'll be safe. Come on." Just then his Airwave crackled.

Murphy's voice said, "We're in position sir. I can see you. Should I join – shit!"

Blair didn't have to ask what was wrong. Even as the three of them staggered towards the exit, while simultaneously trying to scan every direction around and above them, he saw two more werewolves spring from the buildings lining the road and onto the roofs of the two supposed rescue vehicles, effectively trapping Murphy and his men inside their cars. They could possibly get out by exiting the vehicles from both sides at the same time, but it would likely be a suicide move for one of the officers. "Hold on Murphy. We'll shoot the bastards off of you when we get there. Just be prepared to provide covering fire and to get the hell out of here as soon as we're in the cars." A movement in the corner of his eye made him spin around and all three of them fired when the fourth werewolf darted out from behind cover and charged them, bounding from side to side, closing on them at a seemingly impossible speed. Blair saw two of the darts miss and hit an overturned table even as he tried to acquire his target and fire. One of the officers took a step backwards and his shoulder bumped into Blair's rifle, sending the dart upwards and shattering a pane of glass. A loud click and a red LED told him his magazine was empty. He reached for his pistol but then realised that he had lost it at the same time the werewolf had torn into his thigh. The other officer managed another shot, but missed again. Blair gripped his rifle with both hands to use as a basically useless club as the werewolf crashed into them, jaws wide and snarling. The hurtling mass of fur, muscle, and claws crashed into them and sent all three men sprawling on the ground. Blair shouted incoherently and struck out with the butt of his rifle, pounding at the creature's head and shoulder until he realised that the great furry mass was lying unmoving on top of him and the officer who had bumped into him. With a shudder of disgust he pushed free of the limp body and a constable helped him to his feet. Looking down he saw a dart protruding from the werewolf's calf. Patting his ammo pouches he said, "I'm out of darts."

"I'm empty," the man holding him up said.

"Me too," said the third officer.

Growls from deeper in the market hall echoed through the building like distant thunder. Blair pointed at the werewolves crouched on top of the cars that were their only chance of salvation. "All right. We run for the cars. When we get close, you two open fire with your pistols. I know it won't hurt them, but if we can draw them towards us, it will give Murphy and his lads a chance to get out and use their dart guns. It's our only chance."

The two officers looked frightened, but nodded in agreement, knowing that Blair was right.

Blair dropped his useless rifle and drew his fighting knife. It was a gift from John Seward and he knew that the high carbon steel blade was inlaid with a fine network of silver that looked like a decorative embellishment. Seward had offered to supply knives for all of his team, but Blair had declined, knowing that such a clearly expensive gift might raise questions within the force. "All right then. Let's go!" He began to run as fast as his injured leg would allow, his free hand braced on the shoulder of another officer, whose own arm hung limply at his side. They had just cleared the pillars that marked the end of the market hall when a chorus of howls and roars broke out behind them. More werewolves had arrived and they sensed that their prey had been flushed from cover and were running. Ignoring the tearing agony in his thigh he forced himself to move faster, the hairs on the back of his neck tingling as the sound of the werewolves grew ever louder behind him. The werewolves on top of the cars were grinning in anticipation, their tongues lolling wet, fangs glistening in the sunlight. He panted into his radio microphone. "Murphy, we're going to draw the bastards off your cars. Get ready to take them down!" Murphy's voice shouted from the radio, cutting him off. "Sir! Behind you!" Blair twisted around, only to see three more werewolves bounding towards them from the direction of the market. Turning back towards the cars he pointed at the werewolves crouched on their roofs and shouted, "Open fire. Shoot them!" He could see Murphy's pale, strained face through the windscreen, and he knew they weren't going to make it. As the two officers' pistols barked, their gunfire oddly muted and echoing in the open courtyard, he turned to face the trio of werewolves who were approaching so fast that his eyes had trouble focusing, and raised his knife before him in a futile attempt to hold them off. Behind him he heard the werewolves on the cars roar in anger at the sharp sting of the pistol bullets, and then the reverberating thump of their paws on the sheet metal of the cars as they hopped down off of the vehicles to rip the annoying humans apart. But the three werewolves coming from the direction of the market were too close. He knew they would kill him and the others before Murphy and his men could take them all down. He hunched forward, as if bracing against a hurricane, his lips curling into a snarl. A sudden loud hammering made his tensed body jump in shock, and his eyes widened in even greater surprise when the charging monsters tumbled and howled in dismay and agony, large dark patches of blood staining their fur. There was more hammering, and similar howls arose from behind him.

Shocked by the apparent failure of their near complete invulnerability, the werewolves skidded to a confused halt, and at the sound of more gunfire, bounded away in the direction of the London Transport Museum and Tavistock Street, leaving trails and spatters of blood on the paving.

Murphy and his men sprang out from their cars and fired at the retreating creatures, bringing two of them down before they could get out of range or behind cover. "Come on Sir! We've got to get out of here before more of them turn up," he shouted, waving his arm in a beckoning gesture.

Blair looked towards the shaded arch of the Royal Opera House and spotted a feminine figure wearing the familiar silver-grey body armour that he knew was an experimental product of one of John Seward's companies, and realised that his rescuer had to be a member of Seward's private security force, armed with a totally illegal assault rifle firing bullets tipped with a capsule of silver nitrate. He would have dearly liked to arm his own men with such bullets, but since no official study had proven the vulnerability of werewolves to silver, it would be impossible to explain the use of silver impregnated bullets by the police at the autopsy of a dead and technically sick civilian. The military had been pressing for tests on captured werewolves, but the Cabinet had refused any suggestion of experimentation on humans, especially experiments aimed at causing them harm. If such a thing had been leaked to the United Nations or even the World Court, Britain would have been roundly condemned, especially since the Government continued to maintain that they were dealing with an epidemic and not werewolves. Unofficially, more detailed – and truthful – information had been given to friendly governments, but everyone was agreed that the public reaction to an announcement that werewolves existed and were spreading nearly out of control would be too awful to contemplate. He realised that Seward must have assigned someone to watch over him and he saluted towards the shadowy figure. He would have liked to thank his rescuer, but he suspected that more werewolves were probably on their way, and even the ones wounded by the silver bullets would heal since they had not been killed outright. The longer he hung around, the greater would be the risk to his men as well as Seward's personnel, so he gave the masked and helmeted woman a nod and limped towards the waiting cars.

When he was inside the van, a duplicate of the one in which he had arrived, Blair remembered the phone call he had been unable to answer during the fight in the market. When the log showed that the call had been from John Seward, he frowned. He knew the industrialist wouldn't have called him while he was on duty unless it was something important. He had not received any police reports of an attack on the Houses of Parliament, so he knew Seward couldn't have called about that. He winced when the officer attending to his leg wound tightened the bandage, and then touched the screen of his mobile phone to return the call. "Seward? What is it? I'm rather busy right now." Blair had strong suspicions that Seward was more than human, although he still couldn't bring himself to think the word "vampire", and normally would have been more polite, but at the moment he really didn't care.

"So I gather," John replied dryly, having received a text message from Karen Duncan, the head of his corporate security team and the person who had just saved Blair's life.

The same thought went through Blair's mind and chagrined he said, "Whoever it was, give her our thanks. We wouldn't have made it without her intervention."

John nodded, even though Blair couldn't see him. "I'll do that. Back to the reason for my call. I just had a rather nasty thought, call it a hunch if you want to. But this organised disruption feels like a distraction."

"To keep us away from Parliament?" Blair said, wondering why Seward was bothering with such an obvious observation.

"No. To keep you from responding to an attack on New Belmarsh," John said grimly. He felt increasingly certain that his hunch was correct.

Blair's face went pale. He didn't need Seward to draw him a picture. Thousands of angry werewolves unleashed upon the country en masse, possibly led by the cunning and ruthless Viktor. It was a nightmare scenario. "I understand. I'll alert New Belmarsh immediately," he said and hung up. It took him a minute to find the direct number to the New Belmarsh control centre. When no one answered, he tiredly leaned back against the side of the van and closed his eyes. After a moment he sat up again and called Central Communications Command. He identified himself and asked to speak to a senior officer. "I need you to send a mobile unit to New Belmarsh to ascertain their status. Yes, I've tried contacting them. Yes I know your men are busy, but this is urgent. Critical. Yes, thank you." He ended the call and then turned to Sergeant Murphy, who was in the van with him. "Get in touch with HQ and recall all our people. I don't care if they're on leave or down with the flu. Unless they're in hospital or pregnant I want them in and geared up ASAP."

***

Viktor had just received news of the failure of the ambush at Covent Garden when the call from Commander Blair appeared on the telephone display, and his claws dug deep grooves in the hard plastic-coated surface of the table. He suppressed a surge of anger and gazed out of the control room window at the interior of the prison. "How are we doing, Jenny?"

"The last group is being collected now. Another ten minutes," Jenny replied, her attention focused on the cell gate controls and the video displays.

"Good, good. All right, get everyone ready to pull out. You all know your assignments and what you have to do," he said looking around the control room at his followers and grinning at the chorus of enthusiastic growls and acknowledgements, depending upon the form each of them held at the moment. He bent down and patted the inspector's shoulder. "Don't worry. Me and my people will be gone very soon. As promised, I'm letting everybody go unharmed."

"Everybody on the list is out and is on board, Viktor," Jenny said, a disturbingly anticipatory smile dancing on her lips. The smile widened into a grin when she saw Viktor's nod. Silently she tapped the commands that would unlock all the remaining cells, thousands of them, and would also unlock all the internal security doors that separated the inmate section and the separate sections occupied by the guards and service staff. Of equal significance, she unlocked the double gated entrance to the medical facility. The inmates never required medical treatment because of the alien nanites infecting their bodies, but the medical wing also housed the equipment that attached and removed the tranquillising arm bands that prevented the inmates from changing into their werewolf form. With that done, she ripped out the cables and wires that connected the work stations to the main control system and servers.

Viktor gave the orders that started his followers silently leaving the control room. He counted them to ensure that none were missing and then gallantly waved Jenny ahead of him. When they were in the slaughter house that had been the visitor's processing hall he said casually, "I wonder if any of the policemen will get free before the inmates find their way to them."

Jenny laughed. "Even if they do, I very much doubt any of them will get far before they are run down and killed. The inmates will enjoy the hunt." She knew that all the vehicles that were being left behind had been disabled, and no unarmed human was going to outrun the thousands of newly freed and enraged werewolves that she had just unleashed on the unsuspecting population of Southern England. But they were just a distraction. They were the ones who either lacked the mental strength and discipline needed to even partially control themselves when in werewolf form, or had refused for whatever reason to sign up with Viktor's new army. They would soon find out that the humans wouldn't see or care about their motives or morals. Those who survived would realise that only by joining them, joining Viktor, would they have a chance of freedom instead of the life of a hunted animal.

Viktor sprang into the coach that held the first group released, the ones handpicked by Ed Barlow. Spreading his arms he shouted, "I promised you freedom! And here you are, out of that miserable cage!"

"Damned right!" Ed shouted back, waving a fist in the air.

After a moment, another man shouted, "Free!", and then another and another, until the coach vibrated with their shouts and the pounding of their hands against the backs of the seats in front of them. But when the shouting subsided, one of the men, a tough looking character with a scar dividing his eyebrow said, "Why are we still wearing these fucking things?", raising his arm and pointing at the tranquilliser band. Several others growled in agreement.

Viktor held up his hands. "Most of you have had little experience or practise in controlling your change. We can't have you changing during the drive and getting … rowdy. As soon as we're at our destination, I promise you they'll come off." He watched his own followers board and smiled when their grim confidence silenced the doubters.

When all the other coaches had departed, Jenny boarded the coach too and nodded to the driver, who was also one of Viktor's pack. As the door hissed to a close behind her she frowned at the bloodstain on the driver's seat. "That was careless."

The driver shrugged. "He got suspicious and hit Mark with a tire iron. You can't blame Mark for being pissed off."

Jenny bit her lip and then pointed. "Cover it with

that newspaper. We can't risk an observant copper spotting it. She moved up to stand beside Viktor. "We're ready."

"All right then! To the Palace of Westminster! It's time for Parliament to hear what we, the people, have to say," Viktor cried, grinning at the eager expressions on the faces of the passengers filling the tour coach.

Chapter Six

Commander Blair listened grimly to the recording of the police patrol car's transmission.

The reporting constable's voice said, "The car park's empty except for vehicles belonging to the Belmarsh staff. Wait ... it looks like ... all of them have had their tyres slashed." There was a muffled conversation between the two constables in the car and then, "The main entrance looks to be open. In fact, it looks like it's ... yeah, it's broken, like it was hit by a battering ram, but from the inside." There was more murmured conversation, and then, "I see movement inside. It's a woman. She's in civilian dress, no injector cuff on her arm, a visitor maybe. She looks like she's in shock. We're exiting the car to assist."

Blair listened as the sounds of uniform shod footsteps crunched across the parking lot and then the voices of the constables calling out to the woman.

Faintly, there was the sound of the woman's reply, then, "Fuck! She's changing!" followed by the snapping sound of dart rifles being fired. "She's down! She's down! We're OK." There were more indecipherable noises. "There's more of them! Dozens! They're all around... get back to the car ..." There were more snap-crack sounds of the dart rifles firing, and then the screaming began.

"Shut that off," Blair snapped angrily. "We need to get a helicopter or a camera drone over Belmarsh ASAP," he said to the communications officer.

"Sir, they say they're all busy covering the situation in the city," the constable replied after a moment.

"I don't care if we have to requisition some hobbyist's drone or get the MOD off of their arses. Tell them we're most probably faced with a mass breakout from New Belmarsh! This could be a national disaster!" Blair shouted back. Then he remembered John Seward and Parliament and a chill burned down his spine like liquid nitrogen. He had Seward on quick dial and seconds later he was speaking to the industrialist and possibly the only being he knew who could stand up to the werewolves. "You were right. There's been a breakout at New Belmarsh. Expect company soon. I'm gathering what's left of my team and I'll alert SO17. But since I still don't have definite proof of a specific threat to Parliament, all they can do is heighten security, which will be less than useless against an army of werewolves. "I don't know what you can do Seward, but thank you."

***

John put his mobile phone away and turned to his companions. "There's been a break out at New Belmarsh, just as I had feared. Monica, perhaps you should go home now. Things are going to become very dangerous in a little while."

The guide shook her head. "You still need me to help you get around easily. I know some small rooms with really thick doors and no windows. When something bad happens I'll hide in one of them. No one's going to bother with a tour guide when there are much bigger fish to fry."

John prized bravery and loyalty, and he was impressed with the woman's determination. He nodded and gently squeezed her shoulder. "Can you find us a private room to get changed. We can't walk around with weapons, but we can at least get into our armour. With our coats on we'll just look a little eccentric but not alarming.

Chapter Seven

Ian Werner, CEO and owner of Werner Aerospace and Robotics frowned when a notification popped up on his monitor screen. When he clicked on the notification box a text message appeared. "Satellite images from New Belmarsh, UK. Your eyes only." He clicked on the link provided and leaned forward when a series of photographs taken by a top-secret US Government intelligence satellite appeared on his screen. It was illegal for him to have access to such images, but laws were only for ordinary people, peasants, although he would never utter that word in public. He clicked through the sequence of images and hummed thoughtfully when he saw the stream of inmates flowing out of the main entrance and into the fleet of waiting tourist coaches. He leaned back in his chair and smiled. "So, it's begun," he said to himself. Both he and his think tank had agreed that the Brits would inevitably suffer a major werewolf incident in the not very far future, most likely instigated or aided by their ex-agent Viktor Tiranul. Werner was determined to find a way to control or otherwise utilise these amazing creatures, although his scientists had shown a frustrating lack of progress. He was tempted to summon Dr Wright simply for the pleasure of shouting at him, but he was too good a manager to demotivate his staff simply to ease his own frustration. He had given the researcher a deadline and all the funding he required. Instead he called the head of Human Resources. "Have a shortlist of potential replacements for Dr Wright prepared for my consideration by the end of the week."

***

Apart from being a brilliant scientist, Dr Wright was no slouch at office politics too, and he had taken care to cultivate a friend in the HR department, so he was almost immediately informed of the instructions to begin a search for his potential replacement. He also knew that it was a not so subtle hint from Mr Werner that his patience was wearing thin. The trouble was, he had nothing at all to report. He had tried chemicals, including outright poisons, physical trauma, electrical shock, x-rays, retroviruses, but nothing seemed to affect the test subjects when in werewolf form. In human form they could be injured, but the injury triggered the change and subsequent rapid healing. Of course there were many possible chemicals and allergens to try but they would take time, and they would be unlikely to give him any insight into the factor that was causing the entire werewolf phenomenon. He had already tried external beam radiation, but the damage caused by the focused radiation exposure quickly healed just like every other injury. However, he had yet to try systemic radiation, injecting radioactive iodine into the test subject's body at extreme doses. The trouble was, even if this did manage to affect the unknown agent, the massive damage done by the radiation would also kill the subject, which would be basically self-defeating. But there was the faint possibility that at some stage he might gain some insight into how the mysterious alien treatment worked even as it was destroyed by the radiation.

Through the high definition monitors, Dr Wright studied the wildly struggling werewolf that was strapped down to a motorised operating table with steel bands in the lead shielded room. A large cannula and IV line was attached to the creature's arm and the plastic tube led to a remotely controlled device which would allow Dr Wright to inject controlled doses of the mixture of radioactive materials which he had specially designed to flood the subject's entire system. Since the dosages he intended to use would almost certainly be fatal if it worked at all, he had to handle the actual procedure himself to avoid stupid lab assistants spilling all on social media or to the alternative news. After a final round of checks to ensure that all instruments and recording devices were working properly, he pushed the slider that would begin feeding the radioactive isotopes into the test subject. He knew nothing about the male subject other than the fact that he was middle aged and of average health, nor did he care. Getting the right results were literally a matter of life or death – for him. A display linked to a radiation detector showed the highly radioactive material flowing through the roaring monster's veins as glowing green threads that were rapidly spreading and diffusing into the test subject's flesh, organs, and bones. The whole-body dose which was in excess of thirty Gy was invariably fatal within one to two days in a normal human, but incredibly, the werewolf's enhanced metabolism actually seemed to hold its own against the deadly radiation. The thought of disease and radiation resistant troops, and the commercial possibilities it presented made his mouth water. But as the radioactive isotopes continued to flow into the werewolf's veins, there seemed to be a turning point after three days. Abruptly, whatever had been shielding the werewolf's system against the radiation seemed to fail, the first sign of which was that the subject unexpectedly transformed back into human shape. In a tightly controlled frenzy, Dr Wright began taking samples from the subject's highly radioactive body using remote controlled manipulators and computer operated equipment, tissue, blood, fluids, photographs, video, x-rays, MRI images, everything in his scientific arsenal that might possibly capture the elusive element that had transformed this person into a biological miracle. Then just as suddenly, the subject died. Every function of the body simply ceased. But at that moment Dr Wright didn't care. He had masses of raw data to analyse and interpret, from which maybe, just maybe, he could catch even a glimmer of what had resided inside the subject's body. He watched as the samples were moved via a conveyor belt to the next room, which was a laboratory, while the body was moved off of the work table and into a lead shielded coffin. Since all the physical samples were radioactive, they would have to be handled by remote manipulators and specially designed testing equipment.

***

Unknown to Dr Wright, he had indeed managed to damage the semi-intelligent alien nanite swarm residing inside the subject's body. But the designers of the nanites had built their medical products well. The core purpose of the nanite system, to preserve body integrity, and basic autonomic functions, were hard coded into each nanite's physical structure, impervious to being corrupted by accident or intentional attack. However, in order to make the basic nanite matrix capable of being configured to clients of various species and sub-species, the specific biological templates had to be stored in a writeable and modifiable form, similar to what Earth technology would call Random Access Memory or RAM. Even this element was incredibly stable and resistant to corruption. However, exposure to constant and high levels of radiation injected into the host's bloodstream over a period of days was beyond what the alien creators considered likely, in the alien environments or battlefields that they faced, and eventually the non-permanent memory matrices degraded and failed. However, the designers were thorough, and they had provided for exactly such an eventuality. It only required the host to be exposed to a few intact and uncorrupted nanites and the lost information would spread through the damaged system of nanites, acting as reset to a default factory standard, but of course this did not happen. In its degraded state, the nanites couldn't flush the host's body of the radioactive isotopes quickly enough to prevent severe damage, so instead it put the entire body in a state of death-like stasis, while it struggled to filter out the radioactive materials and to slowly eject them from the body through every means possible, such as urine, tears, sweat, and saliva, these secretions appearing very much like decomposition fluids from a dead body. Once the levels of radiation fell to a non-fatal level, the damaged nanites sprang into action restoring the basic life functions of the host. But without the physiological templates, the nanite colony could only restore simple cell and tissue damage, the host's pulse, respiration, and the most primitive of brain functions. Six hours after the body was placed in the unsealed lead-lined container, the subject's eyes opened.

***

Dr Wright rubbed his eyes tiredly, and tried to force away a growing sense of panic. None of his samples and scans revealed anything other than dead and dying tissue. He felt as if the alien technology was actively mocking him, and the loose items on the control panel rattled when he slammed his fist down on the enamelled metal surface. For a moment he thought he had damaged something when a yellow warning light began to flash. Rolling across the long console on his chair, he moved in front of the monitor that displayed the morgue where the deceased test subjects were stored before being cremated. Although the lead lined case was still intact and the lid closed, according to the display there was a significant amount of radiation leaking from it. It wasn't at a dangerous level at the moment, but it wouldn't be safe to move the container through the halls to the furnace room. He was almost glad of the distraction from his fruitless work and donned a light radiation suit before swiping his key card over the lock and typing in the security code. He passed through the air lock and walked cautiously towards the coffin shaped container. The simple hasp lock appeared to be intact, and he pulled at the lid. He frowned when he felt a slight movement. These containers weren't intended to be absolutely air tight, and the lid must have shifted or warped very slightly during transportation. He unfastened the hasp and then took a two-handed grip on the lid on the long side opposite to the hinges. Being lined with lead, it was quite heavy so he had to bend his knees and lean into the lid to push it up and back. He grunted in satisfaction when the folding struts locked, keeping the weighty lid upright and open. Before performing a check of the lid's edges for dents or warping he looked down at the corpse. He frowned when he saw one of the hands of the corpse twitch, although he wasn't surprised. Dead bodies often displayed minor movements even twelve hours after death. Out of reflex he reached into the box and checked the flexibility of the corpse's arm, testing for the onset of rigor mortis which should have been clearly detectable after so many hours. When the arm bent easily at the elbow he frowned and leaned closer. If he had not been wearing the suit's heavy gloves he would have noticed that the corpse's arm was still warm. Too warm for a corpse that had been dead for so long. But as it was, he mentally shrugged the anomaly off as an effect of the radiation or the werewolf condition and returned to inspecting the edges of the lid and then the rim of the container itself. He was leaning over the open box to examine a dent on the far side next to the hinges when he felt a subtle vibration. Before he could react, something closed with crushing force on the flesh of his upper arm. He shouted in alarm and pain, and tried to pull back and straighten up, but his eyes widened in disbelieving horror when the corpse's hands grabbed his wrist and shoulder, holding him in place like steel hooks.

The fabric of his suit ripped, and his voice rose to a shrill scream of sheer terror when teeth clamped down upon his exposed flesh. The heavy container began to rock and slide as Dr Wright fought to break free of the subject, which was very definitely not dead. His struggles were given greater energy by the thought that the subject might at any moment turn into a werewolf and tear him limb from limb. With a maddened effort he managed to brace a foot against the side of the box and throw himself back and away. But he screamed again when he failed to break free of the subject's grip and instead simply pulled the non-corpse out of the box to land on top of him when his back slammed down on the resin-coated floor. The impact of both the floor and the impossibly alive subject drove the breath from his lungs and stunned him, and his arm burned in pain where he had been bitten. He tried to struggle, to fight free of the subject's crushing weight, but he froze in terror when the subject reared up above him, teeth bared and eyes empty of all but the most basic animal intelligence. He managed a hoarse "No!" before the subject plunged down to fasten its teeth on his throat, tearing and ripping.

***

The radiation detection system in the morgue wasn't only linked to Dr Wright's laboratory, but also to the building's main security system. A leak of radioactive material could threaten every occupant of the building, including Mr Werner himself. So when the subject tumbled out of the lead case it only took seconds for the alarm to sound in the main security office. Six minutes later two specially trained security guards in radiation suits pounded down the corridor that led to the laboratory, guns drawn. Upon hearing the alarm, the Chief of Security had overridden Dr Wright's shutdown of the video camera system. He had watched in horror at what appeared to be a naked man biting and scratching at Dr Wright and he immediately despatched a team of men to deal with the situation.

Using security master key-cards the guards charged into the morgue. The first guard to enter, who had the name Brad stencilled on the breast of his suit, shouted "Get away from Dr Wright! Hands on your head! Get down on your knees, now! Do it or I'll be forced to fire."

Jake, the second guard, drew a Taser, and when the person attacking Dr Wright didn't respond, he fired. Trailing fine silver wire the twin barbed darts shot across the room and embedded themselves in the attacker's back. There was a crackle of high voltage electricity, and the man shuddered and arched his back in a rigid spasm. But only for a moment. Jake watched in shocked surprise when his target, instead of falling to the floor, swept his arm across the wires, snapping them free of the Taser's body. The re-animated corpse turned clumsily around and snarled at the new threats.

Brad recovered quickly. He drew his gun and fired twice, hitting his target in the abdomen as he was trained. But his target didn't go down. In fact he wasn't noticeably inconvenienced by the holes in his body. Before Brad could fire again, he found himself in a tug-of-war over his pistol. His opponent's grip on the gun prevented him from finding a target, and then he screamed when the nameless man lowered his head in a strange darting motion and clamped his teeth upon the base of Brad's thumb through the leather of his glove, and bit down hard. Brad slammed his fist into the side of the man's head, but it had as much effect as hitting a store dummy. A moment later the gun was wrenched from his grip at the same moment as his thumb was bitten off of his hand, leaving the glove dangling from his attacker's mouth. Brad stumbled backwards staring in horror at his mutilated hand, his mind reeling at the possibility of dangerous radiation exposure. "Take him down! Take him down!" he shouted to his partner.

Jake dropped his Taser, drew his pistol and fired, emptying his magazine. He cursed when one round passed through his target's arm and hit Brad, grazing his chest just below the armpit. At least three of his shots hit the target dead centre, but it hardly slowed the attacker. All it did was make him turn towards Jake. He ejected the empty magazine and snatched for his reload, but the loose-fitting radiation suit made him clumsy, and the living corpse was on him before he could finish reloading. Jake shouted in fright when his apparently bulletproof attacker threw himself forward and sank his teeth into Jake's right thigh, biting right through the tough fabric of the suit and tearing a chunk of flesh from his leg.

The most critical damage the radiation had done to the medical nanite system was that it had affected the safeguard which prevented it from infecting a non-intended host, in this case humans, except in life or death situations. Since the nanite system was effectively blinded, it went to work on any living host it found itself in that was injured and matched a very generally advanced biology. So it wouldn't work in a dog or rabbit, even now. But it did work on Dr Wright, who was rapidly bleeding to death from the wound in his throat. The torn veins and arteries clotted and healed and flesh formed on top of it, but a jagged scar remained, as if cauterised. The nanite system had no template to base any more complicated repairs upon, but it was enough to keep the body alive. Sadly, the same couldn't be said for Dr Wright's brain. Oxygen deprivation had caused extensive damage and no trace of the superbly trained scientist's mind remained when the body sat up.

Brad was too distracted by his injury and the ongoing attack on his partner to notice Dr Wright's impossible recovery, or at least until the Doctor crashed into him, jaws and teeth snapping at his face like a hungry shark. Brad expertly threw the Doctor to the ground despite his injured hand, but staggered in panic when the Doctor twisted around like an eel and sank his teeth into Brad's calf, once more biting right through the fabric of the suit. Before he could bend over to strike at his new attacker, a violent pull on his lower leg threw him backwards onto the floor. His head struck the ground, stunning him.

***

The Security Chief gaped in horror at the scene in the morgue and then his hand slammed down on the panic button that silently summoned all the senior security officers and notified selected members of management, including Mr Werner. By the time he had finished explaining what had happened and looked back at the screen, the morgue was empty.

The huge monitor screen on Werner's office wall mirrored the image of the empty morgue as he listened to the report from the chief of building security, who advised him to get into his panic room, which had recently been upgraded and reinforced after the disturbing late-night visit by an unseen intruder. But unlike the company's research facilities and factories, this office building couldn't be sealed off floor by floor through remotely controlled emergency doors, although the alert would lock all the building's external entrances. If he entered the panic room, he would be trapped there until whatever had escaped from the morgue could be re-captured or destroyed. Instead, he grabbed his mobile phone and his emergency brief case containing his passport, various important documents and flash drives, a large amount of cash, and an automatic pistol complete with spare magazines. Speaking into the intercom on his desk he said, "Get the car ready. I'm leaving."

"Yes Mr Warner," his secretary replied, knowing

better than to ask questions. If Mr Warner had thought she needed to know more he would have told her.

A touch of a button opened the door to Werner's private elevator that led to the basement car park. If there were one or more werewolves loose in the building his staff would deal with them, and notify him when the problem had been solved. Until then he would work from his penthouse apartment. The elevator reached the parking basement with a smooth bump and the doors slid silently open. Werner started to step out, his eyes searching for his armoured limousine, and then he realised what he was looking at and came to a frozen halt. He had found his limousine, two car lengths to the left of where it should have been. Eddie, his driver, was stretched backwards over the long polished front of the vehicle with his uniform jacket and shirt torn open and his belly a gaping red pit. Squatting over the driver's dead body was the blood-soaked figure of Dr Wright. A loud female scream made Werner jump, and his frantically searching eyes spotted a woman running across the huge car park pursued by a man in the torn remnants of a radiation suit and the uniform of the building's security officers. He realised that Wright and this guard must have pursued the woman down here, and that Eddie had merely been unfortunate enough to be at the wrong place at the right time.

At that moment the creature that used to be Dr Wright spotted Werner standing in front of the entrance to the private lift, and the CEO's face triggered a burst of rage in the scientist's ravaged mind. Uttering a wordless shriek of rage, Dr Wright clambered off of the car and charged.

Shaking off his shock Werner stepped back into the elevator cage and jammed his finger against the "close" button. He watched the doors smoothly close while Dr Wright ran unsteadily towards him. He forced himself not to flinch when the elevator rumbled from the impact of a body running full tilt against the outer doors just before the elevator began to move. He pulled out his mobile phone and selected the number of building security. "This is Werner. Have your men seal off the basement. Tell them it's full of – "

"Zombies, sir?" the security chief replied. "We can see them on the monitors."

"Then why isn't the basement already sealed off?" Werner snapped, ignoring the guard's use of the word "zombie". The elevator glided to a halt and the doors opened to his office again. Werner stepped out as the guard replied. He frowned at the sight of his secretary standing with her back to him. "Clara, what are you doing in … " his voice trailed off when she turned around to reveal her pale face and the gory bite wound just above her left breast.

The security chief's voice buzzed from the phone, "The zombies … they're all over the building, sir. I'm in the security office to get more ammo. I'll come for you as soon as I'm reloaded. Sir? Sir? Are you all right, sir?"

Werner knew he couldn't get back into the elevator before she was on him and being trapped inside a moving elevator with one of these things would be even worse. He was many things, but a coward wasn't one of them. "Get your ass up to my office now!" he shouted before putting the phone down on his desk and picking up a heavy decorative letter opener. Holding it out in front of him he edged around the desk, his free hand searching for the pistol he kept in the drawer without taking his eyes off of this horrible remnant of his secretary. Because he wasn't looking down, his foot kicked the castor of his chair with a loud clunk and made the chair slowly rotate. He saw his secretary tense and a fleeting flash of thought illuminate her eyes. He lunged towards the drawer, all thought of stealth abandoned, but before he could claw the drawer open his secretary hopped awkwardly onto the desk top and then threw herself at him, teeth bared in a hungry snarl.

***

Viktor knew that at the first sign of a real emergency or threat to the government the military would be mobilised to help the police, which would be a major obstacle to his plans. He was not so foolish or overconfident as to think he could eliminate the army, air force, and navy elements in and around London, but he didn't need that, or even want it. He just needed to keep them busy. So he had arranged for two or more coach loads and car loads of very bitter and angry werewolves fresh from New Belmarsh to be despatched to each of the major military bases and barracks in London, including the Duke of York Barracks, home of the 21 SAS and, it was rumoured, units of The Increment, the black operations teams assigned to the SIS, popularly known as MI6. He was quite sure that fifty to a hundred pissed off werewolves all of whom had been promised cash rewards and membership in Viktor's rapidly growing werewolf society, would be more than adequate to keep all the soldiers at each barracks occupied with simply staying alive long enough for his actual objectives to be accomplished. Most of the werewolves would be either killed or captured eventually, but Viktor saw it as an audition of sorts. Those that survived and didn't simply run away would be valuable additions to his growing werewolf army. He held high hopes for them because unlike newly turned ones, these werewolves had had time to adapt to their condition and they knew full well what awaited them at the hands of humans. If they survived the attack, they had all been given assembly points where they would gather in human form to be taken to safe hiding places by Viktor's people.

***

The uniformed sentry ran under and past the huge triangular lintel with its ornate clock and horses, waving his arms and shouting when the huge tour coach hissed to a halt in front of the Hyde Park Barracks on South Carriage Drive. "Oi! You can't stop here! Keep moving!" he cried, waving his arm vigorously as he squinted, trying to see through the vehicle's windows to no avail due to some kind of dark coating on the glass. He pounded on the folding door with his fist when the coach just sat there unresponsively. "Come on! You can't block the gate like this!" For two minutes nothing at all happened. He could hear the crisp tread of what had to be an officer coming up behind him and he began to sweat. When he saw the door start to move he grabbed the edge and pulled, relieved that he might be able to resolve the problem before having to explain his failure. The door folded open with a metallic clunk and rattle, and he opened his mouth to shout at the driver. But whatever he had intended to say was lost when a huge hairy paw slammed into his chest, sending him staggering backwards to collide with the person behind him.

***

One of the horses of the Life Guards on duty at the gate leading to Horse Guards Parade shifted uneasily when a tour coach swerved sharply from the road towards the open black iron gates that lay between the two mounted cavalrymen. Its rider patted its neck soothingly, but then cried out in shock when the bulky vehicle accelerated and roared through the gate, filling the air with acrid engine exhaust. The horses went wild and the guards were totally occupied with preventing their mounts from bolting and couldn't do anything to impede the completely unexpected intrusion.

The Changing of the Guard happened to be in progress, and the screech of the coach's brakes made the neatly arrayed and helmeted heads snap around in surprise and alarm. It was almost inevitable that the first thought that came to everyone's mind was of a car bomb or ramming attack, and the ranks of horsemen turned into a swirling mess of individual riders and horses, all trying to put as much distance as they could from the threatening coach. At the same time, assault rifle armed soldiers ran across the huge courtyard in the opposite direction.

Then the coach doors opened with a hydraulic hiss, and a moment later every horse in the courtyard went mad, rearing and bucking, throwing their riders or galloping madly away and carrying their helpless riders with them. When the werewolves began to stream out of the coach like a horror film parody of a tour group, the panic spread to the dismounted cavalrymen and uniformed soldiers. Some of the cavalrymen drew their sabres as they backed away from the growing cluster of furred monsters gathering at the gateway. The rifle armed troops formed up in a loose row, their faces strained and nervous. They knew that their weapons would be largely ineffectual against the werewolves except for direct head shots, and even those were usually not fatal. But they had to try to give the cavalrymen what cover they could, as well as to defend the entry to Buckingham Palace and Whitehall until the Queen, who happened to be in residence, and all the other important personages had a chance to evacuate, which was why all of them, including the archaically armed and armoured cavalrymen, were there in the first place.

Suddenly, terrifyingly, a concerted roar broke out from the mass of werewolves, and as one they all started bounding towards the white-faced soldiers, fangs bared in hungry snarls.

The troops with guns opened fire, their rapid,

staccato bursts sending some of the werewolves tumbling and twisting in a spray of blood, tripping others behind them. The entire group of soldiers edged backwards, hoping to reach the gateway behind them, which would prevent the werewolves from flanking or even surrounding them. For a moment, the hail of bullets seemed to offer a chance of at least slowing the werewolves, but then one after another the soldiers' magazines emptied and their guns fell silent. Empty magazines bounced and clattered against the ground as the soldiers snatched frantically for reloads. But it was too late, and the mass of werewolves, enraged by how they had been treated, and by the searing pain of the bullets ripping through their alien modified flesh, crashed into the ranks of soldiers and incongruously colourful cavalrymen, and the killing began.

Just like every other military installation in Britain, Horse Guards Parade had been supplied with the automatic dart rifles and the unique tranquilliser, but they were stored in the armoury and not in daily issue based on the recommendations of the Tourism authorities, who deemed that such obvious reminders of the werewolf threat to be unwise. When the alarm sounded, armourers scrambled to locate the padded metal cases containing the air rifles as well as the insulated boxes of pre-loaded dart magazines, unlocked them, and courageously ran with them towards the sound of battle. When they arrived at the gateway, it was a scene of slaughter-house horror, blood splashed all over the old stone archway and coating the ground in slippery, sticky pools. Amazingly, the troops still held the entranceway against the massed werewolves that snapped and clawed at them. The surviving soldiers in combat fatigues had pulled back to the rear of the ragged formation, those who still had ammunition taking aimed shots at the werewolves whenever they could. Surprisingly, it was the cavalrymen's armour and sabres that had allowed them to last as long as they had. Packed tight in the gateway, they were not so easily dragged away and ripped apart by their werewolf assailants, and their cuirasses protected them to some extent from the werewolves' disembowelling blows, even though their diamond hard claws actually punched through and ripped the polished steel.

Using the deadly sacrifice of their fellows, the soldiers gladly snatched up and loaded the dart rifles, but despite the armourers' valiant efforts, it was too late, and the last surviving cavalrymen were hurled out of the gateway as if thrown by an explosion, and the werewolves broke into the inner courtyard. The battle broke into dozens of individual skirmishes, with the werewolves running down everyone they saw, while the dart gun armed soldiers fired and ran in pairs, covering each other's backs. However with each shot they became a target of more and more werewolves, and the air was filled with the screams of men and several women as they were literally torn apart by the enraged werewolves all around the massive enclosed space where so many martial parades had been held in the past. Although at least ten werewolves went down at the first oddly flat sounding volley of dart rifle fire, it became far more difficult for the soldiers when the furred monsters scattered across the open space and even smashed their way into the surrounding buildings through windows and doors. Men armed with dart rifles began to go down under ripping fangs, hurling torrents of blood everywhere. It quickly became a war of attrition, a battle of survival between the dart rifle armed soldiers and the werewolves. Incredibly, more and more men were throwing themselves into the unequal battle, picking up blood soaked dart guns from where they lay next to eviscerated soldiers and shooting at the nearest werewolf, often only to die, torn limb from limb moments later.

The worst carnage happened inside the buildings around and adjoining the parade ground. Individual werewolves prowled through corridors, offices, and meeting halls, virtually unopposed. Some of the civil service workers who somehow learned what was happening without actually running into a werewolf, sounded the fire alarm in the hopes of evacuating the buildings without causing a panic. Unfortunately this resulted in people calmly gathering in the corridors just in time for one or more werewolves to plough into them like maddened threshing machines. This naturally resulted in a panicked stampede and even more casualties, as well as a disastrous pile-up at the exits which provided the grinning and vengeful werewolves with what the military called a "target rich environment". The result was massacre on a truly horrific scale, hundreds of people being literally shredded and torn limb from limb in great gory piles that blocked the doors to anyone who had not joined in the initial rush to escape.

If all of the werewolves had remained in the parade ground, the dart gun armed soldiers would have been quickly overwhelmed, but because the majority of them had gone after easier prey inside the buildings, which was what Viktor's people had encouraged them to do in order to maximise the carnage, the surviving soldiers found themselves the victors in this mad replica of an ancient Roman Colosseum spectacle of humans versus predatory animals. If unlimited numbers of dart rifles and ammunition had been available, the subsequent battle to capture or kill the rest of the werewolves would have been fairly one sided, if not exactly bloodless on the human side. But due to the limited number of effective weapons and the puzzling lack of help or reinforcements, the subsequent room to room, floor to floor, hunt was far more bloody and terrible. Never before had the police or military been forced to face large numbers of werewolves in combat, especially in an environment that favoured the werewolves' speed, agility, and advantages in close quarters battle.

With the unfamiliar shape of the automatic dart rifle gripped tightly in his hands, Lieutenant Philip Ward peeked around the corner. The Admiralty Extension was a maze of intersecting corridors and it felt like an insanely realistic first person shooter game, with roars, growls, and screams filling the air from every direction. Behind him he felt Corporal of Horse Tony Ballard's hard steel cuirass press against his back.

Ordinarily, Ballard would have divested himself of the clumsy ceremonial armour before entering combat, but he had discovered that the steel armour was actually more useful against the claws of the werewolves than modern body armour. Unlike Ward, he was armed with a standard L85A2 rifle complete with an under-barrel grenade launcher, but with only one grenade. That wasn't a serious disadvantage, since firing a grenade in a corridor was close to suicidal. The assault rifle's ammunition would be only marginally effective against the werewolves, but there were too few dart rifles to equip everybody with them. His job was to watch the lieutenant's back and hold off attacking werewolves until Ward could turn and fire a dart. He had also retained his cavalry sabre, despite the risk of it getting in the way or rattling. With his eyes to the rear, he felt the lieutenant tap his arm, indicating that he had seen something. There was so much noise echoing through the corridors that it was hard to tell if a werewolf was nearby simply from the sound. He glanced over his shoulder and saw the lieutenant point around the corner and then hold up one finger. One werewolf spotted. He turned back to the rear, made sure that there were no threats visible, tapped Ward on the shoulder once, and followed him around the corner, rifle raised to his shoulder.

The lieutenant had been so focused on the moving

figure of the werewolf that he hadn't seen what was behind the tall deadly creature until he had taken several quick paces forward and looked down the sights of the dart rifle. Then suddenly the reality of what he was looking at struck him. It was not a pile of bodies, so much as a heap of bloody flesh, organs, and long sickening loops of intestines. It was worse than any scene from a slasher film, the wet glistening of raw tissue mixed with the ghastly smell of opened bowels. He froze, his gorge rising in a painful rush, even as the werewolf snarled and paced towards him.

"Shoot it! Shoot the bastard!" Ballard shouted as he took a long sideways step so that he could fire his rifle without destroying Ward's eardrums. Even so he mentally winced when he pulled the trigger. The repeated triple hammer blows of sound made his head ring, but he forced himself to ignore the pain and emptied his magazine into the approaching horror. "For god's sake Ward, shoot!" he shouted when the werewolf staggered and then kept coming, its jaws open in a wide malevolent grin. The creature was on him before he could extract a magazine from the belt pouch strapped incongruously around his waist so he dropped the rifle, letting it hang from its sling, and drew his sabre in a slashing cut that caught the werewolf's forearm, the edge jarring against steel hard bone.

The enraged werewolf roared and lunged towards Ballard, ignoring the sabre and the rapidly healing wound on its arm. A clawed hand lashed out in a ripping, disembowelling blow which hit the cavalryman's cuirass. The blow dented the steel and claws harder than tungsten-carbide cut grooves into the armour, sending fine spirals of steel flying into the air.

The force of the blow sent Ballard tumbling backwards to bounce off of the wall and onto the floor. Before he could sit up, a huge hairy foot slammed into his head, sending his helmet rolling away down the corridor and pinning him down. He almost peed himself in terror when the werewolf doubled over in a way that no Earthly wolf could ever have accomplished, lowering its gaping jaws towards his throat. He screamed when the entire weight of the monster landed on him and he pushed his hands against the creature's chest, trying to keep the fang filled jaws away from his face and neck, knowing that a single bite, even a shallow one, could infect him with whatever had turned his attacker in the first place. It was only when Ward helped to roll the heavy body off of him that he realised the werewolf wasn't moving. "Well it's about bloody time!" Ballard said, only half in jest. He was shaking and his legs were wobbly, so he lay flat on his back breathing heavily, until he saw the lieutenant pick up his sword and head towards the drugged werewolf. He pushed himself upright and said, "What are you doing … sir?"

Ward burned with shame at his display of weakness that had almost cost both of them their lives. He had barely recovered from violently throwing up in time to shoot the werewolf before it had torn Ballard's head off. He hefted the sabre in his hand and then pointed it at the werewolf. "I'm going to cut the fucking thing's head off. We don't have the necessary restraints, and there's nowhere to lock the bastard up that would hold him. It won't be long before it wakes up, and I'm not giving it a chance to do that again!" he said, swinging the sabre in an arc to point at the pile of raw human flesh at the end of the corridor.

Ballard flinched when the tip of the sabre swished past his face. "Watch it!" He climbed unsteadily to his feet, his hand exploring the dent in his cuirass. He held up his other hand placatingly. "I'm all for beheading the sodding thing. But you know it's against standing orders and the law. We'll both be in for it if they hold an inquiry later on."

Ward spat at the werewolf. "I don't care. You can

leave if you want. I'll tell them we were separated and you didn't see me do it."

Ballard tapped his armour. "It nearly opened me up like a tin can," he said and held out his hand. "May I have my sabre back, sir?"

Surprised, Ward raised his eyebrow at his subordinate. "Are you sure about this CoH Ballard?"

Ballard picked up his helmet and clapped it on his head, fitting the metal linked strap to his chin. "Absolutely Lieutenant," he said, extending his hand again. With the sabre in his grip he said, "You'd better stand back sir. This is likely to be messy."

***

The attack on Horse Guards Parade produced even worse casualties, especially amongst the cavalry horses since there was much less space for men or horses to manoeuvre, or stampede. In addition, the armourers were brought down by the werewolves before they could unlock the armoury and issue the dart rifles or even ammunition for the L85A2s. Tourists and local Londoners in Hyde Park stared in shock disbelief at the sight of armoured horsemen fleeing desperately through the park, pursued by packs of werewolves, before they themselves were slaughtered by more werewolves. Some even managed to upload photos and videos onto the Internet before being torn apart.

Because the werewolves were not operating as a disciplined force, the surviving soldiers eventually managed to gain access to the dart rifles, and a counter-attack that more resembled a big game hunting party commenced. Again because of the close quarters of the combat inside the buildings and in the park, the casualties amongst the troops were terrible, many of the dart rifle teams being lured into ambushes while others were surprised and blind-sided by the far faster and stronger werewolves while the soldiers were trying to bring down another pack of the creatures.

***

This chaos was repeated in every military barracks in and around London and Viktor chuckled as the reports came in from his non-werewolf observers supplied by the underworld gangs that he controlled and the Chinese Triad gangs that had voluntarily allied themselves with him. Despite the terrible casualties, both military and civilian, he knew that no permanent harm had been done to the Army. However, for the moment, both the police and the military were totally incapable of doing anything other than protecting themselves and any civilians that had the misfortune of being in the vicinity. Which left the way open for the main event. He looked across the floor of the rented warehouse and the select team of twenty werewolves including Ed Barlow, plus Jenny and two of his trusted followers. They had all been dressed respectably and supplied with mobile phones and cameras so that they would blend in with all the other tourists that would be at the Houses of Parliament. Each of them still wore their injector bands, but they had been unlocked and could be removed with the flick of a finger. But apart from the mass terror that the released werewolves were causing he had another operation in progress. Viktor was nothing if not practical, and at that very moment, his human gangsters were carrying out robberies all throughout the city on a scale never before seen anywhere in the world short of an actual war or revolution. After today's carnage, he was confident that not a single one of the criminals would even dream of withholding his tithe of the proceeds. He would be the richest man in the country after this. He glanced at the clock display on his phone and nodded to himself. He looked around and waved for Ed Barlow to come over.

"Start gathering everyone together. Let those who are with the women finish up, and then have them gather over there." He had organised a load of good food, alcohol, and prostitutes, supplied courtesy of the Triad. The escorts had been promised double their normal rate to make the men, and some women, happy.

When Ed indicated that everyone was present and the escorts had been taken away by their Triad minders, Viktor climbed up on a table and clapped his hands loudly for attention. "All right, into the buses! It's time to make history. We're going to accomplish what Guy Fawkes failed to do. We're going to destroy Parliament!"

Jenny walked up to him as Ed ushered the volunteers onto the coach. "Brodie hasn't come back to us on the tour guide schedules and security procedures that he said he could get. Do you think we should be worried?"

Viktor frowned as he considered the information. "He might have been careless when kidnapping the guide, or it may have been something completely unrelated to us. But if he has been taken by the police, he doesn't know enough to be dangerous, and if there had been a security alert at Westminster we would have been informed. Besides, neither the police nor the army are in any position to interfere. But just to be safe, make sure our people are ready to pull out at the first sign of trouble. Don't let them get carried away in the excitement. That goes for you too."

She pouted. "But I want to bag myself a few MPs or even a minister or two!"

Viktor grinned and put his arms around her. "I'm not telling you that you can't hunt. Just keep an eye out for threats and be ready to drop everything and run if things somehow go bad." He kissed her.

Jenny stiffened for a second, the instincts developed during her years as a prostitute cutting in, and then she relaxed and kissed back. She had come to honestly love

Viktor, and strangely enough his viciousness and utter ruthlessness aroused her in a way she could never have imagined before she became a werewolf. "Don't worry. Ed and his lot can take the risks."

Viktor gave her bottom an appreciative squeeze and nodded towards the coach. "Time to shake this country like nothing before."

***

After receiving Commander Blair's warning, John called Karen Duncan. "It's definitely on. I can't get you into Westminster, but bring your team over here as we discussed. It's likely that there will be a lot of people charging out of Parliament pursued by werewolves. I'm counting on you to protect them. You have Blair's number. If his people are there, try to coordinate with him. But be careful. Legally you're vigilantes and under the current law the werewolves are innocent civilians with an illness."

Duncan looked around at her team, dressed in a modified version of the high-tech body armour that both John and Tara wore. It wasn't as strong or comprehensive, since the weight would have been impractical for humans, but it was better than anything even the military possessed, especially against werewolf claws and fangs. Nor did they carry dart rifles. The large calibre semi-automatic rifles fired fragmenting bullets coated with silver. Unlike John and Tara, whose vampire reflexes were superior even to the werewolves, humans were at a serious disadvantage when fighting werewolves at close range. Dr Rowland Harker and Emily Palmer, his lover and assistant, had been working on ways to counter this, and the rifles were equipped with their latest attempt at a solution. Inspired by the face and smile detection functions built into modern electronic cameras, they developed an electronic sight for the rifle that could distinguish and recognize werewolves and which controlled the trigger. When activated by a thumb switch, the user could pull the trigger and sweep the rifle's muzzle in the direction of the nearest werewolf enemy. However, the rifle wouldn't fire until the sights locked onto the figure of a werewolf. It was unlikely that the various authorities would approve it for commercial use, since there was a small chance of identification error, but after seeing the system in operation successfully in a wide variety of conditions, including a single werewolf replica in a room full of furry mascot costumes, John had decided to issue them to his security team, with instructions to only use the function in dire need and close quarters combat.

When Duncan was satisfied with their turn out, she stepped back and looked each of them in the eye. "I will say again, this is a volunteer mission only. If you are arrested or captured there will be little that I or Mr Seward will be able to do for you. In addition we are likely to be outnumbered by the werewolves, so I won't blame anyone who wishes to opt out. Those who still want to come along, board the transport now. The rest can surrender their weapons and resume their ordinary duties. She had worked hard to train this group of men and women, who were ostensibly security personnel for all of Mr Seward's operations, but who were covertly trained and equipped to combat werewolves. They had already fought one pitched battle against mercenaries sent against them by the American W.A.R. corporation who were trying to monopolise all traces of the alien technology that Tara and Viktor had accidentally discovered, as well as Dr Rowland Harker's unique aircraft technology. But now for the first time they would come face to face with werewolves in what might be pitched battle. She had to hide a smile of pride when all of them filed silently into the disguised armoured personnel carrier, which appeared to be a sleek prototype commercial transport vehicle for which Mr Seward had managed to obtain legal vehicle registration. Rowland had wanted to install an automated cannon on the roof, but John had pointed out that getting a permit for it would be rather difficult. Duncan wished that Rowland had gotten his way as she climbed up the ramp into the vehicle. As the ramp raised and locked, she called Mr Seward. "We're on our way."

Chapter Eight

Tara looked around at the seemingly endless rows of doors, corridors, and junctions. "Should we try to intercept them before they get inside?" she said, glancing at the bag containing her weapons and the combined helmet and mask, that acted both as protection and disguise. It was inevitable that the existence of vampires would become public sooner or later if they continued to fight the werewolves, so it would help if their faces were not all over the Internet.

"There are too many possible entrances. We can't depend upon Viktor and his people coming in through the tourist entrance, and we would be too far away from the Commons and House of Lords to intervene if they are attacked," John replied. "This isn't the first time that Parliament has been threatened, even by werewolves and vampires over the centuries. But never by what is likely headed our way today."

"You sound … afraid," Tara said, feeling a sudden chill of fear herself.

John shook his head. "Not for myself, or even for you. Yes, we risk death, but that's nothing new, and I'm confident of your abilities. Neither of us will be easy to kill, not even by Viktor's new friends. But I do fear failure. If they manage to kill a majority of Parliament, including the Prime Minister and Cabinet, it could deal a fatal blow to the confidence of the country. People will panic and social order will fall apart. Societies are more fragile than most people imagine."

Tara waved her arms in frustration. "Can't Commander Blair convince Parliament to cancel proceedings, at least for today? If there was a serious bomb or biological threat to the government they would do something!"

John put his hand on her shoulder and squeezed gently. "Viktor has shown a lot of cunning and patience.

The break out at New Belmarsh will simply draw more police resources in that direction. The attacks on the army installations will paralyse the military, and the random ambushes of the police and public will flood all the channels with calls for help. But there is not a single solid indication of an attack here at Parliament House. The government would be a worldwide laughing stock if they cancelled a sitting of Parliament on nothing more than an anonymous tip about werewolves, and Viktor knows this." He chuckled. "Even kings feared ridicule more than the assassin's knife. I know I did."

"So we just stand here and wait until people start to die?" Tara asked. As a test pilot she understood patience and meticulousness, but the waiting had never been easy for her.

"My guess is that they will attack the Commons. It's Question Time today and I think that is Viktor's target. Don't forget, it will be broadcast live, and so would any attack," John replied. "But yes, given the situation, people are going to die, and we won't be able to prevent it. Duncan and her team will be outside soon, and hopefully Commander Blair and his men are on the way. I wish the SO17 command were being more cooperative, but they will undoubtedly respond when the attack comes, so we won't be totally alone."

"Provided they don't shoot at us instead," Tara said ruefully. "Hopefully Blair can convince them that we're on the side of the angels."

***

"But Commissioner – " Commander Blair said, his grip on the phone turning his knuckles white.

"You have your orders Blair. You did well in spotting the break out at New Belmarsh. The inmates are reported to be wandering all over the countryside and I'm ordering you to get your men out there to lead the apprehension of all escapees. I don't want to hear another word about some ridiculous conspiracy theory plot to attack Parliament. Even if there was to be an attack, SO17 will handle it. I've even put them on special alert, so stop arguing and do your job. God knows there's going to be blame enough in this fiasco to go around. You and I will be lucky to hold on to our jobs after this Blair, so for god's sake do as you're told." The Commissioner's voice sounded tired and strained. Reports of disaster were flowing over his desk like a tidal wave, and the escape of the New Belmarsh inmates was the last straw. He had spoken up publicly in favour of the facility as a solution to the werewolf problem, and now that it had all turned to shit, he would be catching more than his fair share of the blame.

Blair sighed. "Yes sir. I understand," he said, careful to keep his tone level, hiding the frustration and insubordination he felt bubbling inside like molten lead. He knew that the Commissioner was wrong, even in a political sense. If even a single MP was injured or killed, and there had been the slightest chance that Blair and his team could have prevented it, the Commissioner's career would be finished. He put down the handset and stared blankly at the wall. He trusted Seward even though he suspected that the man was … more than a man. But he couldn't tell the Commissioner, and even if he did, what good would it do? "Commissioner, a man that I suspect is a vampire is convinced that there is going to be a major attack on Parliament." He snorted in bitter amusement. And yet … the chain of command existed for a reason. Who was he to decide that the lives of Members of Parliament were more valuable than those of the people living and working around New Belmarsh? And yet again … there was the political and social considerations. What would be the consequences of the utter destruction of Parliament? New MPs could be elected, a new government could be elected. But would the country survive such a sudden and public decapitation of its leadership? How many would die in the ensuing chaos and panic? And if he disobeyed a direct order, what would happen afterwards? Blair took a deep breath and turned around to look out through the glass section of his office wall. As he expected, Sergeant Murphy was looking at him. He nodded and gestured to the sergeant, and then waited until Murphy had entered and closed the door behind him.

"Was that the Commissioner, sir?" Murphy asked. He had been with Blair long enough to know that his superior was troubled.

Blair nodded. "It was. He wants us to join the clean-up at New Belmarsh. A direct command."

Murphy knew about the possible attack on Parliament, and looked dismayed. "But sir – "

Blair held up his hand. "I know Murphy, and I know where I have to go. But I can't order the men to follow me in this. Or you. So I'm ordering you to assemble all the men fit for duty and to head for New Belmarsh. A command centre to organise the recapture effort has been set up there. Remember, CC01 is not in the main chain of command. Don't let the men get absorbed into the rest of the search and capture effort. You and the lads will be best employed tracking and taking down those werewolves that put up an organised resistance to being recaptured."

Murphy stared at his superior for a long hard moment, obviously tempted to argue, but then he nodded briskly. "Yes sir."

Blair waited until Murphy and all the field officers had filed out of the office, presumably headed for the armoury to get kitted up and issued their weapons. He had a locker in his office where his own body armour and weapons were stored. He unlocked it and began to strap himself into the more than ordinarily elaborate body armour. It was a new set, the one from the Covent

Garden battle being a total write off. Around the armour he strapped on his pistol. The belt was also new. He checked his pistol, pulled out the magazine and stared at the bullets, his eyes narrowed in thought. Then he spun towards his desk and began to eject the bullets from the magazine with his thumb into a tray. Then he pulled open a drawer and extracted a large box of cartridges which bore no logo or company name, just an indication of the nine-millimetre calibre and an S in brackets. These had been given to him by John Seward as a gift. They looked like ordinary hollow point bullets, except that the deep indentation at the tip was filled with a silvery powder and sealed in with an epoxy resin. These were not the specialised bullets made for Seward and his people, but modified commercial rounds and impossible to trace back to Seward. Blair reloaded all of his magazines with these rounds. If he had to fire his pistol, then using unauthorised ammunition would be the least of his problems – or that of Britain itself. The sound of his office door opening behind him made him cover the ammunition box with a folder before he turned around. "Murphy? What are you doing here? Is something wrong?" he asked, his mind whirling with possibilities.

"Nothing's wrong, sir. Sergeant Green and the lads are on their way to New Belmarsh," Murphy said stolidly. "You got enough of those to share around, sir? The dart rifles are good, but not good enough if we've got to stop the bloody werewolves from killing the PM and the rest of Parliament."

Blair started to order Murphy to get in a car and to head for New Belmarsh, but he knew that Murphy wouldn't obey. "Share around? How many idiots have you convinced to throw away their careers with you, Sergeant?"

"Four, sir. All of them were with us at the hospital where we first saw the werewolves. They all know what those things can do when they're not newly turned and confused. They're not going to leave you to face them alone. Nor will I sir," Murphy said, his jaw set firmly.

Blair was torn between guilt and pride, but he knew that Murphy and the others wouldn't be talked out of their decision, nor was he even sure he had the right to try. "I've got one more box of fifty rounds. Here, share them out amongst you. But make sure they know they aren't magic. The wounds will be slower to heal and cause more pain. But even a head or heart shot won't kill them, just put them down for longer than the darts."

Murphy took the box of ammunition. "We won't have time to restrain them all and still keep our lords and masters alive," he said, looking significantly at Blair's sword hanging in the locker.

"We go for the kill. I'll take full responsibility for it," Blair said with a heavy nod.

Murphy chuckled. "If we save enough of them, we'll be bloody heroes and nobody will touch us. If we don't, there'll be responsibility enough to go around." He paused for a moment, and then said, "Will they be there?" He didn't have to say who he meant.

Blair nodded. "The two of them are already there and waiting. I think more of their people, like the ones we saw at Covent Garden will be outside."

"They're good people, whatever they are. It'll be good to have them with us," Murphy said. He loaded a magazine with his share of the custom-made bullets, and helped Blair tighten the straps of his armour. "I'll give these out to the lads."

"I'll meet you at the garage," Blair replied. When Murphy had left he called Seward again. "We're coming as soon as we can. Six of us. The rest have been ordered to New Belmarsh. Don't start the party without us."

***

Viktor sat in the coach with his arm around Jenny,

151

enjoying the feel of her body pressed against his. He turned his head and kissed her as the coach turned into Lambeth Road. "Nearly there."

"I can't wait to really, finally let go," Jenny said, her eagerness plain on her face. Noticing the minuscule narrowing of Viktor's eyes, she quickly added, "Don't worry. I know what I have to do, and I won't let you down."

He patted her shoulder and kissed her on the cheek. "I know you won't, Jenny." He knew he didn't have to remind her of the consequences of failure, and she had proven her loyalty and her ability to do as she was told. "I'll make sure you have the opportunity to … indulge yourself."

She kissed him back. "You're so sweet," she said. The fact that she meant it surprised herself. He wasn't kind and loving, and she knew he would rip out her throat if she ever crossed him, but he never hit her for no reason, and she knew he would always look after her so long as she was loyal. For the first time in her life, she truly belonged, and she would kill the entire world to stay by his side. And for a start, she would slaughter the high and mighty that had treated her as worse than dirt. She had never minded being a prostitute. No one had forced her into the life. But the hypocrisy of the men, and more than a few women, who had used her services and then called her scum the very next day, filled her with a burning rage. Now it was time for her to let them know exactly what she thought of them. The Americans liked to say, "payback's a bitch", which seemed appropriate to the situation. Well, she thought, this bitch intended to get payment in full on debts that were owed to her.

***

John frowned and turned to Monica. "The Prime

Minister's Question Time is at noon. It's ten thirty now. Can you get us tickets to the gallery?" he asked.

"I can try. There's usually a queue for tickets unless you get them in advance," Monica replied.

"See what you can do. If we can't get in, we'll have to wait at the entrance and force our way in when Viktor arrives," John said.

"What if an attack begins at the main tourist entrance or elsewhere?" Tara asked.

"We'll have to leave that fight to the police. With most of the government gathered in one room, we're going to be their last and only chance," John replied. His warrior instincts urged him to charge into combat, but centuries of war had taught him to pick his battles. There was a time for attack and a time for defence.

Chapter Nine

The Werner Aerospace and Robotics building was located just off Farragut Square, a bustling part of the business district of Washington D.C. Like most modern corporate headquarters, it was not unusual for staff to work through the night. Nor was it unusual for the building to be locked down for security exercises and actual alerts, since W.A.R. dealt with cutting edge military technology with offices all over the world, so when deliverymen and other visitors found the doors locked they just shrugged and turned away. At the top of the building, Werner woke up from a nightmare filled sleep. The bite on his hand throbbed painfully and he reached for the plastic container of pain killers and a fresh bottle of drinking water. The panic room was luxuriously equipped with food and drink, as well as entertainment, an Internet connection, a telephone line that was independent of the building's communications system, and even a radio capable of digital, FM, and short-wave transmissions. The problem was who he could call, or more precisely, who he could trust to handle the situation. He knew nothing about the disease or whatever it was that had infected some of his staff including his personal assistant. For the moment they were all trapped inside the building, but he had lost contact with his security team and he didn't know who else might be infected or how many of the crazed victims were roaming the building. Although he did have access to some of the security cameras' views, he didn't have the level of control that the security office provided. But from what he could see, it definitely wasn't safe to wander around the building. There seemed to be only a relatively few of the infected that he could actually see on screen, and they showed no signs of turning into werewolves so he finally decided to call in a crew of reliable and discreet independent consultants, mercenaries really, to come and get him out. Despite the deaths and his own near demise, Werner was excited. They had finally managed to affect the alien system, whatever it was. Even though the researcher was dead, his records would be on a very secure part of the corporate system, and they would be able to duplicate his work and carry on from where he failed. Once he was clear of the building, he could arrange for a larger team of mercenaries to go in and capture or kill the infected. As for the surviving staff, they would be offered a generous bonus along with a non-disclosure agreement to ensure their discretion and silence. Those who refused or seemed untrustworthy would be dealt with by the same mercenaries. After he made the call and arranged for spare keys and the necessary codes to be handed to the mercs by his lawyers, he settled back on the comfortable sofa and poured himself a generous shot of bourbon, grimacing when his bandaged hand bumped the table. The team wouldn't be able to equip and get to the headquarters building until around dawn, so he turned on the video monitor and switched from camera to camera in hopes of getting a better idea of the number of infected. This proved harder than expected, since the infected looked very much like everyone else unless they were attacking someone or had wounds visible to the cameras, which was how he managed to identify a few of them. And unlike the werewolves, these victims didn't seem to completely heal, although they didn't appear to be hampered by their injuries either. After a while he grew bored with staring at the screen and made himself a meal from the frozen food using the microwave, and then went to lie down to get some sleep after setting the alarm to wake him at six a.m.

When the alarm went off he woke up with a splitting headache and what felt like a hangover. But he took more pills and pushed the discomfort aside. He called the contact number for the mercenary team, who told him that they were about ten minutes away from Farragut Square. A glance at the monitor screen revealed that everyone in sight seemed to be sleeping, which was good. He didn't want to have to deal with a load of panicked questions from stupid office boys and secretaries. Once the mercs had the doors open and got to his office he could make a quick discreet departure, and then seal up the building again. Then he could arrange for a clean-up team to take care of whatever was loose in the office complex before anyone outside of the building became aware that something was wrong. He switched the monitor to the camera facing the main entrance and waited. Although the panic room was as large as a hotel suite, the enforced stay made him claustrophobic, and he jumped up when he saw the group of men appear at the main entrance. It was about a quarter to seven and the street behind them was fairly empty, so Werner had little doubt that they were his rescuers. He rubbed his temple as he watched, and snatched up his mobile phone when he saw one of the men holding his. "Werner," he said when his phone buzzed.

"We're here, sir. Please get ready to move. How should we handle the other occupants of the building?"

Werner didn't hesitate. "Verbal warning if it's safe. If they're too close or appear hostile, do whatever is necessary. What about noise?" They were in the middle of Washington D.C. and gunshots were bound to attract a great deal of unwanted attention.

"Since we're not facing werewolves, or armed and armoured targets, we're using suppressed SMGs and subsonic ammo. Best we can do sir," the mercenary replied.

Werner had to agree. Faced with a building full of possible threats who looked like ordinary people, dart rifles would be impractical and even harder to explain if it ever came to an autopsy. "Agreed. Just be careful, I don't know what the infected are capable of. I'll be waiting. Tell me when you reach my floor so that I can unlock the door."

"Yes sir. Will do. Going dark and affecting entry now. "

Werner nodded when an indicator on the control panel told him that the main entrance had been opened, and then locked again. Although leaving the doors open would have been safer, he didn't want any of the infected or his frightened staff escaping into the street. He switched to the interior main lobby camera. Normally there would have been uniformed receptionists and security guards on station, but after the lock down everyone had been advised to find safety in a room with a lockable door and to stay inside until given the all clear. The rescue team came into view moving carefully in single file, guns covering all approaches and the last man walking backwards. However, since they knew they weren't faced with enemies equipped with firearms, they didn't hug cover as they moved but kept to the centre of the corridors and rooms to avoid sudden close-range confrontations. They had nearly reached the elevator lobby without incident when one of the office doors crashed open. A man and a woman charged out into the hallway, dishevelled and wild eyed, heading straight for the startled team.

The team leader shouted, "Hold fire!" but it was too late. Both man and woman went down in a flat hammering of automatic fire which hit their head and necks, resulting in explosions of blood, brains and skull fragments. Because he wasn't focused on shooting at the couple, he saw what they had been running from and he raised his own weapon, an ST Kinetics CPW, which looked like an oversized pistol and loaded with subsonic 9mm ammunition. "Behind them! Infected!" he shouted, mindful of the earplugs all of them wore and the effect of the gunfire in the confined space on their hearing.

157

Three distorted, blood soaked figures pushed through the doorway, moving quickly but with an odd lack of coordination and horrible twisted faces, as if they all suffered from severe brain damage but retained the ability to walk and move. He lifted his stubby weapon to his shoulder and opened fire, shifting his aim from one target to another as fast as he could and still aim accurately. Due to their odd, jerky gait, he missed the first figure but hit the second, two bullets striking her throat and one grazing her skull. To his shock, the infected woman didn't go down from the clearly fatal wounds, but instead merely staggered and then charged at him in a shambling run. Gunfire erupted beside him, so he focused on his attacker and let his team handle the others. She was closing on him too rapidly for fire control, so he took aim at her upper torso and emptied his magazine. Without taking his eyes off of his incredibly still standing target, he ejected the empty magazine, snatched another from his belt and reloaded in a single motion, and fired again at point blank range. He jerked back and away in disgust and fear when blood and bits of flesh spattered his face and her hand grabbed at his vest. He slammed the short collapsible stock of the CPW against the woman's wrist, freeing himself just in time to prevent her from pulling him down to the floor as she collapsed. He glanced at the transparent magazine and then joined his team in shooting at the other two targets, filling the lobby with flashes of light and flat cracking sounds of the suppressed weapons.

"What the fuck?" one of the mercenaries yelled, staring open mouthed at the still jerking and quivering bodies on the floor. Each of the infected had taken enough hits to put down a rhino, many of them directly to the head, and yet they continued to move, obviously trying to crawl towards them.

"They're zombies! Goddamned zombies!" yelled another of the mercs.

"Shaddup Zack!" the team leader snapped. "We were told they were infected by something. But they don't have claws or fangs, and aren't very smart. They don't heal fast like those werewolf things the Brits have. So we take them down just like anybody else. Got it?"

Zack spat at the still twitching bodies and nodded. "Yeah. I got it."

"All right then. Let's get moving. Our client is still waiting, and we don't get paid unless we get him safely out of here," Coleman, the leader, said, pointing towards the waiting elevators.

***

Werner watched intently as the rescue team stood waiting for an elevator car, feeling as if he was viewing a horror film and expecting more zombies to jump out at them at any moment accompanied by dramatic music. He sighed with relief when they backed into the elevator safely, and then felt annoyed at giving in to his emotions in that way. He switched the monitor to the camera covering the lobby on the penthouse floor and waited impatiently for the team to arrive. He swore under his breath when he saw the floor number freeze half-way up the building. He hurriedly tapped the camera controls to the indicated floor and then cursed out loud when the screen revealed a crowd of at least eight figures crammed against the door to the elevator. Bright flashes of light told him that the mercenaries were still alive and fighting, although the camera didn't let him see inside the elevator itself. Then the doors slid shut and he tapped the controls again to bring the view back to the penthouse level. He couldn't suppress a grunt when only three men stepped out of the elevator when it arrived at his floor. His phone was already in his hand when it buzzed. "I see you. I'm coming out." He was certain none of the infected or his surviving employees had gotten up to the penthouse floor. The elevator required a key card or his approval to rise up to the top level, and the emergency exit couldn't be opened from the stairwell. He picked up his briefcase, checked the Glock pistol in its belt holster, and keyed in the code to unlock the vault-like door. He checked the monitor, now showing the interior of his office, and pushed the lever handle that caused the door to swing quickly and silently open. The body of his personal assistant still lay draped over his desk in a somewhat suggestive posture where she had fallen after he had stabbed her in the neck with a letter opener and shot her repeatedly in the mouth after he had managed to grab his pistol from the drawer while holding her off with his other hand, which was how he had gotten the bite wound. The injury didn't worry him since extensive tests had shown that humans could only be infected by the alien technology when they were close to death at the time of exposure, whether it was through the alien medical applicator or from a werewolf's bite. He warily kept an eye on the corpse, since he couldn't be sure it wouldn't still come back to life despite missing half of its head. His hand reached for the pistol when the door to his office burst open, but he froze and remained very still when he saw that it was the mercenaries. He absolutely didn't want to be shot by his supposed rescuers.

"Mr Werner?" Coleman asked out of courtesy even though he recognised his client from video and photos that had been provided to him.

"What happened to your colleague?" Werner asked.

Coleman grimaced. "We were on the way up when the elevator stopped at one of the lower floors. One of your people, I assume uninfected, had pressed the call button before the … zombies got to him. When the door opened, those things were standing right in front of it. They snatched Morales right off his feet and tore out his throat before we could open fire. They nearly pushed their way into the elevator before we killed the ones in front and kicked the crowd back enough for the door to close again. We should be safe on the way down. I don't think any of them will be pressing any buttons, but we'll be standing well back from the door just to be safe."

"You're calling them zombies?" Werner asked. "They're not really the living dead, you know."

The mercenary leader pointed towards the elevator lobby. "Well they're close enough for me. Have you got a better name? Infected just doesn't cut it."

Werner nodded. "Fair enough. Let's go."

Coleman turned towards the door. "Stay behind me sir. We'll go straight down and out the door and blast anything that gets in our way."

Werner started to follow when there was a muffled thud behind him and something clamped painfully around his ankle. He couldn't help crying out in pained surprise. Twisting around he was shocked to see his supposedly dead PA's hand wrapped around his ankle. His gaze followed her arm up to her head and he choked in disgust at the sight of the eyeball hanging from its socket and then he was shaken by a surge of fear when he saw that the bullet hole in her forehead had crudely healed over, even though some of the white of her skull still showed through the wound. He tried to pull free, but her grip was relentless and he tripped and fell painfully onto his back. He grabbed for his pistol, but an explosion of gunfire blew the reanimated PA's head apart, and his hands went to his ears instead as he shouted in pain, his head ringing from the battering noise.

"Here sir. You better put these on. They're 3M CAG 4 ear plugs. They'll make the noise more bearable without cutting off your hearing," Coleman said, holding out a set of plugs. He helped Werner to his feet after his client had inserted the ear plugs. "Right, let's go." He was having a hard time remaining calm himself, but he was a pro and the team as well as his client was counting on him to lead them out of this nightmare.

Werner silently nodded his thanks and followed the trio towards the elevator. The ear plugs made the world oddly muffled and gave him a feeling of isolation and remoteness. But that didn't stop him from positioning himself behind the mercenaries when the door slid open and they boarded. To his relief, the elevator car didn't stop on the way down. The elevator reached bottom with a "ding" and the recorded female voice said, "First floor". He leaned forward in eagerness to get out of the horror filled building.

Coleman's gun muzzle tracked the movement of his eyes as he scanned the wide, marble floored reception lobby. When he didn't see a threat he stepped out of the elevator. "Go!" He wanted to jog towards the locked doors, but he forced himself to maintain a steady gait, making sure the client remained behind him, flanked to either side with the remaining members of the team. But before they reached the reception desk, he heard sounds coming from both left and right. He glanced to either side. "Shit! Run for it!" he shouted as he led the way. Zombies were coming at them from the corridors on both sides, dozens of them, all moving with an unsteady but terrifying speed. Coleman knew they could never unlock the doors in time, so heedless of the possibility of hitting passers-by in the street, he fired at the tempered glass of the main doors, spraying bullets in a circular pattern that smashed most of the glass from the solid metal frames. With glass fragments crunching under his boots, he paused to shove Werner through the improvised exit before stepping through himself. He moved to one side to let his men out and fired back into the lobby at the closest of the zombies. He didn't have enough ammunition or time to take each of the mob down with head shots so he fired at their legs, hoping to slow them down.

The other two mercs did the same, and when the

swarming mass of zombies tripped and stumbled over the crippled ones in the front row, they turned and ran for the van that had brought them here.

Coleman ushered Werner in the same direction as he reloaded on the run. Glancing over his shoulder he saw zombies tumbling out of the building and into the street. The containment part of the plan was undoubtedly shot to hell. "Get that fucking van started!" he shouted, and then spun around to empty his fresh magazine into the mass of zombies all coming towards him. He was shocked to see more and more of the creatures pouring out of the building and realised that most if not all of the occupants of the building had been infected over the night. Hundreds of zombies were spreading out over Farragut Square, most moving in pursuit of the early morning crowd of people on their way to work. Screams started to replace the tranquillity of the park and streets as he pushed Werner into the van and climbed in himself. "Go! Go!" he shouted pounding his fist against the back of the driver's seat. Looking out of the back window he saw a group of zombies throw themselves at the rear of the van. One of them managed to climb up on the bumper and cling to the vehicle as it accelerated away. "Shake it off!" he shouted to the driver. He was tempted to shoot, but shattered windows and bullet holes might attract police attention. The van violently swerved from side to side, throwing him against Werner. When he managed to look out of the back again he saw the zombie stretched out in mid-air, clinging to the van by its hands, and then moments later it was gone.

"Get me to Dulles airport. I have a corporate jet waiting. I'll arrange for your fee to be paid as soon as I'm at the plane," Werner said. "You did well. There'll be a bonus for your lost man and your performance."

None of the men Coleman had brought with him had been close friends or part of a regular team. Because of the urgency he had called in whoever was available on short notice, so the loss of his man wasn't an emotional blow, and Werner's offer was generous. "Thank you, sir. I'm sure the others will appreciate it." He pointed to Werner's hand. "You're hurt. Do you want me to have a look at it?"

Werner shrugged. "It's nothing serious, but changing the dressing is probably a good idea."

***

The infected, the zombies, spread out across the Farragut Park area, driven by the basic and primal urge to feed. All of the advanced safety precautions and near artificial intelligence in the radiation damaged alien nanites no longer functioned. Without a physiological and biological template to work from, the nanites treated everything other than the most primary body and brain functions as being hostile, and gradually destroyed the victims' higher brain functions, leaving only the most basic instincts to feed in place. Worse still, their basic social instincts were corrupted as well, and the zombies only saw uninfected humans as prey, although the damaged nanites were still able to sense the presence of nanites in another infected human, so they didn't turn on each other. Hard to kill and ragingly hungry, they attacked and infected every human they came across. Unlike the werewolves, they lacked the superhuman strength, fangs, and claws to rip their prey apart, so most of their victims were neither crippled, disembowelled, nor suffered immediately fatal wounds except when bitten in the throat or accidentally having their skulls or necks broken in the initial attack. But the severe bites and severed veins were enough to trigger the damaged nanites into action, simultaneously healing their hosts' bodies and destroying their minds, thereby creating another wave of zombies, although the time the deadly process took varied widely from victim to victim. Their mental abilities also varied to some degree, from almost completely mindless, to others with a basic intelligence that let them open doors and search hiding places. Knowing only hunger and the urge to survive, the zombies spread out in all directions from Farragut Square, drawn by movement and the promise of fresh prey, including Connecticut Avenue NW, leading to Lafayette Square, and the White House.

***

With his mind focused primarily on damage control and a way to blame terrorist biological attack for the disaster, Werner climbed on board the private Gulfstream G650 jet.

The pilot greeted Werner. "A flight plan has been filed and approved to SJC Sunnyvale, California, Mr Werner."

Werner nodded as he seated himself and accepted the glass of Rip Van Winkle Family Reserve Kentucky Bourbon. "Good. Get us off the ground as soon as possible," he said, rubbing his temple. "Get me some Tylenol," he said to the attractive stewardess as he leaned back and closed his eyes. He had been able to erase all the security camera recordings from the control panel in the panic room using a military grade deletion program, so there would be no hard evidence of what had happened. While in the air, he would have to arrange for another team to search the headquarters building and employee homes for survivors. No doubt they would also have to hunt down a few employees who had gone into hiding or were trying to sell their story to the media or publish it on the Internet. His PR department would discredit any videos or interviews that did get out. Now all he needed to do was to find a positive spin for the zombies.

The horde of zombies grew exponentially as they met more and more people on their way to work and opening businesses, as well as tourists exploring the famous area and intending to view the White House. People began to realise what was happening, and despite the seeming impossibility of an actual zombie apocalypse, panic spread rapidly but unevenly down the street ahead of the advancing mob of infected zombies. However, this actually made things worse. The sight of fleeing prey triggered a hunting response in what passed for brains in the zombies and they began to run in pursuit, with new zombies continuously rising at the rear of the mass all the time so that the ravenous throng of zombies filling the street seemed to stretch and flow like some kind of gigantic primitive multi-cellular creature.

The screams and the panicked people running towards Lafayette Square finally attracted the attention of the police. Their natural assumption was that it was some kind of riot, and both foot patrols and squad cars rapidly assembled at the lower end of Connecticut Avenue NW, forming a barrier with their cars and officers with drawn batons while calls went out for riot police. Officers with shotguns took up positions behind the vehicles, while a line of officers moved forward, waving arms and batons and shouting orders for the advancing crowd to halt. The American press, in cooperation with the Government and at the request of the British authorities, had downplayed the incidence of werewolves in the UK, treating it as some kind of disease, like rabies. Even those officers who were better informed about the existence of werewolves would not have automatically associated the shambling crowd descending upon them with those creatures, since they were obviously human. The officers did begin to get more nervous when the zombies came closer and the bites and other wounds became more visible, as well as the strange twitching of their bodies and mindless look in their eyes. Some of the officers in the front row glanced over their shoulders worriedly when their colleagues with shotguns racked their weapons.

A sergeant stepped forward with a megaphone. "Stop where you are! You do not have approval for a protest march. Stop right now or you will be arrested." When the strangely silent crowd, lacking slogans or placards, continued to advance, he stepped back into the line and glanced from side to side.

One of the officers said, "Sarge, those guys don't look right, like they're doped up or something. And there's a lot of them."

Before the sergeant could reply, a woman who had been hiding in a doorway just in front of the advancing mass of zombies, panicked and made a run for it, dashing across the front of the mass of blood soaked infected. She spotted the police barricade and turned towards them, arms outstretched, but before she could change the direction of her run, two of the zombies threw themselves at her with bared teeth.

Several of the street hardened policemen cried out in horror when the zombies started to bite her, ripping off her clothes in search of bare flesh. One of them sank its teeth into her throat and a jet of bright red blood sprayed out, painting the advancing zombies with crimson. "Pull back behind the cars! Now!" the sergeant yelled, realising that what they faced was not a riot at all and that they might all be overrun by what looked like drugged up crazies. Most of the officers had drawn their firearms by this point, abandoning the idea of using Tasers or pepper spray after seeing what had happened to the hapless woman, and the sergeant did the same as he dodged behind one of the red striped cruisers. The woman had disappeared inside the advancing crowd and the sergeant tried one more time. Using the megaphone

167

he shouted, "Halt or we will fire. Stop right there!" He looked around. "Anyone have beanbag rounds?" he asked. When two hands came up he shouted, "Beanbag rounds only. Open fire!" He focused on the advancing mob as the shotguns roared to either side of him, and cursed when the targets went down under the impact of the pellet filled bags but were completely ignored by the rest of the advancing crowd. Under ordinary circumstances a controlled retreat would have been in order, since mowing down rioters in front of the public and possibly the press and citizen journalists with mobile phone cameras wasn't ideal, but the White House was right behind them as well as a growing crowd of stupidly curious civilians. Then his radio crackled.

"This is Captain Jefferson. I've been informed of your situation and I'm watching a live helicopter feed."

"Good to hear from you Captain," the sergeant replied, relief washing through his body like ice water. "They're not stopping Captain, and they've definitely killed at least one person, and from the blood, I'd say there've been more. What are your orders?"

There was a strained silence, then Captain Sarah Jefferson said, "You are authorised to open fire."

"Yes, Ma'am," the sergeant replied, almost shaking with relief. The Captain's order had come just in time as the front row of the advancing mob was less than ten yards away. He raised his pistol and squeezed the trigger just as he shouted, "Open fire!"

Gunfire broke out as if the sergeant had yanked a string, and zombies all across the advancing mass staggered and swatted at their bodies as if they had been stung by wasps. A few fell, hit in the head, heart, or legs, but the noise and the smell of fresh blood only seemed to enrage them and they broke into a jerking, shambling run, their inhuman silence more terrifying than any war cry. More and more fell, but still they came on, and when they were just in front of the first cruiser some of the policemen turned and ran.

The sergeant started to move backwards still firing his pistol, and when the first officer fell screaming under a trio of the attackers he shouted, "Fall back! We can't stop them! Fall back!" When the slide of his pistol locked back on an empty magazine he joined the others in running. He scanned the street ahead of him for something that would allow his officers to reform and take a stand. If the advancing crowd reached Lafayette Square and spread out, it would take the National Guard to stand a chance of stopping them. When two SWAT vans pulled up in front of him and turned sideways to block the street he almost cheered. His radio crackled again.

The Captain's voice said, "Sergeant, have your men join the SWAT team. Do whatever you can to hold them back. The President has approved the deployment of the military, who are on their way, and the Secret Service is taking measures to protect the President. It is vital that those of you on the ground contain these rioters until back up forces arrive on scene."

"Understood, Captain. We'll do our best," the sergeant replied. He could hear the footsteps of the horde behind him as he dived between the SWAT vehicles. Even as he turned and started to reload his pistol, the SWAT officers opened fire, joined a moment later by the shocked and pale faced police officers. Heavy sniper rounds and automatic fire slammed into the advancing zombies, and for a moment it seemed that nothing living could continue to advance into that storm of gunfire. Bullets plunged deep into the mob, some even passing through their targets and knocking down the ones behind them, forming a barrier of bodies across the street. But still they came on, heedless of the bullets, wounds, or of the fallen, and at the rear of the mob, the wounded staggered to their feet, dreadful injuries miraculously if crudely healed, to re-join the unstoppable mass of undead.

Over video feeds obtained from drones, helicopters, and street security cameras, Captain Jefferson watched in horror as the fragile line of her officers was overrun and bitten to death by the cannibalistic mob. Worse still, she could see figures in police uniform striding and staggering along with the rest. She turned to another screen which linked her to the military command and Secret Service. "Were not going to be able to stop them from breaking out into Lafayette Square. Plus I have reports of smaller but growing bands advancing along parallel streets as well. I'm not throwing any more of my people against those ... things. They don't have the equipment, training or the numbers."

On the left half of the screen Colonel Timothy Grey, Joint Force Headquarters, National Capital Region, nodded. "Your people did all they could, Captain Jefferson. We'll be taking over now. The situation has been declared a National Emergency, although it is still unclear if there is any terrorist element, possibly biological, involved. Ground and air forces have been deployed and will be on site very soon. I don't have to tell you that the situation is grave. We cannot tolerate a mob of ... whatever they are, attacking people in the Capitol." What he didn't say was that if the White House was overrun by zombies on his watch, his career would be over. He actually had tanks, helicopter gunships, and heavy artillery at his command, but since the threat was still technically a civil disturbance, a riot, despite what had happened to the police, the use of heavy weapons would cause rumbles all the way to NATO and the United Nations, his response was confined to infantry and armoured personnel carriers – for now. But that still meant he could employ M4 Assault rifles all the way to .50 BMG heavy machine guns. His men were minutes away, but he could already see elements of the cannibalistic crowd spreading out from the end of

Connecticut Avenue NW and mixing with the public, many of whom were still stupidly standing there taking photos and videos with their smart phones, until they were attacked and bitten themselves. There were also more policemen running and driving into the area despite orders to pull back, refusing to stand by and watch civilians being murdered. Most of them retreated in confusion when in many cases they couldn't visually separate the innocent bystanders from the supposed rioters without getting so close they risked being attacked and bitten themselves. Up to this point, nobody had used the word "zombie" over the radio channels, but almost everyone who had seen them and survived was thinking the word.

The zombie mob had almost doubled in size by the time the military arrived. The heavy vehicles couldn't drive into Lafayette Square because of the bollards and trees, so troops poured out of the APCs and trucks, and set out in pursuit of the rioters. Other transports drove to either end of the stretch of Pennsylvania Avenue NW fronting the White House and disgorged troops who took up positions all along the street and especially at the gates that led into the White House lawn. At the same time, harried and frightened policemen worked to usher away all the civilians and tourists in the area. All the while the noise, confusion, and sheer terror continued to grow and spread across the park and the surrounding streets. With the arrival of the troops, the ear pounding sound of gunfire added to the scene of madness.

Lieutenant Lee deployed his platoon along the western edge of Lafayette Square, keeping the Weapons squad close to him and the other three squads spread out in line. This was an unorthodox formation at least for modern combat, but he was facing a scattered and unarmed enemy, with civilians mixed amongst them. However, he had seen the video of what had happened to the well-equipped and well-trained SWAT units and police officers, and he was not going to underestimate the threat he was facing. There would be no warnings, and the men were ordered to shoot to kill. No matter what anyone said, he knew these were not just people high on PCP or something. When he saw that all his men were in position he signalled for them to advance. The operation turned into total catastrophe almost as soon as the line of soldiers came into contact with the milling crowd filling the grassy square. First of all, it was nearly impossible for the soldiers to determine whether they were faced with an injured, terrified civilian, or a vicious, and strangely fearless rioter until their opponents were within grappling range. Since there were many women and some children in the crowd, this made the decision to fire even harder. Second, even when they did fire, aiming as they were trained for the centre mass of the target, roughly the middle of the abdomen, their bullets seemed to have little to no effect, and once again they found themselves grappling with an amazingly strong enemy who seemed immune to pain and determined to claw and bite the unfortunate soldiers to death.

Several men were knocked down or dragged screaming deeper into the crowd and the gaps were immediately filled by more rioters. Within moments, before Lieutenant Lee could order his men to pull back and reform, the entire line was broken up into isolated bunches of troops fighting desperately for their lives. "Pull back! Pull back!" he shouted, driving the muzzle of his rifle into the face of the zombie in front of him, only to have the rifle pulled from his grasp by another, his panicked grip emptying the magazine in a deafening burst that went uselessly up into the sky. He drove his foot into the belly of an attacker and used the force of it to push himself backwards and out of the grip of the blindly reaching hands of the mob. Terrified screams filled the air, both from his fallen men and civilians all across the grassy square. The lieutenant glanced behind the command group and paled when he saw their retreat cut off by another blood-soaked bunch of zombies. Ignoring the possibility of innocent casualties, he slapped the shoulder of the gunner armed with the M249 LMG. "Clear a path for us out of here," he shouted pointing at the approaching zombies to their rear.

The machine gunner didn't hesitate. He spun around, shouldered the light machine gun, and opened fire with short bursts, moving the muzzle in a narrow arc. He had seen the failure of the others to take down the enemy with body shots, so he aimed higher, hoping for either head shots or damage to the spine and heart. Naturally many of his shots missed, or passed through his targets, and cries of indignant shock and panic arose from the direction of the Smithsonian's Renwick Gallery as bullets hammered into parked cars, ricocheted off walls, and smashed windows. Lieutenant Lee turned back just in time to see a zombie bite and rip a large chunk for flesh from the soldier standing next to him. Reflexively he pushed his rifle's muzzle into the zombie's nose and blew its head off with a long burst of fire, showering the screaming soldier with hot shell casings and deafening him at the same time with the rifle going off less than an arm's length away from his ear. Lieutenant Lee grabbed the infantryman's harness with his left hand and dragged him backwards while firing his rifle single handed. Hands reached out to help him and the command group retreated through the gap in the zombie horde behind them, stumbling and stepping on the corpses downed by the M249. As they broke clear he glanced to either side and saw clusters of his men fighting their way free as well, but it was obvious that he had lost over half of his men, and many more were badly injured. One soldier was literally dragging a zombie along, with the creature's teeth clamped immovably on his forearm, aided by two other infantrymen who were too busy shooting at the pursuing zombies to pry the zombie off of their comrade. The bitten soldier hammered at the zombie with the butt of his rifle, but he couldn't use as much force as he wanted to since each blow ground the creature's teeth against his arm, creating waves of sickening agony and actually increasing the severity of his own wounds. All of them were starting to think of the supposed rioters as "creatures", since they were very obviously no longer human. Variations of this scene were repeated all along the army's line, with troops furiously trying to break contact with the almost amoeba-like mass of snarling, biting mouths and bloodied grasping hands.

The lieutenant was on the radio the moment they were clear of the mob and gathered in a tight group whose concentrated fire power was sufficient to at least slow the advance of the eerily silent zombies as the soldiers backed out of the park and into the clear space of the road. He reported the failure of his advance and his current situation. The platoon had deployed with a single Stryker Armoured Personnel Carrier armed with an M2 .50-cal heavy machine gun on a Remote Weapon Station, and the lieutenant instinctively directed the survivors towards the protection of the APC.

Unnoticed by the soldiers, the zombies who had been shot and injured badly enough to fall, were healing and getting up faster and faster as the alien medical nanites learned how to deal with their new, undefined hosts, and shared this information to the nanites in the bodies around them. In addition, the nanites worked furiously to adapt their "patients" to the environment, and without any templates or restrictions, simply modified their hosts as needed, making them tougher, faster healing, and faster moving in response to the gunfire. Of course all this expenditure of energy and materials had to be met with more food, so the zombies became increasingly ravenous as well. Those at the back of the horde turned their attention from the retreating soldiers and headed towards the rear of the square and towards the White House. More infected victims joined the mass of zombies, streaming in from the direction of Farragut Square and adjoining streets, and their bodies immediately began to change as their nanites learned from the others. Hundreds of them stumbled and ran towards Pennsylvania Avenue in search of fresh food even as the original group continued their pursuit of the remnants of Lieutenant Lee's platoon.

The commander of the Stryker watched what was happening from an open hatch and saw that they were being surrounded. He shouted to Lieutenant Lee, "Lieutenant! Get your men inside and we'll drive through them!", pointing towards the open rear ramp which faced the bollards blocking the entry of vehicles into Jackson Place NW. The Stryker could officially carry nine passengers, but a lot more could pack in during an emergency, especially for a short trip. More of them could climb up onto the vehicle. The mounted heavy machine gun could rip the rioters apart, but there was no way he would employ the weapon on unarmed American civilians unless ordered to by someone high up in the chain of command. Very high. He could already see his face on the TV with the word "Butcher" underneath it. Unfortunately, he was so preoccupied with his thoughts as well as watching the backward progress of the lieutenant and the other survivors that he failed to spot the zombies coming up on the Stryker from the other side of the vehicle, his vision being obstructed by the blocky shape of the RWS turret. He only became aware of the threat when he felt the horrible and unexpected agony of teeth sinking into his shoulder, follow seconds later by the screams of the driver.

Lieutenant Lee looked back and up in shock when he heard the commander's yell, just in time to see the man being dragged bodily out of the Stryker by two zombies. The screams of the driver told him that the Stryker was lost. A quick glance showed him that their only chance was to fight their way towards the line of troops in front of the White House. Pointing down the road he shouted over the almost constant roar of gunfire, "The Stryker's gone! Follow me!" His sergeant and RT operator, both of whom were still on their feet, followed him at a run.

* * *

Captain Turner's jaw clenched, the only sign of his shock when he spotted the small group of uniformed and blood streaked soldiers running desperately in the direction of his position, pursued by an equally blood covered group of civilians. He had been listening to radio updates from all over the area in and around Lafayette Square and he had even seen video from drones hovering over the park, but seeing the so-called rioters in person was completely different. Since they were unarmed, none of them even carrying a stick or piece of rock, it wasn't possible to classify them as an armed enemy. They didn't display any organisation, wave placards, or chant any slogans, so they couldn't be called protesters either, so he had been ordered to treat them as violent rioters. It was obvious something more than just social or political anger was behind this, but as yet there was no proof. Some of the more paranoid were already speaking about chemical or biological attack. A CDC medical team was already on its way to try to obtain samples for testing. Just moments ago he had received confirmation that the Governor had declared a State of Emergency and had officially requested military aid in dealing with the situation. He lifted a microphone to his mouth. It was connected to a public-address system with powerful portable speakers at the middle and either end of his line. "By the authority of the

176

declared state of emergency, you are ordered to stop whatever you are doing and to sit down on the ground with your hands behind your head. This is your only warning! If you do not obey my instructions we will have no choice but to open fire!" His heart sank when not a single member of the advancing mob broke stride or made any attempt to obey. "Machine gunner. Warning burst. Fire!"

The gunner had been carefully briefed in advance, and on command he fired a short burst into the ground roughly two metres in front of the crowd. The thunder of the automatic weapon echoed off of the surrounding buildings and the nearby members of the Secret Service protective detail in the White House grounds behind the army's lines stiffened uneasily. The power of his weapon had always given him a feeling of satisfaction, and a certain amount of pride and confidence. His first response when the advancing mob totally ignored it was disbelief. Nobody simply ignored a burst of machine-gun fire right in front of them, especially not a crowd of civilians. But these people did. It was almost as if they didn't care, or thought they were indestructible. "Sir? They're not stopping!"

Captain Turner felt the sweat running down his forehead. "Fire at will!"

The troops in the line had seen what had happened to Lieutenant Lee's men and didn't hesitate when given the command. Gunfire broke out all along the line, three round bursts blending with the longer bursts of the machine guns like heavy metal music from hell. All along the front of the advancing amoeba-like mass of the infected, figures staggered, some fell when hit in the head or leg. Then for the first time a sound, a formless, meaningless growl, rose from the mass of near mindless quivering, jerking, former humans, and all at once the entire mass broke into a weird bounding run. Even worse, the injured and fallen ones quickly staggered to their feet and joined in the charge, the terrible gaping wounds on their body still healing at an unnatural rate.

Several of the non-commissioned officers who had actual combat experience realised what was about to happen and shouted for the men beside them to fall back. The Captain was only moments slower in giving the same order. The entire line started to back up in an ordered formation, the men still firing as they moved, but as the slavering mob closed with them at a nightmarish speed, teeth bared and clawing hands outstretched, the coordinated rearward movement broke like shattered glass and sections of the line scattered and ran towards the White House or off to either side, while the remaining troops were forced back towards the bollards fronting the spike topped steel fence that was twice the height of the troops by a closing crescent of the infected. The machine guns had fallen silent, their ammunition exhausted or barrels glowing red hot, while the other soldiers were firing aimed single shots with the last of their ammunition in a hopeless attempt to create a break in the crescent of attackers through which they could escape. But despite the withering hail of bullets and even a few grenades thrown by desperate men, the mob never seemed to reduce in size nor did they succumb to fear or pain. It was impossible and contrary to everything the soldiers had been taught. Then suddenly everybody was running for the dauntingly high fence. Captain Turner made an effort to rally his men, but even he saw the hopelessness of their situation and pelted after the others. It was obvious that he wasn't going to get past the savage mob at either side, and they were already so close to the main gate that it would be hopeless to run towards it. So his only choice was to try to scale the fence, just like the rest of his men. In front of him, some were climbing the fence on their own, while others boosted another soldier up in hopes of being helped up themselves. The top of the fence was lined

with spikes that prevented anyone from straddling it. In addition, White House security teams were moving up to the fence, shouting and waving their weapons threateningly, adding to the confusion. With the zombies closing rapidly, Captain Turner threw himself at the fence and began scaling it while casting glances over his shoulder. He felt a pressure against the sole of his combat boot and he looked down to see one of his men pushing. He nodded his thanks and reached up between the spearhead-like spikes lining the top. Red faced with effort, he jammed his boots against the railings and gripped the top bar with one hand. When he was as sure as he could be of his grip, he twisted his body and reached down to help the man who had given him a boost. Their hands locked but at that same moment he looked down along the man's body and saw a zombie's hands close around the soldier's ankle. The captain yelled in pain when the weight on his arms threatened to dislocate his shoulder joints and tear his grip off of the fence. Cursing helplessly he watched as the zombie's jaws closed on the soldier's calf. The sudden agonising pain caused the soldier to loosen his grip and to fall back and off of the fence despite the Captain's desperate grab. He closed his eyes when two more of the zombie rioters fell upon the soldier, biting madly at the screaming man. Then self-survival took over and he continued scrambling up and over the fence, scraping his leg painfully on the points at the top. To his shock, when he jumped down and landed in a tuck and roll on the other side, he found himself looking up at the muzzle of an assault rifle held by a man in a black tactical suit and body armour. When he swiftly glanced around he realised that all of his men were being treated in the same way. "What are you doing? Can't you see we're ….
" A threatening move of the muzzle cut him off.

The Secret Service agent shook his head. "Your job was to bring a major civil disturbance under control.

Ours is to protect the White House and the President. You screwed up. Get face down and put your hands behind your back. Now!"

The Captain opened his mouth to protest, but he realised that the agent was not going to listen. They had strict protocols when it came to the safety of the President. He sighed and gave the fence an anxious look as he obeyed. Perhaps those things wouldn't be able to climb. What he saw made him gasp. There were no more soldiers climbing or backed up against the fence. All of them had either made it over and were in the process of being detained, or had been killed in the most horrible ways. But that wasn't what had made him gasp. It was the solid mass of zombies pressed up against the fence from end to end. For some reason, none of them were trying to climb it. Instead they were simply pressing against the heavy metal ironwork as if they thought they could just walk through it. In fact the entire mob was pressing so hard that some of the zombies in front were being crushed, bones and tissue being horribly snapped and pulped against the unyielding steel. Then his eyes widened when he saw the top of the fence begin to sway. "They're coming in!" he choked, his throat tight with terror.

The Secret Service agent dropped a knee into the small of Captain Turner's back. "I told you, I'm not interested in your excuses. Now lie still and shut up before I .... " His threat was cut short by a loud cracking and creaking of breaking steel and he finally looked up, just in time to see a section of the White House fence collapse under the pressure of hundreds of bodies that didn't feel any pain. His captive completely forgotten for the moment, the agent snatched up his assault rifle and fired into the flowing mass of zombies striding across the White House lawn.

Seeing that the agent had more urgent things to attend to, the Captain slipped his hands from the loose loops of the zip tie handcuffs and sprang to his feet in a crouch. Looking around he saw several of his men lying helplessly trussed on the ground, their captors also now engaged in the hopeless effort to stop the onrushing zombies. He pulled out a folding knife clipped to his pocket and set about freeing his terrified men. When he had freed everyone he could see, he pointed in the direction of the White House itself, directly away from the advancing zombies. "Stay together and follow me!" he called out and started jogging towards the famous white structure. Just then, there was a roar of rotor blades and three helicopters took off. He recognised Marine One, and realised that the President was being flown to safety. He wished he was in one of the machines, but was also glad that his failure to stop the zombies hadn't put the President at direct risk. He twisted his head around when he heard another roar, and saw an F-16 fly past. "Run! Incoming air strike!" he shouted. He couldn't be sure that they would really bomb or launch Hellfire missiles at the White House grounds, but he wasn't going to wait around to find out if he was right. The explosions began behind him just as he reached the famous white columns, followed by the distinctive sounds of mini-guns and heavy machine guns being fired from helicopters. Hell had come to the White House.

Chapter Ten

Viktor smiled politely at the security personnel as he passed through the metal detector gate at the public entrance to the Houses of Parliament. The gate remained silent since he was not carrying any weapons. Not metal ones at any rate. He noted the presence of extra armed constables standing at a discreet distance. Given the havoc he had unleashed upon the city, this was exactly as he had anticipated, which was why he and Jenny were the first ones in. He took her hand and gave it a warning squeeze when he felt the eager shivering tenseness in her grip. The prospect of blood, especially the blood of that class of people she hated, tended to make her reckless. He saw her nod and smiled at her. "We're nearly there," he said casually, as if speaking of a tour stop or the promise of a cup of tea. He let go of her hand and drifted off to the left side of the hall, nodding pleasantly at the armed security officer as he passed. When he was sure that he was out of the range of the constable's peripheral vision, he stopped walking and willed his body to change, a skill only a few of his followers had mastered. Most still needed a jolt of pain and the associated rush of adrenaline to deliberately start the transformation. He savoured the familiar ache and almost pain, as well as the rush of heightened sensory input. A million new scents and sounds, a flood of visual details from the shadows. He willed his body to change from the ground upwards, making the terrifying transformation less noticeable until it was too late. A flick of his head let him see that Jenny had undergone the same change and was in turn watching him for the cue to burst into deadly action. Viktor was wearing elastic trousers and top under his coat, and they held up under the drastic changes to his physiology, so there was no dramatic ripping of fabric as he turned into a werewolf. He felt the change reach his head and neck and he nodded to Jenny just before spinning towards the sub-machine gun armed constable. Although the police officer's body armour would have presented little resistance to his incredibly hard claws, Viktor wanted to delay the spread of the alarm for as long as possible so he lashed out with his claws at the officer's right forearm and then his throat, disarming him and sending a fountain of blood shooting into the air from the man's sliced carotid arteries, almost meeting and crossing with the jet of blood coming from Jenny's victim.

Triggered by the slaughter of the armed guards, Viktor's followers pounced upon the other officers and security staff at the entrance. Two of his followers went around helping the recruits from New Belmarsh deactivate their injector cuffs, and used miniature cattle prods to trigger the change to werewolf form in those who lacked the ability to transform even under the excitement of the massacre or simple blows of their own hands. Cries and screams from the tourists and visitors already in the hall filled the air, most of whom ran in a terrified stampede towards the nearest exit, while a few cowered behind whatever hiding places they could find. Moments later the acute hearing of the werewolves caught the sound of alarms going off elsewhere in the huge palace complex and the sound of running booted feet as the security forces responded to the attack.

Viktor nodded in approval when his hairy followers sprinted for the exits rather than staying back to finish off the tourists. His plan was to spread havoc and panic throughout the venerable cluster of huge buildings that made up Westminster Palace, rather than fighting a pitched battle at a single spot. This way, the limited security personnel would be forced to scatter in an attempt to protect everybody, leaving the way clear for him and a select group of followers to head to the dignitaries gathered in the Commons. He loped over to Jenny and opened his jaws in a canine grin before changing his head back to human shape. "You know what to do."

Jenny didn't change back but simply nodded her elongated head before signalling to two followers and bounding off towards the Television Control Room. Viktor wanted the attack to be seen by everyone in the nation, and it was the job of the pair of followers to ensure that the transmission wasn't cut off. When she had taken the Control Room she would join Viktor for the main attack. She dropped onto all fours and sped down the corridors in a blur of muscle and fur.

Viktor took a moment to smile, inhale deeply, and hum a bar of the Beachboy's "Fun, fun, fun," before changing fully into werewolf form again and loping away towards the Commons. He was in no hurry. The chaos his followers caused would prevent the people in the Commons from making a quick and orderly evacuation since no route could be determined to be safe. Besides, he had promised Jenny that he would wait for her, and he knew how much she wanted to be a part of the climax for this part of his convoluted plan. However it went today, it was not going to be the end here. There was an entire world waiting for him and his kind.

**

Monica frowned and looked towards the door leading to the Visitor's Gallery. "Far be it for me to be telling you how to do … whatever you do, but you do know that there is a bloody great sheet of bulletproof glass closing off the Gallery? You won't be able to get down to the main floor from there."

John was just about to reply when a burst of faint noises made his head twist from side to side. "They're here. You need to go and hide Monica. Lock the door and stay very still. You should be safe, although I wish you had left when I asked you."

The guide smiled. "Everybody has to do their bit if we're going to beat the villains, not just you hero types," she said before turning and trotting off towards her chosen hiding place.

"That's a brave woman," Tara said. "Do you really have a way through the bulletproof glass? Maybe we should go around to the Press Gallery or the VIP area."

John shook his head. "We'd have to talk our way past guards, and Viktor won't expect us to come at him from this direction." He picked up his bags and nodded at the entrance to the gallery. "We've got to time this just right. We're going to cause a panic amongst the real visitors and eventually attract the attention of the security forces. We have to be through the glass and down in amongst the benches just as Viktor or his people arrive."

Tara nodded her understanding. "The werewolves will be an obvious threat and they will be more willing to accept us as rescuers without asking inconvenient questions."

John put his hand on her arm. "We'll be doing this in front of the whole country, the whole world. They may not figure out that we're vampires, but they'll know that there are more than just werewolves amongst them. I've had centuries to prepare for this, but you … "

"This day was coming no matter what. At least it will be for a good cause … not that I necessarily think that those people down there are good in themselves," she replied with a grin.

John nodded. "I know. There have been many times in my life when I wondered why I should care about those who would gladly hunt me down and kill me. But then I was in the same situation when I was Voivode. My enemies vastly outnumbered those who were truly my friends." He stared at the wall for a long silent moment. "But in the end, if I do nothing, then I will truly be the monster they imagine me to be. When power, fame, and fortune are gone, all that remains is my honour."

A distant muffled scream of terror and agony made Tara grimace. It was hard, terribly hard, not to run towards the sounds of slaughter. To do something, if only to inflict the same slaughter in return. For a fleeting second she saw her mother's smiling face, a comforting memory from her childhood. From the corner of her eye she saw the ancient vampire that she now thought of as John looking at her. She shook herself and nodded. "I'm ready," she said, pulling her weapons out of her bag. Their vampire sonar was useless in detecting the werewolves through the sturdy walls and muffling wood that filled the palace, but it wasn't hard to discern that the attacking monsters were getting closer to the Commons from the shouts, screams, and occasional gunfire. Suddenly the hubbub of voices in the Commons fell silent.

Weapon slung across his body, John tilted his head as he focused upon his hearing, his fingers slowly opening the glass panelled wooden door that led into the Visitor's Gallery. He knew there were no guards in the corridor or inside the Gallery as they had been called away by the high alert that the city-wide attacks and the urgings of Commander Blair had managed to trigger. He nodded towards the centre of the Commons floor. "You stay near the Prime Minister and the Cabinet if you can. Viktor will try to draw us both away from them by attacking the other MPs. You can't let that happen. We're here to protect, not hunt werewolves. I'll try to take down as many of them as I can."

Tara nodded back. "Bodyguard detail. Right." For a fleeting moment she felt a twinge of resentment. She wanted to get another crack at Viktor, and it felt as if John didn't believe she could handle her ex-copilot and werewolf, but the ingrained self-control and discipline of her test pilot training and experience crushed the surge of emotion. John had vastly more experience than her in these matters, and only one of them could lead. She pressed her prototype electronic rifle against her chest in a non-threatening manner and followed John through the door.

"Security officers! Remain calm and stay in your seats. The Parliament is under attack, but you should be safe if you stay right were you are!" John shouted in the command voice he had learned and used in hundreds of armies and in dozens of languages. Looking towards the balustrade he grunted in satisfaction at the sight of the bulletproof screen that had been erected to prevent visitors from throwing anything or even shooting at the Members of Parliament below. Although it served its purpose well, it was far from being a military grade installation. The metal frame holding the thick sheets of laminated glass and plastic was strong, but not built to sustain a direct assault itself. Looking through the screen and down to the floor of the Commons he saw two werewolves standing at the left side entrance behind the government benches. His eyes narrowed as his vision zoomed in on the furred intruders.

"It's Viktor and his girlfriend Jenny!" Tara rasped, her throat tight in anger and anticipation. Both werewolves were focused completely upon their intended prey, and the bullet resistant glass wall stopped them from catching the scent of the two vampires up on the Gallery, so for the moment she and John held the advantage. But they would lose the element of surprise as soon as they tried to break through the glass barrier. They could have dashed out and then back in through one of the ground level entrances to the House of Commons, but that would mean losing sight of their opponents at a critical moment.

The same chain of logic had previously run through John's mind, and he could only hope that the shock and surprise would be enough for them to get in place to defend the humans below. With every step he took towards the glass barrier, the urbane modern industrialist faded and the ancient warlord that the world knew and feared as Dracula came to the fore, and by the time he was in arm's reach of the glass his body had fully taken vampire form. He drew back his arm, palm held outwards. His mind and body focused completely upon the strip of light metal that framed the super tough laminated glass. With a motion that started all the way from his feet his body whipped around, driving his palm forward with all the superhuman power of his vampire form, coupled with deeply ingrained skills acquired over centuries. The heel of his palm struck the metal strip with force sufficient to have shattered a concrete block, creating a sound that made the occupants of the gallery cower in panic.

From the floor of the Commons it seemed as if a bomb had gone off above their heads, and everyone looked up in shock before diving for cover. Viktor's head snapped up, lips drawn back in a snarl. The huge glass structure bulged outwards with a deep, almost bell-like tone accompanied by the squealing of twisting, tearing metal. Broken rivets, wooden shards, and spiderweb patterned glass panels exploded outwards from the Visitor's Gallery, followed moments later by two silver clad figures who leaped from the high gallery in apparently suicidal dives down towards the green leather benches below them. Viktor recognised the threat before Jenny or the six other werewolves that had followed him into the famous chamber and threw himself down and to the side. A series of supersonic cracks came from the falling figures and two of the werewolves staggered, one with its head completely blown off of its shoulders, the other with a huge gaping wound in its shoulder.

Jenny dropped down beside her lover and leader. Using the code cum language that Viktor had invented to suit their werewolf forms she made the growling sounds that meant "Fucking vampires!"

Viktor nodded with a jerk of his long muzzled head in the direction of the middle of the chamber. "Get near the humans. They won't be able to shoot." He followed his own advice and darted forward, hurdling benches and dodging from side to side at a speed that made him a blur.

Tara swore when she fell too fast to take a second shot at the werewolves that continued to pour into the Commons chamber from both entrances. However, her inhumanly acute hearing told her that even more werewolves continued to prowl the palace complex in search of prey and were fighting the surviving security guards, which meant she and John wouldn't be completely overrun by the slavering monsters, at least not yet. She landed on her feet, balanced perfectly like a gymnast upon the varnished wood back of a bench, the force of her landing cracking the timber beneath her. Because of her vampire's heightened vision and sonar mapping she didn't need to look around to locate every human in the chamber, as well as John and the werewolves. Better yet, the alien nanites in her body used the flight system interface to project this information onto a radar-like display similar to an aircraft's HUD, an advantage that even John didn't possess. To her relief, her sonar revealed that no one had been crushed by the falling glass panels, although a few had been injured or knocked down to the floor. Leaping from bench to bench, she headed towards the Prime Minister. She knew little about PM Richard Grayling, other than that he and most of his Cabinet seemed to have more centrist policies than many in the recent past. However, his politics mattered little at the moment. Good or bad, left or right, she knew that having the Prime Minister of Great Britain ripped apart by werewolves on live super high definition television would most definitely not be a good thing. "Prime Minister! Stay where you are. I'm here to protect you!"

She followed up the instruction with a snap shot that sent another werewolf stumbling backwards from the impact of the massive silver coated bullet. However the werewolf's amazing speed in dodging and her lack of solid footing sent the bullet smashing into its shoulder instead of its forehead, wounding instead of killing it. Even with the silver, she knew it would be back in action sooner or later unless she finished it off. But her objective was to bodyguard the PM and any of the others that she could convince to gather near her, so she left the hunting to John and continued leaping from bench to bench towards the centre of the Commons where the PM and many members of the Cabinet stood milling around the Table of the House in terrified confusion. A werewolf leapt up at her from between the benches, but her sonar and nose had already spotted it. She sprang into the air in a high rolling somersault and fired down into the top of the creature's head when she was upside down. The werewolf went down, but the heavy recoil of her weapon, which might have broken the shoulder of an ordinary person, changed her trajectory and she crashed down onto the benches with an impact that would have broken a human's ribs. She grunted in pain but flipped upright and continued her run across the benches towards the Prime Minister, the bruise across her back already fading. There was absolute chaos in the large chamber and she realised that the werewolves were deliberately mingling with their human prey so that she and John couldn't easily shoot at them without risk of hitting the constantly moving humans they had come to save. A final leap put her atop the Table of the House and right next to the Prime Minister. "Get everyone to gather around the Table!" she shouted to him as she fired at a charging werewolf, hitting it in the thigh and knocking it to the ground. But the monsters were edging ever closer, some even holding an MP in front of them as a human shield. She held out her right hand like a pistol and reached over her shoulder to draw her short silver inlaid sword, a touch of her thumb unlocking the scabbard lengthwise and allowing a quick draw. Spinning clockwise she fired at every werewolf that was close, even when they didn't present a clear target, desperately trying to keep them away from the people clustered around her.

"Who are you?" the Prime Minister shouted, his back pressed against the table. "How could this happen?"

"We're an experimental strike team. Unofficial. But we were all that was on hand to respond because of the breakout at New Belmarsh," Tara replied tersely as she reached into her backpack for another magazine.

"New Belmarsh? Bloody hell!" the Prime Minister exclaimed, his face going even paler. He immediately realised the dreadful implications of a mass escape of thousands of very angry and aggrieved werewolves, most of whom had no control at all over their actions once in werewolf form. He winced when Tara's rifle cracked right over his head, the heavy projectile whipping past the shoulder of an MP and smashing the head of the werewolf holding her hostage, splattering her with bone, brains, and blood. She screamed in agony when an involuntary muscular contraction of the dead werewolf shattered the bone of her upper arm. "What about the Palace security force? Why aren't … "

"This is a carefully planned attack involving a large number of werewolves. They're all over the Palace, killing everyone they meet. The guards have their hands full, and I suspect that the ones guarding the Commons are all dead," Tara said, swearing under her breath as the werewolves edged closer. She wanted to shout out to John to do something, but she knew he would already be fighting for his life at close quarters with more werewolves than she had ever seen in one place. Her vampire senses and the pulsating white dot on her HUD told her where he was in relation to herself and that he

191

was still alive. An "Incoming" indicator and a moving red dot behind her on the HUD made her duck and pivot, her short sword humming through the air at near supersonic speed just in time to sever the neck of a leaping werewolf.

***

John practically rode a pane of bulletproof glass down to the benches like a flying transparent surf board, his super-fast vampire reflexes allowing him to actually steer the falling glass to a small extent, the result of which was that the edge of the thick laminated glass and plastic pane sliced into the torso of a werewolf as the pane landed with an ear-splitting crash. John threw himself off of the glass just before it struck, his booted and armoured feet slamming into the side of another werewolf who had its teeth sunken deep into the throat of a male MP. The tremendous impact slammed the werewolf against the back of the bench in front of it. Ribs and bones snapped and cracked, but even these horrific injuries would have healed in minutes had John's rifle not exploded its heart with a silver coated bullet. John's momentum was too great for the impact to stop him and he bounced off of the dying werewolf, and only his vampire fast reflexes and strength, as well as centuries of combat experience, allowed him to perform an arcing double somersault that ended with him landing feet first on the Speaker's chair, which collapsed in a cloud of dust and splinters. Without taking a second to recover from the impact, he sprinted in the direction of the nearest werewolf that stood between him and where his vampire senses told him Viktor was located. While the werewolves were stronger, vampires were faster, in his case, very much faster.

The werewolf was using two people as shields, holding them by the scruff of their necks and jerking them from side to side tauntingly, waiting for John to get close enough that it would negate or reduce the advantage of his weapon and allow it to use its fangs and claws to best advantage. But it was one of Viktor's newer followers and had never faced a vampire before, although Viktor had warned them. All the werewolf saw was a fast-moving human figure with a gun. It knew it was stronger and its instincts were to close in and rip the enemy apart. But in holding on to the hostages, it made a fatal mistake.

Jumping higher and faster than any Olympic gymnast, John sprang into the air, his body twisting and spinning so that he came down behind the werewolf facing its back. The werewolf started to turn its head, jaws gaping, only to receive a bullet just below its ear, causing its skull to explode in a shower of gore. Its dying spasms flung its hostages to either side, the men crying out in terror and pain as they were slammed against the floor and heavy wooden benches. John's sonar senses told him that something had popped up from behind a bench and was leaping towards his back. He ducked, but a clawed foot hit him between his shoulder-blades like a sledge hammer. However, his sonar and incredible reflexes meant that he was already throwing himself forward when the werewolf's blow struck, and his armoured suit stopped the claws from ripping his back open. He was sent hurtling forward diagonally across the backs of the benches like a surf board hitting a rocky shore, and landed upside down between two benches. Deeply ingrained combat reflexes told him that to remain still was to die, and despite the pain and disorientation he tucked his legs in and rolled forward along the floor, hearing the werewolf land with a furious roar where he had been just seconds ago. He reached the aisle between the blocks of benches and jumped to his feet in a spinning twirl. Even as he was rolling he knew there was no time to raise and aim the mass driver rifle held across his chest by its elastic sling, so instead his sword was in his hand as he spun around to face the slavering werewolf which was in mid-leap, its snarling jaws spread wide. Powered by the weight and momentum of John's spinning body, the tip of his sword struck the werewolf's head with a ringing hollow "thwock", slicing through its super tough hide and cracking the bone of its jaw. Normally the werewolf would have shrugged off even such a savage blow, healing completely in less than a minute, but the silver not only interfered with its natural healing ability, but triggered a massive allergy response that even the alien medical nanites had trouble suppressing without putting the creature into an induced coma, which would have been fatal in any kind of a fight. The werewolf whined in pain, staggered, and tripped on the broken corner of a bench. John dashed forward to finish the creature off with his sword, but was forced to drop into a slide and roll to avoid the charging leaps of two more werewolves who simultaneously attacked from either side of him. The werewolves collided in a snapping, snarling tangle and he managed to snap off a shot that killed one of them before the second dived out of sight behind a group of humans. He swivelled his head around, searching for Viktor. If he could kill or capture the werewolf master, he knew it was likely the others would lose heart and run. Although he didn't have a visual HUD like the one Tara possessed, over the centuries his mind and body had developed a smooth and powerful working relationship with the alien medical nanites, and he could physically feel where and how far Victor was from him in the chamber, the way a homing pigeon knew its way home, even though the mechanism was different.

Viktor lifted his head over the back of a bench and saw John looking directly towards him. "Kill! Kill them all!" he roared, using simple words in his self-created werewolf tongue that he had taught his followers and a few useful words to the most angry and invested escapees from New Belmarsh. Although he would never admit it, even to himself, he was afraid of the grim-faced man who had powers that matched or even exceeded his. But he knew that John would be forced to try to save every human in the room, which would leave him free to go after his main targets. He could see that Tara was guarding the Prime Minister and the other senior Ministers and members of the Shadow Cabinet who had been seated near to the PM prior to the attack. He had a healthy respect for Tara's capabilities too, but his outrage at her refusal to die at his convenience and his personal antagonism towards her blinded him to her full abilities. He was going to kill her, and that was all that mattered. He could sense Jenny nearby and his jaws formed a lupine smile. She would attack the Prime Minister and all the others near to hand, and Tara would be forced to defend them, providing him the opportunity to take her down while she was distracted. In addition, Tara's plight might draw John's attention too and allow his massed followers to overwhelm him as well, or at least keep him occupied until he and Jenny had done what they had come here for. Jenny had taken the television control centre without difficulty and his followers now controlled it, ensuring that his attack upon the centre of government in the country would be seen by everyone. If he demonstrated publicly and undeniably that neither their leaders nor the military could protect themselves against the power of the werewolves he led, the public would lose all hope that the authorities could defend them. They would fear him and their mindless fear would force the government to give in to all of his demands. He cursed when a silver bullet smashed the edge of the bench just above his head and coughed when he inhaled a few grains of silver dust. When he heard the roar of attacking werewolves he jumped over the bench followed closely by Jenny, and then ran on all fours towards the aisle furthest away from the direction that the shot had originated.

When John saw the werewolves change from hiding amongst their human victims to attacking and killing them, he switched his tactics as well. With his sword in one hand and his mass driver rifle held like a pistol in the other, he leapt over the benches towards the nearest of the monsters. He knew Viktor was trying to distract him or to paralyse him with too many victims needing rescue, but age and sheer experience with the horrors of combat had taught him to accept that casualties were inevitable on the field of battle, and that he couldn't allow the fact to affect how he fought. The werewolf had its teeth sunk into the unfortunate man's shoulder. John sprinted up to the werewolf and without slowing, chopped down with his sword at the back of its neck. He couldn't cut the creature's head off without the risk of cutting the throat of the man beneath it, but the severe damage caused to its neck and spine by the silver coated sword would keep it out of the fight until he and Tara had won or they were dead. His sword became stuck in the werewolf's body and he kicked against its torso as he pulled it free, and then roared in pain when crushing jaws closed around his right forearm. The werewolf had crept up on him, staying low on the floor and crawling forward, unwittingly reducing the ability of John's sonar to detect it. If he had been an ordinary man, and not wearing the unique body armour developed by his companies based upon his specifications, it was likely his forearm would have been ripped right off by the werewolf's powerful jaws, neck, and shoulder muscles. Despite the crushing pain, he kicked off against the wounded or dying werewolf and used the momentum to throw himself towards the second creature, reducing the ripping, shearing force of the monster's attack and pushing its head up and back. That same momentum rammed his sword forward like a silver-laced horn, which stabbed up and into the werewolf's lower jaw and through to its brain. A twist of his hand severed its spinal cord, and not even the incredible toughness of the werewolf species could stand up to that kind of treatment. The monster's jaws went slack and fell off of his arm. With a powerful thrust of his shoulder he broke free of its grip and sprang to his feet. He cursed angrily at the screams of dying and wounded men and women, bent his legs and sprang into the air, going higher than any gymnast or pole vaulter, almost taking flight. Looking down, a werewolf which had been leaping at his back, passed right under him. Reaching the peak of his leap he grabbed the pistol grip of his thick-barrelled rifle and fired a three round burst downwards along and into the werewolf's body. He landed with his knees bent and feet together, vampire claws protruding from slits built into his armoured boots, dropping like a pile driver on the werewolf's shoulders and crushing it against the floor, its legs splaying out with the nauseating sound of snapping bones and rupturing organs. He sensed a movement by several of the werewolves in the chamber to surround him, and instead of waiting for them he ran towards the area covered by the sheet of bullet-resistant glass which had created a gap in the circle of attacking creatures. There was no way for him to save or defend every person who was not part of the cluster formed around Tara, but if he could draw the others into attacking him instead of the humans, that would serve just as well – even though he would risk being overwhelmed. Once he broke through the encircling movement he leapt up upon the thick laminated glass panel lying across the backs of several rows of benches. The platform protected him from werewolves coming at him from below or from the cover of the benches, as well as providing level footing. The smell of werewolf blood and the seeming inability of the werewolves to harm him had enraged the survivors to the point that most ignored the remaining humans and converged on him. He raised his sword and rifle, his grin made savage by the full extension of his fangs.

***

With the vantage point of the very solid table, and with the people she was protecting crouched all around it, Tara was able to use her rifle to maximum effect. The combination of her extremely sharp and sensitive vision that caught the tiniest flicker of movement, along with her sonar, the military-grade alien nanite system, as well as her father's interface implant in her brain, allowed her to literally see each of her attackers as glowing red dots on the heads-up display that was overlaid on her field of vision. She was spinning and firing faster than the normal human eye could track and she noticed that the Prime Minister was sending startled and puzzled glances at her in between trying to look in all directions at once. As fast as she was, Tara couldn't actually face all directions at once, and when she crouched and swivelled to fire at a werewolf which was in mid leap, her shot came too late to prevent the creature from sinking its fangs into the throat of the Finance Minister, who was unable even to scream before her head was gorily severed from her body. The werewolves were coordinating their attacks, and Tara knew that she was going to start losing more and more of the people she was trying to protect despite her best efforts. Again she wished John was at her side, although she knew, and could even see on her HUD, that John was hard pressed himself, and that he was in fact drawing many of the werewolves away from her. Spinning into a crouch, she shot one of the monsters in the belly, while severing the leg of another that had leapt at her over the head of the Prime Minister. The creature fell at her feet roaring in pain and she flipped her sword so that it was point down and drove it into the werewolf's chest. A flashing icon on her HUD made her wrench her sword free, spring upright, and fire, the muzzle blast making the Prime Minister stagger and clamp a hand over his ear in pain. The round counter display on her rifle went red, showing zero rounds in the magazine even as the attacking werewolf dodged, the silver alloy bullet grazing its shoulder. A moment later the icon on Tara's HUD changed to a triangle with the word "Jenny" displayed over it, a dotted line connecting it to the friendly icon that indicated the Prime Minister. The nanite combat system recognised Jenny and judged she was headed for the PM. A millisecond scan of the HUD revealed no other werewolves that were an immediate threat, so Tara let the elastic sling pull the empty rifle to her chest and leapt over the Prime Minister and towards Victor's second in command. Although the risk she was taking wasn't fair to the others, the public death of the Prime Minister, ripped apart by a werewolf in the middle of Parliament House and on live TV would be a fatal blow to the moral of the nation.

**

Viktor had been momentarily dismayed that the obstacles he had put in Tara and John's way had failed to kill or, apparently, even inconvenienced them. He was also violently angered that they had seen through his plans and were here to try to stop him. On the other hand, it also meant that it gave him the opportunity to eliminate these nuisances once and for all. He saw that Jennie was dealing with Tara, so he gathered two of his more experienced followers and began to make his way towards Tara's friend and helper. If he could eliminate John Seward, Tara would not be able to survive long without his support. The inexperienced werewolves from New Belmarsh were having little luck against Seward, who Viktor knew from bitter experience, was inhumanly deadly with every kind of weapon or even with his bare hands. But they did serve as a distraction, allowing him and his two followers to get behind Seward. He pointed at the wood panelled wall and started to climb.

***

John rammed his sword in the chest of the werewolf in front of him, suffering a hammering blow to the head in return. His tight helmet and mask protected him from the terrifying hooked claws that raked across the side of his head, but he spat blood from the impact of the blow against his face. Despite the fact that he didn't heal as quickly as the werewolves, the alien medical nanites almost immediately suppressed the pain and the ringing in his head, and his arm was rock steady as he twisted to shoot the second werewolf charging him from the rear and side. His rifle clicked empty and with another pair of werewolves charging directly at him he let go of the rifle and drew the silver laced fighting dagger from his side. Despite not having an interface like Tara's, he had so integrated with the alien military grade medical implant, he was able to use its capabilities on an instinctual level. He could feel that Viktor and his two followers were getting into position to attack him from above, the way a person could feel the warmth of sunshine on their skin, or the direction and movement of a chill draft. He rushed forward to meet the pair of werewolves who were obviously relying on sheer force and numbers to overcome him. But just before he collided with the onrushing monsters he darted to one side, sword raised high like a matador. Because of their momentum and the slick surface of the glass, the werewolves were unable to stop and turn to face his new angle of attack. The closest werewolf twisted its head back over its shoulder and snapped its fangs closed around John's plunging sword, but even the massive strength of its jaws couldn't grip the high carbon steel tight enough to resist John's thrust, driven by all his vampire strength. The sword made a squeaking, grinding sound as it slid through the werewolf's fangs, past it's ribs and into its heart. The other werewolf leapt over its dying comrade and John was forced to let go of the handle of his sword to avoid the second werewolf's fangs closing on his fingers. He dodged a clawed slash at his face, grabbed the werewolf's wrist, and pulled it towards him using the creature's own momentum against it. The werewolf tripped over the dead werewolf's body and John drove his dagger into its belly, ripping it open. Again he couldn't afford the time to finish it off, relying on the silver in the dagger to slow the healing of the devastating injury until the main fight was over, one way or another. Instead he launched a forward kick that threw the groaning werewolf backwards and away. He reached down to retrieve his sword and spun around, just in time to see Viktor and his two werewolf companions leap down from the wall and land heavily on the glass in front of him, making the thick glass vibrate and the werewolves slip and stagger, their clawed paws scrabbling at the slick and unyielding surface. For a fraction of a second he locked eyes with Viktor, and he saw the rage and hate that literally made the werewolf's eyes turn red. His sonar gave him the advantage of being able at the same time to watch the movements of the other two werewolves and even to sense which of his three opponents was preparing to attack at any given moment. John saw Viktor's muscles tense and he sprinted towards the werewolf leader, knowing that the other two would instinctually hesitate as Viktor sprang into motion to meet him. But instead of crashing into Viktor, he threw himself to the left at the last moment, driving both his blades into the surprised werewolf while Viktor skidded past him. He kicked against the ribs of the wounded monster and used its mass to rip his blades free and to throw himself towards the werewolf on the other side of Viktor, who was already turning to face him. The werewolf in front of him leapt into the air, claws extended intending to crash into the approaching vampire and to take advantage of its greater strength, fangs, and claws. However, John had anticipated this and twisted in mid-air to land and slide on his back, his dagger held edge up as he passed beneath the flying werewolf who was unable to change its trajectory in time to avoid the silver blade that slashed down along its chest and belly.

The werewolf yelped in shock, landing with a crash on the glass and sliding off of the edge to crash into the benches below, its belly sliced open and unable to rapidly heal because of the silver embedded in the dagger's blade.

John sprang to his feet, only to have Viktor's clawed paws hammer against his shoulders and chest like spiked clubs, flinging him onto his back. His suit stopped the werewolf's claws from ripping the front of his body open, but the impact was like being struck by a car. The diamond hard claws of his feet extended through the slits in his boots and screeched as they dug into the glass surface, cutting parallel grooves into it as he fought to remain upright while simultaneously fending off the massively powerful blows of Viktor's paws in a blur of blocks and strikes. Because of the blades in his hands he was able to block Viktor's blows using their silvered edges, sheer speed, and centuries of experience rather than trying to match the werewolf's raw strength. Finally, he dodged to the side and managed to slash a hairy forearm with his sword, forcing Viktor to back away, clutching his injured arm.

However, Viktor wasn't seriously hurt and he started to circle his opponent, knowing that time was on his side. If he could keep the vampire occupied, his werewolves would move in and take Seward down from the back and sides, and he would have the satisfaction of ripping the vampire's guts out. His forearm hurt, the silver making the wound burn like fire and he snarled.

While all the time watching for an opening to attack, John witnessed the disconcerting sight of Viktor's face as it changed back into a twisted, distorted human shape. He could sense more werewolves creeping up on them and he knew he had to finish this fight quickly. Undoubtedly Viktor wanted to talk in order to distract him, but the werewolf leader would have to shift his focus from the fight as well in order to speak, and that might provide him with the opening he needed.

Viktor worked his neck and jaw and then said, "Give up. Run away now and I'll let the two of you live. You know you can't face all of us. Keep fighting, and I'll make sure Tara dies in the most horrible way possible."

John's fangs lengthened, his face twisting in a snarl of rage at the threat, but he knew that Viktor was trying to play on his emotions, to weaken his resolve by threatening Tara, and although he let his fangs remain extended, he smiled coldly at the werewolf leader. "It doesn't seem to be us who are doing the dying," he retorted, simultaneously circling to his left to frustrate a werewolf that was sneaking up behind him.

Viktor grinned confidently and matched John's circling movement. "Remember that I gave you a chance to save her when you watch me tear her apart – "

While Viktor was still talking, John threw himself forward at the full speed that his vampire body was capable of, accelerated even more by the alien nanites. It was this speed that had given birth to the legends of Dracula disappearing into thin air. He was upon the werewolf leader before Viktor could even begin to react. But instead of trying to close in and kill the surprised Viktor, which is what the werewolf expected, John launched a whirlwind attack with his blades, moving them so fast in front of himself that they were a humming blur, each stroke aimed at Viktor's hands and forearms, and not his head or body.

The werewolf master managed to block some of the strokes with his elongated claws, but the blades were moving too fast for him to grab or beat them aside and he couldn't pull his arms away without exposing his body and head. Within seconds his hands and arms were covered with dozens of deep bleeding cuts. With his face back in werewolf form, Viktor roared in agony and frustration as he jumped backwards to save his hands, which were now practically useless. They would heal, but it would be long minutes before the bleeding would even stop because of the silver in the blades, instead of the near instant healing that would normally occur.

But before John could drive in and finish Viktor off, three more werewolves sprang up onto the glass platform and attacked. Spinning around in a low crouch he managed to hack the back leg clean off of one of his attackers, but the other two crashed into him, clawing and biting furiously and knocking him off of his feet. Although his body armour saved him from being ripped apart, the blows and bites still seriously hurt, and he had to battle in order to keep their jaws from closing over his face or throat. Through it all he could still sense Viktor approaching. He drove his sword into the chest of one of the werewolves, but it became jammed in its ribs and was ripped out of his grip. He immediately extended his claws to full length and grabbed the injured werewolf by the neck, his claws digging into the creature's throat like miniature daggers. He grinned savagely when the monster yelped in pained surprise. Inspired by fashionable glitter nail polish, both he and Tara had coated their claws with an epoxy resin that contained microscopic flakes of silver. With the dagger in his other hand, he simultaneously fended off the jaws of the second werewolf who was pinning him to the ground with its own body. He was confident that he could fight them off, but at the same time he could sense Viktor moving towards his head, and although the werewolf leader's hands and arms were injured, he still had his jaws and feet. He managed to drive the dagger into the werewolf's body just below its neck and he used it to force the monster off of him, but then when he looked up he saw Viktor's gaping jaws looming over his head, ready to bite his face off. The helmet and mask-like goggles would only provide so much protection. The two werewolves pinning him saw it too and redoubled their efforts to hold him down despite their injuries. Saliva dripped onto the goggles and his jaw opened inhumanly wide, baring his own fangs as he prepared to fight back with the only weapons he had left.

***

Tara wondered whether she had made a mistake in leaping at the werewolf she recognised as Jenny. She could have pulled the Prime Minister up onto the table, but that might have been too slow and could have resulted in the human being clawed apart. As it was, Jenny moved faster than she had anticipated and Tara was forced to twist in mid-air to avoid slashing claws that were aimed at her throat. The tuck and twist of her head and shoulders saved her throat from being ripped out, but the claws caught the side of her face instead, ripping right through her cheek. The immediate burst of agony sent a blast of cold through her body while her face and head felt like she had been doused with boiling water. However, the nanites in her body damped down the pain almost as soon as it appeared and the bleeding had stopped by the time she landed on all fours just short of the end of the benches, her diamond hard claws cutting furrows in the floor. Instead of slamming against the solid wood and leather of the benches she used them to kick off, literally bouncing back towards the werewolf, drops of blood running down the front of her tight-fitting body armour from her torn cheek. As she moved, she flipped her short sword around to grip it with the blade projecting from below her fist and lying along her forearm. Instead of directly attacking Jenny, she swerved at the last second and dived past the raging werewolf. Claws raked painfully along her back, but her body armour prevented more of her flesh from being ripped open. However, the edge of her sword sliced across the front of Jenny's fur covered thighs.

Jenny shrieked in rage and pain but staggered two steps back, the deeply cut muscles of her thighs making her wobble unsteadily instead of continuing forward to kill the Prime Minister who cowered against the side of the huge table, frozen in terror at the sight of the raging and bloodied werewolf.

Tara brought herself to a halt by running into a bench, and jammed the point of her sword into the seat while simultaneously drawing a fresh magazine from a dispenser in her backpack with her other hand. For a few seconds there were no other werewolves closing in on her, and Jenny was slowed just enough by her injuries. She pressed the magazine catch and dropped the empty one from her rifle, inserted and seated the new one while she spun around to face the direction that she had just come from. Although the mass driver rifle used caseless ammunition, it was still possible to jam the weapon by shoving the magazine into the receiver too hard at the wrong angle, and she absolutely couldn't afford a jam. Just as she raised the heavy rifle to her shoulder, Jenny dropped onto all fours behind the benches and sprinted towards the Prime Minister. If she had switched to full automatic fire and simply sprayed the line of approach that Jenny had to take to get to her victim she would almost certainly have hit the female werewolf, but there were people on the other side of the walkway who might have been hit by the heavy silver impregnated bullets. Instead, she ran forward towards the Prime Minister, the rifle still at her shoulder, and after two long paces she sprang high into the air, seemingly taking flight. This lifted her high enough so that she could look down into the corridor between the benches. Sighting her rapidly moving target with both vision and sonar, she fired downwards, the hypersonic rounds sounding like a single ear-piercing cracking sound, resembling the snapping of a brittle column of glass, the powerful recoil actually slowing her descent. The magazine emptied and Tara let go of her rifle and extended her claws as she fell the final metre, landing just behind Jenny. She saw that only two of the bullets had hit the werewolf, and neither had inflicted immediately fatal wounds. However, along with the sword cuts they had weakened Jenny considerably. Tara was absolutely determined to finish off Viktor's closest follower, and she felt a surge of predatory rage the likes of which she had never felt before. She darted around the snarling werewolf, dodging massive swipes of her claws and snaps of Jenny's bloodied fangs, all the while lashing out with her own silver painted claws, ripping at the werewolf's body and limbs, forcing the creature back and away from the Prime Minister. Despite her injuries, Jenny managed to slam Tara to the floor several times, and only her incredible speed and her sonar enhanced senses saved her from broken bones or being grabbed and crushed. She was also aware of John's predicament, but she had her hands full against the pain maddened Jenny. She still had the silvered dagger on her belt, but Tara was so filled with rage and memories of the many times Viktor and this female werewolf had tried to kill her and those she loved that she wanted to rip her opponent to shreds. In one corner of her mind she wondered how much of this rage originated from the vampire nature of the being which had been the basis of the alien implant that had taken over her body, albeit with her willing cooperation. She jerked her head back to dodge a claw that threatened to rip out her throat, and which caught her brow instead, forcing her to blink away blood that ran down past her goggles and into her eye. The momentary jolt of pain only served to further fan her fury to a blazing madness and her attacks sped up to where her movements were a blur and wounds appeared over Jenny's hirsute body almost as if by magic. She bit back a scream of agony when Jenny's jaws closed crushingly on her wrist, but instead of fighting to free her arm from the werewolf's fangs, she jerked her trapped arm upwards and used the leverage to drive the tips of the fingers of her right hand into Jenny's exposed throat. Her claws pierced the werewolf's super tough hide and flesh with an awful pop. Using all of her vampire strength, she clenched her hand into a fist, rammed her knee into Jenny's chest and ripped the female werewolf's throat out.

Jenny's eyes widened in horrified shock, the traces of silver on Tara's claws preventing her body and the nanites from reacting effectively. There wasn't enough silver to stop her from recovering, and the alien medical nanites could prevent even such a ghastly wound from being fatal, but for the moment she couldn't breathe properly or move her head and jaws. Her injured thighs gave way and she fell to her knees, her hands clutching the gaping wound in her throat.

Tara yanked her arm free of the werewolf's suddenly lax jaws. Working her numbed fingers she snatched her silver inlaid dagger from her belt with her other hand and then rammed the heel of her palm under Jenny's jaw, forcing her head up and exposing her already savaged throat. Driven by her vampiric strength she slashed the werewolf's exposed and torn neck, the edge of the blade grating against the creature's spine before ripping it free in a gushing spray of blood. She wrapped her arms around Jenny's head and her body twisted and spun like a dancer. With multiple cracks of snapping tendons and ligaments, Jenny's head tore free of her torso and flew across the chamber, trailing a stream of crimson liquid that splattered the stunned and horrified members of parliament that still survived.

***

As soon as John had set down his bags outside of the entrance to the Gallery, which Rowland Harker, Tara's father, determined from the tiny cameras and microphones built into the bag, he tapped the activation code which launched a swarm of insect sized drones that quickly spread out under his control all over the hallways and corridors around the Commons and the route leading to the main public entrance. Although each drone's computing capability was quite small, they worked in a network, forming a grid of processors of near supercomputer ability. The network allowed each insect-like drone to identify werewolves or even individual people using facial recognition. The combined imaging provided Rowland's base system with a three-dimensional image of the area covered by the swarm. He turned to his assistant and girlfriend, Emily Palmer. "Time to deliver the package to the good Commander and his friends," he said, handing her what looked like a lightweight notebook computer. Duncan had spotted the unmarked police van slowly circling the area and had described the vehicle to Rowland. He in turn had sent out a tiny drone with a built in GPS tracking system to the police van as soon as he had spotted it, which had landed on the van's roof and attached itself with its magnetic base.

Emily kissed him on the cheek and hopped out of their own van when Rowland found a spot to momentarily stop, holding the notebook device in her hand. She had already picked a spot on the pavement next to the Westminster complex that the police van had repeatedly driven past, and she headed for it now.

Rowland dialled the number that John had given him. "Commander Blair? I'm calling on behalf of Mr John Seward. I have something for you. The werewolves are inside Westminster. You must act now."

***

Commander Blair had just received some semi-incoherent alerts and calls for assistance from Westminster when he got Rowland's message. Following the instructions given by Seward's friend, he scanned the pavement over the driver's shoulder and spotted the woman waving to them. "Come to a stop in front of that woman. We need what she is holding. Once we have it, bring us up to the public entrance to Westminster." He turned to the volunteer team. "Use the special ammunition given to you. Unless you run out of bullets, shoot to kill. Bring the dart rifles and ammo just in case one of the MPs or Parliamentary Staff are turned."

"Can't we shoot them too?" one of the men suggested.

Blair turned his head to hide a grin. "You are not authorised to use deadly force on members of the Government or civil service unless you are given no choice and your own life is threatened." He was not about to send his men into an already suicidal situation with one hand tied behind their backs. As the van pulled up at the gate leading to the Cromwell Green entrance, he tried calling the SO17 Palace security unit, but no one replied. "Looks like we might be alone in there ... except for our friends. Anything new on the screen?" he asked, nodding at the constable assigned to carry and operate the display unit that showed moving icons in a three-dimensional map of the area in and around the House of Commons.

210

The constable shook his head. "A cluster of hostiles in the Commons, and more moving along the corridors, apparently hunting."

Blair checked his weapon once more out of habit. "Move out on my lead. Don't let yourself be split off or isolated. These werewolves went in willing to die in order to get revenge for how they were treated, plus a core group of Viktor and his followers. Take them down if you can, but our primary mission is to save lives, whether it is the Prime Minister or the janitor." He pointed at the scanner operator. "You stay with me. That scanner is our best chance not to get ambushed or herded into a trap. Let's go!"

* * *

The scent of werewolf blood, Jenny's blood, made Viktor's head jerk up from his death gaze at Seward. He roared in absolute fury when he saw Tara holding Jenny's severed head.

Taking advantage of the master werewolf's distraction, John turned his gaze towards the werewolf who was clinging onto his arm with its jaws. Taking a deep breath he blasted the monster with a brain scrambling blast of ultrasonic sound to which the werewolves were particularly sensitive.

The werewolf's eyes rolled upwards and its jaws went slack in agony, the super high frequency sound feeling like iron spikes being driven into its eardrums.

With his arm free, John jabbed his claws into the side of the neck of the werewolf that was still lying on top of him and trying to rip his bowels out with its hind claws, prevented only by the prototype body armour which was reinforced over his abdomen for that very contingency. With the other werewolf temporarily stunned, John drew up his knees and planted his boots in the belly of the werewolf on top of him and kicked

211

upwards, bucking and rolling the weight of his body onto his shoulders. The werewolf was flipped off of him, pivoting on John's silver coated claws that were buried in its neck, ripping its throat wide open.

The gargling and choking werewolf arced through the air like a huge club and smashed into Viktor, who was still trying to decide whether to continue his attack on Seward or to give in to his blazing rage and to charge towards Tara with the intention of ripping her into shreds. His werewolf reflexes should have allowed him to dodge the unorthodox weapon, but distracted by his rage he moved too slowly and was swatted to the ground by the copiously bleeding werewolf's body.

John rolled to the side and sprang up onto one knee, his hands closing on the handle of his sword. With two prying motions he worked the silver impregnated weapon free of the werewolf's body, lifted it high and hacked through the neck of the werewolf before springing to his feet and turning towards Viktor – only to have the limp body of the werewolf with the torn throat hurled at him by the master werewolf. John pivoted and deflected the large hairy body to one side with such smoothness and coordination that the werewolf's body struck the leather clad back of a bench hard enough to shatter the sturdy wooden structure, sending splinters of wood flying in all directions like shrapnel from a bomb. He knew that Viktor would be right behind his werewolf shield and he was right, except that he was caught by surprise when Viktor slashed at his face, but then dodged past him and bounded towards Tara. John yelled to her in their supersonic voice, "Watch out! Viktor's coming your way!" He tried to follow, but three werewolves threw themselves in his path one after the other, and though he cut them down with a fury and skill that the world had not seen since Dracula had stood on the battlefield, sword in hand, facing the Turkish hordes, he was unable to catch up with the rage driven master werewolf.

However, Tara had been expecting Viktor's attack, hoping for it, as she stood defiantly with Jenny's severed head raised in her left hand. John's warning gave her several seconds to brace herself, and then suddenly Viktor appeared before her.

Viktor's claws swept up and across in a savage disembowelling stroke aimed at Tara's belly while his other hand stabbed towards her face. Even though he knew he couldn't simply rip her open because of her suit, his claws might still punch through to her flesh. But when Tara hurled Jenny's head at him, he was forced to abort his strike and awkwardly bat his girlfriend's bleeding head away, which also made him slow his lunging attack.

Tara employed this opportunity to step to the side, drop down, and braced by her hands on the seat of the government Front Bench, kick out at Viktor's knee from the side.

Even though Viktor had slowed slightly, when his leg was kicked out from under him he was thrown onto his side, momentum making him helplessly slide forward until his claws could stop his movement, allowing him to spring up onto all fours and spin around to face Tara. His knee had been badly damaged by Tara's kick, but since there was no silver involved, the damaged joint had almost completely healed by the time he had turned, bones and tendons popping and snapping back into place. Snarling in bare fanged fury, he threw himself at his nemesis, totally ignoring the threat of Tara's sword, fangs, and claws.

Equally determined to destroy her former co-pilot, Tara rebounded off of the bench and hurled herself at Viktor in a blur of speed, almost flying over the huge table towards the werewolf leader. She collided with Viktor in mid-air, twisting and slashing with her sword, claws, and even her extended vampire fangs. Tara had been training hard in anticipation of this almost inevitable confrontation, studying under the tutorship of a warrior who had been alive for centuries, and who had developed fighting techniques specially suited to the speed and strength of a vampire. In her past encounters with Viktor she had barely held her own through speed and agility, but this time she had the skill and the knowledge of her vampire abilities that enabled her to fight him toe to toe.

But Viktor too had gained in skill and control over his werewolf abilities, and driven by rage and hate, he abandoned all caution in his determination to tear Tara to limb from limb, both in revenge for Jenny's death and to see the anguish and suffering in Seward's face. He lashed out with his claws, aiming at Tara's goggle shielded eyes, intent upon ripping her face off of her skull.

Tara dodged and deflected his blow, and instead of digging into her face, the werewolf's claws hit her chest and ripped across her breast. Her body armour prevented them from cutting into her flesh, but it still felt like her breast had been struck a grazing blow by a sledgehammer. Yet even as she was hit, she had lashed out with her sword, raking its tip up and across Viktor's ribs, leaving a gory but non-fatal gash that exposed bone.

The cut made by the silver-coated sword felt as if his entire side was on fire, but Viktor pressed forward and grabbed hold of Tara's wrist, preventing her from striking a backhand blow with her sword as he rammed his shoulder into her chest.

Even though her medical nanites were rapidly suppressing the pain and shock, the sheer impact staggered Tara, and the battering ram impact of Viktor's shoulder threw her onto her back on top of the huge table, sending a dispatch box and several heavy tomes flying. She twisted her head aside just in time to dodge Victor's clawed hand which slammed down onto the table hard enough to crack the heavy wood and bury his claws into the table top. Tara felt a thick shaft under her free hand and realised it was the Royal Mace. No ordinary human could have gripped and lifted the heavy ceremonial weapon at that angle, but Tara managed to grip the end of the shaft, raise the mace, and swing it simply by twisting her forearm and wrist. The ornate head of the mace struck Viktor's skull with considerable force and a metallic clunk, stunning the werewolf and allowing her to rip her sword hand free of his grip. She pulled the sword down and out from between their bodies and struggled to get the point against his chest.

At the same moment, Viktor swatted the mace out of Tara's grip and then drew back his hand in order to drive it down and crush her throat.

Suddenly, both of them froze when the sharp flat cracks of a military firearm hammered their sensitive hearing, and Viktor yelped in pained surprise when his shoulder was grazed by a silver bullet, with a second smashing into the front bench above Tara's head. Viktor twisted his head around and saw a man in police tactical uniform framed in the doorway. He recognised the human as the leader of the anti-werewolf unit, Commander Blair, and snarled in frustrated rage. With Seward rapidly closing in, and now the police armed with silver bullets, it had become too risky to finish Tara off.

Viktor's tiny hesitation gave Tara the opening she needed to drive her sword up into his chest, but her thrust hit empty air when the werewolf suddenly sprang up and bounded over her head, disappearing behind the benches. The sonar display on her HUD told her that he was headed for the exit at the opposite end of the Commons. She heard him bark what sounded like a command as he ran, and she guessed that he had ordered the other werewolves to flee if they could. She flipped herself upright on the table, pointed in Viktor's direction, and started to run in pursuit.

John hesitated a second, scanning the chamber with

215

his sonar and vision. Commander Blair's men were pouring into the Commons chamber and most of the surviving werewolves were trying to flee, some even climbing the walls to reach the galleries. The MPs seemed to be relatively safe, so he turned and ran after Tara. Even if Tara could take Viktor down on her own, there were still werewolves roaming the huge maze of corridors and rooms that comprised the Palace of Westminster. Though he couldn't see them on a visual display like Tara, he still could sense the nearness of a werewolf through the military grade alien nanites that had integrated with his body centuries ago.

***

Tara loped along the classically decorated corridors, a red arrow-head in her HUD indicating the way that Viktor had gone whenever there was a choice of exits or turnings. She knew from the glowing green display in her vision that she had passed several werewolves, but she was determined to finish Viktor once and for all. An icon on her HUD also showed that John was not far behind her. She knew that he could have easily caught up with her, but instead he was giving her the opportunity to have the final confrontation that she wanted so badly with the man who had shot her in the chest, tried to kill her father, and turned her world upside down. She entered a long straight corridor and saw Viktor running on all fours ahead of her. From behind her she heard John's supersonic voice say, "He's heading for the clock tower!". For a moment this seemed too melodramatic to be possible, but she realised that Viktor must have assumed that any ground level exit might be guarded by a constable armed with silver bullets. However, if he could reach the roof, he could pick an unguarded spot to climb down and escape unseen. She lost sight of her prey when Viktor reached the end of the corridor and turned a corner. Several strides later she heard the cracking and ripping of wood and squealing of fractured metal, which she guessed was the werewolf tearing open the door that led to the clock tower.

***

John accelerated, fearing that Tara might be ambushed by Viktor inside the tower, and she was just a few turns of the spiral staircase above him when he passed through the shattered door leading to the tower and started to climb the three hundred and thirty-four steps to the clock chamber and above it, the top of the tower holding the actual bell and the wide openings leading out of the tower which were protected only by a heavy wire mesh grating. He knew the tower well, having visited it several times in his life for various reasons. He heard another crash of wood breaking, and he knew that Viktor had entered the belfry that housed the massive and world-famous bell. He uttered an ultrasonic shout. "You follow him out of the belfry, I'll go out on the opposite side so that he can't just dodge around the tower as he climbs down."

***

Tara saw Viktor rip the wire grating from the belfry window as she dodged around the central shaft that housed Big Ben. She sheathed her sword as she approached the gaping hole in the grating, knowing that she would need both hands as well as her feet to pursue Viktor down the outside of the clock tower. She wondered if some tourist would capture her on video as she hesitated at the hole, just in case Viktor had remained near the opening to ambush her when she climbed out. Then a tiny sound of claws grinding into the exterior stone of the Elizabeth tower and the icon on

217

her HUD indicated that Viktor was more than a couple of metres away from the opening. Wire squealed and thrummed behind her, indicating that John was on his way out as well, so she clambered out of the belfry in pursuit of the werewolf master. The diamond hard claws on her hands and feet dug into the stone as she moved head-down across the tower's vertical surface. At the same moment she saw Viktor edge around the corner to her left side, noting that he was climbing down the tower head-up, like a miniature King Kong. She didn't try to warn John, knowing that he would sense the werewolf's approach, and though Viktor wouldn't know what she said, he would hear her ultrasonic utterances and realise that John was on the other side of the tower. She skittered rapidly in pursuit across the stone surface almost like a giant spider, angling downwards, betting that the werewolf would try to get down off of the tower as soon as possible. If she was wrong and Viktor ended up above her it would give him the advantage in any confrontation. When she rounded the corner she saw Viktor below her in the middle of the tower wall. He had stopped moving and she understood why when she glanced at the far side and saw John's head and shoulders. "He's mine!" she shouted to John.

The powerful ultrasonic burst made Viktor's head twist around and he snarled at the sight of Tara. Then his jaws opened in a canine grin when he saw Seward stop moving and realised that Tara intended to fight him alone. If he could finish her off quickly, his chances against the male vampire would be greatly improved and he chuckled at their stupidity. He moved towards Tara to put more space between him and Seward, as well as climbing back up to bring him level with the woman. He fancied his chances even though she was faster and more skilled than in their previous encounters. Clinging to the vertical stone surface, she was deprived of much of her agility and speed, while he was still much stronger than her.

Tara's eyes narrowed when she saw Viktor move towards her instead of heading down and away. She hid her smile of satisfaction as she moved to meet him. It was obvious he was confident his greater strength gave him an overwhelming advantage. She felt her fangs extending as she darted towards him, almost gliding across the ornately carved stone wall which provided her with an almost perfect surface for her bat-like claws and grip.

Viktor relaxed the grip of his right hand on the tower wall while bracing himself with his other three limbs in preparation for a powerful swipe at Tara that would knock her off of the tower, and to fall to her death on the manicured lawn below. He was surprised when she didn't slow down but instead charged towards him at full tilt, but since her momentum would only make his planned attack more effective, he merely pressed himself against the stone wall and braced against the impact when he struck out at her. Then she was almost within reach and he twisted his shoulders, while hooking his clawed hand towards her neck and chin. But his jaws gaped in surprise when his claws swished through empty air.

Just as Viktor had lashed out at her, Tara let go of the wall with all but her left hand, and her body had swung down and around like a pendulum, all of her weight held momentarily by one hand. As she swung she drew her short sword from over her shoulder and thrust it into Viktor's ribs, driven by the momentum of her falling, swinging body.

The master werewolf roared in agony, but the sword had missed his heart and other vital organs. When Tara's body collided with his he drove his elbow into her sternum and grunted in satisfaction when the blow ripped her free of the tower's surface and she fell, tumbling head over heels. With another grunt of pain he ripped the silvered sword from his body and let it fall. With luck it might impale Tara on the way down, he thought. He was badly hurt, and the silver prevented his werewolf body from healing with almost miraculous speed, but all the severed blood arteries and tears in his body cavity were crudely knitting and sealing, so he wouldn't bleed to death. He glanced up and to the side, and to his surprise, Seward was still at the same spot and not moving to avenge Tara's death. He tried his best to disguise the ripping pain in his chest and started to climb downwards and away from Seward, heading for the roofs of the Palace complex. Once there he could move in several different directions and avoid any police gunmen.

***

When the hammer blow of Viktor's elbow struck her chest and ripped her single-handed grip free from the stone of the tower, Tara felt a jolt of pure terror as she began to fall straight down. Her fright increased when she felt her body start to twist and move seemingly independent of her will. Then she noted the text on her HUD flashing "Glide Mode" and she realised that her vampire flight instincts were taking control. The time and distance were too short for her to change into the bat-like form that would actually allow her to fly, but instead she merely took advantage of the wind and air currents flowing around the tower. Without really trying, she glided back against the tower. Without her vampire strength and claws, she might have been slammed senseless against the stone surface or have broken and arm or leg, but instead she landed smoothly on the wall like a bat returning to its place in a cave. Guided by her sonar, her arm shot out at the perfect moment and snatched her falling sword out of the air. Tara grinned when she looked up and saw Viktor clambering down towards her. The bloody werewolf was in for a surprise, she thought with a grim smile. The medical nanites had almost completely suppressed the pain in her chest where Viktor's elbow had rammed into her body like a hydraulic piston, but the nanites had left some soreness in order that she would remain aware she wasn't a hundred percent in that area. She silently climbed upwards, shifting as necessary to remain right underneath the werewolf's descending body and practically invisible as far as Viktor was concerned. She was glad that her armoured suit was skin tight, otherwise the wind would have created flapping noises that Viktor would easily have heard. All other sounds as well as her scent were carried away by the gusting wind. When they were about two metres apart she carefully drew her sword again, gripped the stone wall tightly and waited for Viktor to come within range of her blade.

Watching the strangely immobile Seward, Viktor climbed downwards as fast as the deep wound in his chest would allow. He could have gone around the corner and out of Seward's view, but then he would have been equally ignorant of any movements that Seward might have made, and he was too badly injured to be sure of victory against the male vampire, especially if Seward managed to surprise him. The wind was fairly strong, and he had to be careful not to be blown off the wall when he released the grip of a hand or foot. He was forced to press his body against the wall when the wind changed direction, and then his nose twitched when a familiar and hated scent reached his nostrils. Shocked, he pushed himself away from the wall and looked down the front of his body. He tried to swear when he spotted Tara right beneath him, but all that came out were high pitched growls. He realised that he would be just exposing his legs to her sword if he tried to climb down, and he had already seen she was faster than him so he couldn't out-manoeuvre her, especially with his chest wound. Whatever his faults, Viktor had never been one to hesitate or give in to fear. He only saw one chance and he immediately took it. Still looking down, he relaxed his grip on the wall and let his body slide downwards and fall, the claws of his right foot aimed at the top of Tara's head. Even if she managed to cut or stab him, his falling weight would hit her like an avalanche and with luck he could break her neck with his hind claws. As he fell he bent his left knee, preparing his leg for a kick if Tara managed to dodge his right leg which was plunging down at her like a pile-driver.

Since Tara was already looking up at Viktor, she instantly spotted his realisation and intentions. There was no possibility of stopping his descent, even if she managed to strike him with her sword. Mass and gravity were on his side. His clawed foot was less than a metre away from the top of her head by the time she was able to react. She could have dodged to the side or dropped off of the tower, but in doing that she risked letting Viktor reach the rooftops. Instead, she duplicated what the werewolf had done and let herself start to slide down the face of the tower, actually increasing her downward acceleration with a thrust of her arms. Viktor drifted closer to her as they fell, the carved stone of the tower whizzing past her face like an insanely coarse grater and just as dangerous. If something hit her jaw or face, the impact could rip her head off. She momentarily misjudged their relative speeds and allowed Viktor's claws to drift too close. His claws lashed at her face, cutting a deep furrow in her forehead between her helmet and visor-like goggles, and blood ran down into her eyes, blinding her and forcing her to rely upon her sonar to keep track of the werewolf above her as they both continued to fall, like skydivers without parachutes. Still blinking the blood out of her eyes, she let herself drift closer to Viktor again, strands of her hair streaming upwards and whipping around in the airstream. Then his foot flexed and kicked out at her head again. But this time she pulled her head back and away from his claws and for a second his foot extended in front of her face. Her left hand shot up and grabbed his ankle, simultaneously straightening and streamlining her body so that she fell faster, and letting all of her weight hang from his leg. As she hoped, Viktor responded instinctively to the tug on his leg by reaching out to grip the wall with his claws and slowing his fall, which in turn caused his body to be stretched taut by her falling weight and immobilising him. She pulled herself up with her left arm while her right hand, holding her sword in a downward grip, arced up and across, deeply slashing the backs of Viktor's thighs and splattering her face with more blood. Placing the sword between her teeth, she released her hold on Viktor's ankle, regained her grip on the wall and scuttled to the side. Panting from the exertion, she looked up and across to stare into his eyes as she climbed up until she was level with him. Taking the sword from between her jaws she shouted at him over the fluttering roar of the wind, "Die, you bastard!"

Maddened by the pain of his wounds and the nearness of his mocking enemy, Viktor threw himself at Tara, determined to totally destroy her once and for all. They would both fall, but they were more than half way down the tower and he bet on his werewolf constitution to let him survive the impact. His eyes widened in horror when his badly injured legs failed him and his leap fell short of his target, his claws just missing Tara's body as he plummeted towards the ground.

Without hesitation, Tara threw herself off the wall, swooping down like a diver. Her streamlined form and aerial coordination allowed her to catch up with Viktor's tumbling body. Using the force of the rushing air, she made her body whip around like a propeller blade just as she caught up with him. Guided by her sonar aided senses, her sword struck Viktor's neck with irresistible

223

force, taking his head cleanly off of his shoulders. She slid her bloodied sword back into its sheath and ripped at two hidden tabs on the front of her armoured suit. Extending her arms and legs, she willed her body to transform and wing-like membranes extended under her arms, sliding out of the special slits in her suit and slowing her fall like a wing-suit, letting her glide down and land on the roof of the Palace with a painful but survivable thud. She willed her wings to retract and then scrambled to the edge of the roof to peer down at the lawn below that faced the Thames. Viktor's body lay half on the grass, the incredibly tough werewolf body mostly intact save for a horribly twisted and broken leg. It took her a moment to find his head, which lay a number of metres distant. She continued to stare, almost expecting the body to get up like some film monster.

***

John headed back inside of the Palace as soon as he saw Tara behead Viktor. The mini drones couldn't cover the entire complex and any attempt to evacuate the survivors from the Commons or any other part of the palace could risk an ambush unless he could ensure that the route towards the nearest exit was free of werewolves. He called Commander Blair and Tara's father on a conference call. "Viktor's dead. Keep the civilians together under guard inside the Commons until I can make sure the path to the exit is clear of werewolves. Some of them may feel trapped and suicidally aggressive."

Commander Blair sighed in relief. The monitor displaying the information from the mini drones still showed werewolves moving inside the building and within striking distance. He had been resigned to hunkering down inside the Commons until reinforcements came or all of the werewolves left. But that held the possibility of a further attack from the remaining werewolves, especially if they felt trapped and desperate. He had not relished trying to explain the situation to the Prime Minister and a gaggle of frightened and angry ministers and MPs. "Your rifle?" He looked around and spotted a very non-standard weapon lying on the floor. "I think I see it. I'll have someone bring it to you. I think it best we're not seen working together."

John raised an eyebrow. "So it's like that is it?" He had half expected it. Never rely on the gratitude of politicians, or warlords, he thought with a smile. The Prime Minister was very aware that the assassination attempt had been televised and probably spread worldwide via the Internet by now, and he couldn't afford to seem beholden to rescuers whom he couldn't identify, or control.

"I'm sorry," Commander Blair replied gruffly, honestly embarrassed and angry. "They won't learn anything from me. You have my word."

John had lived too long and seen too much ingratitude based upon political expedience, some of it his own, to be surprised or even truly angry. "I appreciate it. At any rate, we still have to get everybody safely out. I'll let you know when the path is clear. Have your man place the rifle near the entrance to the gallery next to my bags. I'll stay out of sight so that he won't have to lie about talking to me." Although he trusted Blair, the Commander still had to obey orders, so he climbed up the wall overlooking the entrance to the Gallery to wait. Before long he heard footsteps. One of Blair's constables appeared carrying his mass driver rifle which had been ripped off of its sling during the fighting. The constable looked around, placed the weapon on the floor beside the entrance, and then turned and left. But John remained completely still in his elevated perch even after the sound of the constable's

225

footsteps and breathing faded. Nothing happened for about three minutes, and then two more armed constables in the special tactical gear of Commander Blair's unit appeared, one behind the other, weapons shouldered, muzzles sweeping in controlled arcs. They reached the spot where the unusual rifle was lying and ostentatiously studied their surroundings, which included peeking into the Gallery.

"Do you see him?" said one constable in a voice that was just a little too loud.

The other constable replied in a similarly theatrical tone, "Nope. Not a trace of him or the woman. The PM isn't going to be happy."

"Well we don't have enough men to lock down the Palace, not when we have to protect and evacuate everybody, so this was our only chance to take them into custody and it looks like they aren't going to take the bait."

The other constable shrugged. "We might as well get back to the team." He looked down at the weapon and bags on the floor. "The crime scene people can take custody of the evidence when the Palace is secured."

The constables walked away, carefully not looking back, and John almost laughed out loud when one of them held out his hand in a thumbs up sign. He sighed and shook his head. It seemed that his mistrust of politicians had once more been justified. The Prime Minister was obviously looking for ways to cover his posterior, and if he couldn't deal with the werewolves, he could capture his erstwhile rescuers and spin some kind of story that would make him and his government look less hopeless. When he was sure that the constables were gone, he dropped down and recovered the weapon and bags. The micro drones were equipped with self-destruct systems which would prevent their technology from being copied, so they could be left in the air until he and Tara left or they ran out of power, instead of trying to recover all of them. He activated the radio system built into his suit to warn Tara to avoid the police.

***

Tara pulled herself back from the edge when a gawking civilian looked upwards. She longed to climb down just to touch Viktor's dead body. He had escaped so many times before and his death felt almost unreal. However she couldn't risk being seen crawling down the wall and her armoured body suit would make her stick out like an advertising screen. John's voice made her start just as she stepped back. She listened to him and bit her lip. "I'm on my way to you. Viktor is confirmed dead." Despite her words she couldn't resist peeking over the edge one more time. Her eyes searched for Viktor's head and zoomed in until his staring dead eyes filled her vision. She stared fixedly for several seconds, then she spun around and headed for the nearest rooftop entrance.

***

One of Duncan's spotters cried out "Werewolf!" as the surviving monsters began to flee the Palace complex after the death of their leaders and the arrival of armed police with weapons that actually hurt them.

Duncan smiled. "All right, time to earn your pay. Remember, only shoot if you have a clear line of fire. For god's sake don't hit a civilian. Keep moving and don't get spotted or caught on some teenager's video. Let's kill the bastards!" she said, slapping her rifle.

***

The werewolf leapt out from behind a pillar towards Tara's exposed back, claws extended and its jaws aimed for her neck. Heart pounding, she dived towards the ground and raised her rifle as she rolled to her right. The werewolf's head exploded followed milliseconds later by the oddly distorted hypersonic crack of John's rifle. She winced as gobbets of brain and bone splinters splattered her hard enough to hurt. "You're going to be the bait for the next one. Oh wait, according to the drones, this part of the Palace is clear of werewolves. Blair should get his sheep moving."

John nodded and called Commander Blair. "The way is clear for now. You better get your charges moving. Don't bother searching for us, we're leaving too. Good luck."

Tara heard what he said and went to retrieve their bags, her eyes and ears still searching her surroundings. The drones weren't infallible inside buildings like these, filled with niches, alcoves and pillars. "We need to exit where we won't run into anyone."

John pointed with his rifle. "That way. We'll go up and out onto the roof and leave the way we came."

"The werewolf problem isn't over with Viktor's death you know," Tara said as they ran along the silent, deserted corridors.

John, who was leading the way, glanced over his shoulder at her. "I know. In fact, Viktor's death may have created a whole new problem. He at least kept a leash on the most troublesome werewolves and kept them working towards a single goal, or too frightened of him to make trouble. With him and Jane gone, things are just going to go to hell. In addition, the werewolves that escaped from New Belmarsh have had the time and experience necessary to learn how to use their werewolf powers. Those tranquilliser cuffs actually taught many of them how to control their transformations, so we won't be facing confused and almost mindless monsters, but werewolves who are much more like Viktor and his followers. And despite being killed, Viktor achieved at least part of his goal. Confidence in the government's ability to control the werewolf threat will plummet, and we may be looking at the beginning of a civil war of sorts, especially if new and competent werewolf leaders arise."

Chapter Eleven

The private jet bearing Werner corporate markings sat dark and silent at the end of the runway of San Jose International Airport's private jet terminal. All attempts at communication from the tower were ignored, and airport security and fire services were alerted. When the column of vehicles had rolled to a halt at a safe distance, an air marshaller walked to the front of the private jet and attempted to signal the pilot or other crew members in case there had been some kind of accident or illness that was preventing the crew and passengers from disembarking. When there was no response, the emergency crew moved forward to open the aircraft's door.

***

Werner watched the police team enter his jet from the roof of one of the low buildings lining the private runways. He grinned when the panicked shouting began and he could still taste the blood of the crew in his mouth. He wasn't thinking as clearly as normal, but he had been cogent enough to know how to exit the aircraft through one of the emergency escape windows rather than the main exit, and he knew that he had to get away from the airport. When he realised during the flight that he had been infected by the zombie variant of the alien medical virus or whatever it was, he had almost despaired. Then fifteen minutes before landing at SJC, he had realised that he still had one sample unit of the alien artefacts in his briefcase. He had no idea if using it on himself would help, make things worse, or kill him outright, but he had nothing to lose. He had retreated to the aircraft lavatory, telling the attractive stewardess not to disturb him, locked the door, and pressed the medallion shaped thing against his arm. Then he sat down upon the toilet seat and waited. The semi-intelligent alien nanite medical system had immediately recognised the presence of a corrupt form of itself which was killing its host and had set about remedying the situation. Because Werner wasn't actually under the threat of imminent death from a wound and still conscious, he retained much more of his rational mind as the nanites transformed him into werewolf form. Despite appeals from the stewardess, he remained inside the toilet until after the aircraft had landed. He even managed to restrain himself until the jet had come to a complete halt, but then had burst out of the toilet, ripping the door from its mountings and tearing out the stewardess's throat before she had the chance to scream. Then he had sprinted to the cockpit and killed the pilot and co-pilot. However, he was careful not to draw any blood from the co-pilot, killing him by breaking the man's neck. Then he had opened the escape window, dumped the co-pilot's body out of the aircraft and exited the jet himself. Taking care not to be seen, he carried the dead body away in the dark for later disposal. He changed back into human form on the rooftop and had to restrain himself from laughing out loud in triumph. He had escaped dying and changing into a zombie, and he was now imbued with the powers of a werewolf. He would take the co-pilot's body somewhere very private and eat it, especially the parts that might allow the authorities to identify the corpse. Then he would stagger dramatically into a police station or hospital in human form and declare that he had narrowly escaped from the co-pilot who had turned into a zombie. There would be an investigation into the zombie outbreak, but access to all records of the research into the alien artefacts were highly restricted and encrypted. He would arrange for the appropriate non-confidential records to disappear along with the incriminating portions of security video tape. Any of the guards and lab staff who had witnessed the start of the zombie attack and who had survived would have to be dealt with, but that would be trivial. Now that he was a werewolf, the focus of his efforts would have to shift. From what he had learned from the werewolf outbreak in Britain, he would be able to create new werewolves without using the alien artefacts, presenting him with many new options and possibilities. Plus there were the zombies. He knew more about them than anyone in America, so there surely would be a lucrative commercial opportunity in dealing with them as well. He grinned as he punched the concrete of the building. The sharp jolt of pain triggered the transformation back to werewolf form. It was time to go.

***

Back at John's home, Rowland Harker hugged his daughter tight. "I ... " He found himself unable to express the joy he felt at seeing her safe and the terror he had experienced watching her fight for her life through the drone network. He grunted when she hugged him back with more than human strength. Having her in his arms, he felt the trembling tension finally flow out of his body. "Welcome back," he said softly.

Tara kissed his cheek and gave him another squeeze. "I'll always come back. Promise."

"You saved everybody today. I'm so proud of you," Rowland said, smiling at her fondly.

"The PM doesn't think so, and we didn't save everybody. We may be facing more trouble from the authorities than werewolves in the coming days. And John says I can't cut the PM's head off," Tara said, shaking her head sorrowfully. She gave him another peck on the cheek, and then turned to give Emily a hug. "I'm going to take a hot bath and get some sleep. The past days have been exhausting."

Her father's face turned serious as he held out his

hand. "Before you go, there's something I think both you and John need to see."

Just then John walked into the living room holding a mug of brandy laced coffee. "Something wrong, Rowland?" he asked.

Rowland shook his head. "Not right now. But I think it's definitely going to come our way sooner or later." He picked up a remote control and activated the hard drive recorder and the TV. "This is a news feed from the United States." A news broadcast, obviously taken from a helicopter or drone appeared on the screen. Everybody recognised the familiar shape of the White House. There was a moment of shocked silence as they all watched the losing battle. The reporter gasped. "My god! The White House is under attack by ... by what look like zombies! There's no official word of who these people are, even though you can see on the screen that the military as well as the police are trying to stop ... " The reporter broke off in shock when she saw the military lines dissolve into a panicked retreat, and then the broadcast went black.

Rowland reversed the video until an image of the initial confrontation of the military line and the mob of attackers was on screen and pointed. "They're definitely not werewolves, but they're clearly not worried by gunfire. In fact, they don't seem concerned by anything at all."

John pointed at a spot on the screen. "Watch the figure in the blue shirt. She gets shot several times and falls down. See how the crowd walks over her and she doesn't react. I would say she's dead or dying." He skipped forward about a minute. "Now watch this," he said, pointing at the same figure. A moment later the figure in the blue shirt got up and began walking forward again, seemingly no worse for wear. "Whatever they are, they seem able to heal almost as fast a werewolf, if not as well." He pointed at figures with gaping wounds and horrific scar tissue.

Tara nodded. "But they don't seem very smart. Even if you can heal nearly instantly, you don't just calmly walk into massed machine-gun fire. None of them seem afraid, not even the children."

John nodded grimly. "They don't even seem aware of the danger. I can't believe that some new virus or drug could appear right at this time that could mimic the effects of the alien nanites. I think somebody has been tinkering with the nanites and had their work get out of hand."

"Werner's people!" Rowland exclaimed. "They're the only ones with samples of the alien technology and the capability to perform the experimentation without anyone being aware of it. The silly buggers must have damaged the nanites somehow, and let it escape from their labs."

Emily touched Rowland's arm and said, "I think you're right. I've been searching social media for videos of the event, and the earliest images of these … whatever they are, appeared here, on the street near to the Washington headquarters of W.A.R." Manipulating the remote control, she caused a map of the area encompassing both the White House and the W.A.R building to appear on screen.

"It's not proof, but I wager it was Werner's doing. The only question is whether he created these things deliberately or by accident. It's obvious he lost control of them either way. I wonder if he survived the outbreak," John said.

"Are we looking at a zombie apocalypse?" Tara asked only half in jest.

Roland frowned in thought. "Not in the end of the world sense, I don't think. Hollywood has always exaggerated the speed of the spread, especially if it is only transmitted by fluids and not simply scratches, and that assumes that the attacking zombies don't eat too much of the victim in the first place. The US military and police should be able to contain mass outbreaks. However it's obvious from the news video that many more infected were not in the main mass attacking the soldiers and the White House, so just like the werewolves here, there are going to be small outbreaks, spreading slowly across the city and then the country. On occasion the circumstances will be right for a group of them to form before anyone notices and they'll have to be put down with military force. The Americans will have the advantage of not being concerned about killing the creatures, since they are unmistakeably dead already and won't change back to normal human form."

Tara shook her head tiredly. "There's a good chance this zombie version of the nanites will eventually spread outside of the US and even to Britain as well, depending on how long it takes from first bite to complete transformation. As if we didn't have enough trouble with the werewolves and our own government."

John, who had learned to look at things over the long term, the very long term, clapped Rowland and Tara on the shoulder. "We can only prepare ourselves as best we possibly can, and take things as they come. Don't worry. I've had a very long time to make plans and provide for any kind of disaster I and all manner of expert advisers could think of. As for the authorities, if we have to, we can completely change our identities. I even have someone groomed to take over my businesses and properties who looks just like me. See you tomorrow."

Tara nodded. "It's been a long day. We can talk about this tomorrow," she said, waving at the TV screen.

"Yes, there's nothing we can do right now. I need to review the performance of the micro drones and make sure that all of them issued their self-destruct confirmation," Rowland said, putting his arm around Emily's waist. "Let's go to the lab and do some analysis."

Emily bumped her hip against him. "Good idea. I could do with some in-depth analysis."

Tara rolled her eyes. "Just remember to turn off the security cameras. The guards don't need to see your scientific explorations." She made her way towards her room, barely noticing that she was navigating through the huge mansion, which was John's second home on the outskirts of London, using her vampire sonar senses as much as her vision. It was her sonar that alerted her to the fact that the door to John's room was very slightly ajar and she caught a glimpse of John's bare back. When she paused she heard his voice say, "Come in." Her hand reached out for the door but stopped before pushing it open. She sensed that if she went in, something would completely change and she wasn't sure if she was ready. Suddenly her HUD flashed into view, and she looked around herself searching for a threat, but the corridor was empty and quiet. Then she saw the bio-feedback readings on the display. Her blood pressure was up, as was her heart rate. The display switched to the detailed medical readout and she blushed at what she saw. The alien, or perhaps not so alien now AI was trying to tell her something. She smiled and pushed the door open with her fingers. She stepped into the room, and came to a halt with a gasp. She had seen John topless from the front before, but had never glimpsed his back full on. She hadn't thought anything of it till now, but she was shocked by the pattern of scars that flowed across his shoulders and all the way down to the waistband of his trousers.

John didn't need his sonar to tell him what she was looking at. "The Turks were fond of flogging as a method of encouraging enthusiasm and obedience. Unlike my brother, I wasn't very cooperative. I didn't have the benefit of an interface which could provide the nanites with details of a normal human form, and the system must have assumed that the scars were a natural

236

part of my body. I could probably make them fade away with a little effort, but they tie me to the man I was, when I was still human, so I keep them. Do they disturb you?"

Tara closed the door behind her and stepped closer to him. She lightly ran her fingertips over the pale lines and keloid scars. "No, they don't bother me at all, in fact I find them comforting in a way. They make you … "

"Human?" John finished for her, his tone expressionless.

"Real, tangible somehow. Count Dracula is such a figure of legend, and knowing you've lived so long … but these marks, they belong to a man who was once a young boy." Her hand was still stroking his back, far longer than curiosity deemed proper, but she didn't, couldn't take her hand away. Her vampire senses could feel the power that flowed through his body, and she realised that even though she was able to work with the alien nanites more directly than he could, somehow he had adapted and grown, perhaps even used the alien system to grow and develop powers the bat-like creators of the nanites had never imagined. She felt something inside of her reach out to him and connect. When he turned around and took her in his arms she knew that he had felt it too.

John didn't ask if she was sure because her desire reverberated through his body like a giant crystal chime. The oldest vampire on Earth undressed the newest female vampire with ancient skill and confidence, and without a word, led her to his bed.

Tara took a moment to wonder how he had gotten out of his own clothes, and then their mutual lust and passion enveloped her like dark giant wings as she lifted her legs to draw him tightly to her own heat.

THE END